UNWANTED SISTER

Book Five of
The Unwanted Series

Also by Sandra Denbo and Tamarine Vilar

In *The Unwanted Series*

UNWANTED SISTER

Book Five of
The Unwanted Series

by

Sandra Denbo

& Tamarine Vilar

Book Lamp and Chair, LLC
Portland, Oregon

Scan this QR code
 to learn more about
 this series or visit our website at:
www.theunwantedseries.net

Copyright © 2020 Sandra Denbo and Tamarine Vilar

Editing by Adele Brinkley

Cover art by Diane Avenoso

Photography by A C Denbo

ISBN- 978-0-9967895-9-2

Published in 2019 by Book Lamp and Chair, LLC

Printed in the U.S.A.

Acknowledgements

We want to give a personal thanks to Adele Brinkley, our editor, for numerous suggestions and help with our manuscript. It would be another beast entirely without your help. Thank you, for all of it.

Most importantly, to Emery Denbo, who became so enthused after reading our first book that he became an integral part of our writing process. He gave us numerous ideas and suggestions on the plots of all succeeding novels. He has made our stories more complex and interesting, and for that we want to express our deepest gratitude.

I want to acknowledge my daughter and co-author. Although I could have put the story to paper by myself, I could not have made it flourish into the series it has become without her. She has provided today's youthful voice, and added her own as well. In addition, she has helped to pare down some of the rambling scenes I suggested. For that, I thank you, Tamarine.

Writing these books with my mom has been such an honor and a blessing. I will cherish each and every moment of the process and how much it brought us even closer together. Even when I had to "kill her babies" (ideas or sentences she was especially proud of but just couldn't be used), she took it in stride (eventually) and we worked to make every bit of our books better, together.

Finally, we want to give a special thank you to all our friends and family that gave support and encouragement from the beginning of our venture.

Chapter 1

Even for Portland, it was cold for mid-February. A polar vortex had settled in; thankfully without the snow.

Callie Cooper dressed quickly; she was late for her run. She'd have to cut it short in order to get back in time to take a shower and make breakfast for her dad's parents. She lived with them, and loved being their caregiver.

She put her red hair into a ponytail, the long waves draping her neck. She put on her warm jogging suit and pulled on a headband to protect her ears. She grabbed her phone and locked the door on her way out, and stretched. She puffed mini-clouds of steam as she headed towards the hill.

This part of the city had no curbs, so she ran along the edge of the pavement. At least there was that much; a lot of the roads near here were merely rutted, dirt lanes. Several of the roadside mailboxes had their flags up; the neighborhood still felt safe enough that no one worried about mail theft.

Running was her time to think. Lately, she couldn't think of anything else but that pivotal conversation with Gary just a few months ago. He was the same age as her older brother, Mark. With him living next door when they were growing up, the two boys spent a lot of time together. Callie, of course, tagged along as often as possible, so she always looked at him as a best friend. But when Gary's mother died of cancer when he was ten, Callie's parents became his surrogate parents. He managed pretty well, and even landed a full scholarship to college. By the time Gary left for college, he was happy to be leaving his father's house.

Gary's father, Billy, had been so grieved when his wife died that he couldn't function, and basically left Gary to fend for himself. Billy turned to alcohol to dull the agony, and Gary grew more distant from him. Any love he had felt for his father as a child morphed into pity, disgust, and resentment.

Due to an accident the previous year, and the desire to watch his son walk across the stage at his college graduation, Billy managed to get sober. He was still alcohol-free, and Gary was only beginning to reconnect with him.

For all those years growing up, Callie had come to think of him as another brother. So, when he confessed his romantic feelings for her seven months ago, the revelation had hit her like a ton of bricks. She'd never suspected he felt that way. She couldn't recall anything she'd done to encourage him or give him the impression that she thought of him in any way other than as a brother. Since it had been so unexpected, she was still sorting out her feelings about him. When she looked back on all those years of practical jokes, banter, and teasing, she tried to recall any hint of a crush growing. Was he really in love with her or was it just infatuation? He was shy, so maybe he just felt comfortable around her? Callie had been burned by love before, so maybe that was part of what was holding her back.

She shook her head thinking how it was actually a new acquaintance who'd noticed his feelings for her, and she hadn't picked up on it. *Some detective I am* she thought as she ran past the park. *I couldn't even figure that out on my own. And poor Gary, he was so shy that he never acknowledged it until I asked him if what Vera said was true.*

A bit of resentment moved her faster as she rehashed that conversation with Mark at the bowling alley when they were on that double-date – him with his fiancée, Marci, and her with Gary. She had agreed to the date to give Gary a chance, to see if there might be a spark. Marci had left to get drinks for everyone, and Gary was getting ready to roll the ball when Mark confessed that he had known about Gary's feelings for years and he'd never said a word. Gary had turned around just in time to see her punch Mark's arm; not an unusual thing between them. She had barely noticed that Gary's smile turned to worry when she growled at Mark, "Why didn't you say something?"

"Hey, it was between you and him. It would've been weird coming from me. And you might have thought I was reading something out of nothing. Besides, how weird would it be pimping out my own sister?"

Laughing, she knew he was right, and she reluctantly agreed. Then she noticed Gary approaching. She'd never felt more embarrassed, date or not.

Reliving the red face, she muttered angrily as she ran, "I'm so stupid! How could I not see it? Even mom knew! And Marci! And Rudy! Did the whole city know?" Frustrated and embarrassed, she pounded the pavement even harder. She cut across the parking lot at the convenience store to head back.

Regaining her senses, she decided to look at the positive, as mom and dad taught her. She had already started a sheet of positives and negatives at home to figure out this new relationship. Well, new to *her*. She went over it for the umpteenth time, *Gary is already a good friend, I trust him, I like him as a person, I enjoy his company, and he makes me laugh.* Then she moaned inside as she reminded herself that he knew all her secrets. *I've told him things I haven't even told Mark. And I certainly haven't told mom or dad. And he can be so irritating! He always manages to rile me up. I think he even enjoys it!* Could she change the way she thought about him?

They had already had a few dates since that embarrassing moment at the bowling alley. Yes, they had fun, as usual; but that transition to a relationship – could it really happen? *It's already become awkward. And what happens if things don't work out with him? I could lose my best friend.*

She thought about his troubled past. Although Billy was alcohol-free now, he'd spent more than twelve years as an alcoholic. Since Callie's parents basically raised Gary as their own since his dad wouldn't, or couldn't, they had become his Mom and Dad. Her mood softened as she remembered his words, "They saved my life. I don't know what would have happened to me if they hadn't taken me under their wings." Suddenly, she wanted to give him a comforting hug. But that was from sympathy, right? Or was it more than that? She still had a lot of thinking to do.

She slowed to a trot when she saw her grandparent's house beyond the trees. Cooling down during the last few blocks had been a habit, but with all the distractions, she'd forgotten. She slowed down and walked past the driveway. She'd have to pass the house and return. *That's all I need, another delay,* she berated herself.

She let out a sigh of relief when she approached the gravel driveway again, and she pulled out her key. She stopped at the front to stretch again.

When she entered the house, the familiar feeling of belonging wrapped its arms around her and her anxiety waned. She looked around her grandparents' living room and the comfortable, eclectic feel Grandma had given it. Nothing matched, yet it all fit together. She wouldn't change a thing, except maybe a bigger TV.

It felt good to be a caregiver for those you love. Cora, her grandma, was pretty self-sufficient, but Grandpa had needed more help, especially after she moved in. Years of alcoholism, thankfully addressed and curbed a couple years ago, had taken its toll on his health. On top of that, years of poor eating habits had resulted in type-2 diabetes, and all the health issues that came with it. Nobody knew how long he lived with diabetes before it was diagnosed. He had always resisted doctors with a vengeance, and he still did.

Determined to stop the escalating damage to his body, Callie tried to cook whenever possible. Although she only knew the basics, she was trying. It was difficult getting him to change his eating habits after decades of junk food and alcohol, and he invariably managed to sneak in poor choices.

Yesterday was a shock. Cora had discovered an angry sore on the bottom of his foot. Of course, Ralph had lost all sensation in his feet due to the diabetes, so he didn't realize it was there. They immediately made the appointment with the foot doctor for today. Callie had been berating herself ever since. *Some caregiver I am! But then, he resists most of our efforts to help.*

She showered, got dressed, and gently knocked on their bedroom door to wake them. Her hair was still damp from toweling it dry as she went to the kitchen to start breakfast. She put on the coffee pot and a pot of water to boil. Cora had insisted on oatmeal for breakfast every morning, so the routine was mindless. By the time she set the table, they were dressed and coming out of their room. He looked up, saw her, and said, "Trouble's here."

Ralph said this every time she walked in the door. On the surface, he gave the impression of being a curmudgeon, but she knew that was his way to say he loved her. She smiled.

Despite getting sober, Ralph had aged more quickly in the last couple of years. More wrinkles appeared and they became deeper, looking like etchings. Heavy bags sagged under his grey eyes; even the color seemed to have faded. He had gotten weaker which emphasized his limp, forcing him to use a walker outside the house. Hairs on his bald pate had thinned even more, and that actually gave him an excuse to avoid combing his hair. He argued that nobody noticed, so why bother. But Callie could tell, and she figured Grandma just didn't bother to make an issue of it. No sense in causing an unnecessary stir. That was another lesson from her parents: pick your battles. Callie's dad had probably learned that from Grandma. She certainly had to pick her battles during Ralph's years of alcoholism.

They sat down just as breakfast was ready. Cora was dressed comfortably in pink sweats, her favorite color. She still sported the pixie haircut she'd gotten as Ralph was getting sober. The dyed blonde color was perfect for her round face, enhancing her soft brown eyes. Since their menu had better choices, Cora had lost weight, and that made her more perky and cheerful.

Since Ralph was getting better nutrition, his attitude had improved too; although, he still had his cranky moments. Callie's uncles came around more often now that Ralph wasn't always on their case; and that relieved Callie's dad from having to do most of the household repairs.

Cora seemed to examine Callie's face as she adjusted her chair. Cora placed her hand on Callie's arm and said soothingly, "It's not your fault. He wouldn't even let me look at his foot until yesterday."

"But I'm responsible for his care." Callie pled.

Cora shook her head. "It is what it is. It's not your fault if he won't let you see it."

Feeling uneasy, Callie urged, "Let's eat, we don't want to be late."

All through this, Ralph seemed detached, disinterested. Callie wondered if he was purposely ignoring them. A closer look confirmed the third possibility. "Grandpa, did you put in your hearing aids?"

When he didn't answer, she got up to fetch them. She placed them on the table next to his applesauce.

He looked at them, surprised, "Ah guess Ah fergot. Thanks." He poked them in his ears and kept eating.

Chapter 2

Callie had borrowed her mother's van for the trip to the doctor's office. She pulled the van into the handicap spot at the hospital parking structure; it was the closest spot for the doctor's office which was next door to the hospital. She dutifully put the handicap tag on the rearview mirror and stepped out. Cora, who was in the back seat, also got out so she could help Ralph.

When Callie shut the driver's door, she saw that someone had pulled into a handicap spot across the lane from them. But he didn't have a handicap license plate and he didn't put up a tag. When he stepped out of his SUV, she called out, "Excuse me, I think you forgot to put up your handicap tag."

He frowned at her and barked, "This is a hospital vehicle!"

What does that mean? So, she asked, "Do you have a handicap tag?"

He glowered at her and walked towards them, raising his voice, "I said, it's a hospital vehicle. I drive patients!"

"Oh, sorry. I didn't know that when I asked you," she apologized.

His eyebrows pushed down over his ice-blue eyes. "And where's your tag?!" he demanded.

Confusion made her step back. "What? It's right there," she said defensively, pointing to the rearview mirror. Shaking her head, she started to turn the corner at the bumper, so she could get Ralph's walker out of the rear of the van. She could hear Ralph grumbling to Cora about not needing help.

She stopped abruptly when the man had approached and blocked her way by standing next to the rear door. He leaned forward, almost nose to nose. He was slightly shorter than she was, so he had to look up to her, revealing creepily large pupils. "And what right do *you* have to ask *me* anything?!" he shouted. He reminded her of an angry dog baring its teeth.

Stepping aside and maintaining self-control, she said, "I was concerned because when people park here without authorization, then handicapped people can't use it."

Glaring, he said, "And who are *you?* The parking *Nazi?!*"

Goosebumps prickled her arms. "No. I was just trying to be an advocate for the handicapped."

His face got red and the veins in his neck start to pulse. "Well, you're *not!* You're only making *trouble!*"

His demeanor made her nervous. Hoping not to aggravate him even more, she squeezed by him to get into the drive lane.

Following her with his arms wide, he demanded, "Just butt out next time!"

"Excuse me; I have to get my grandfather's walker." Her hand had to pass close to the man's shoulder in order to reach the door handle

"You're avoiding the issue!"

She bit her tongue. *Just get the walker and leave,* she told herself.

"So, you admit you're wrong. Go ahead. Admit it."

She felt her anger boiling, so she decided to leave before she lost control. She pulled out the walker, shut the rear door, and walked towards the passenger side to get some distance from him. Using all her self-control, she paused at the back corner of the passenger side, and calmly counseled him, "You need to work on your customer service."

His eyes widened in rage and pointed angrily at her. "*You* need to work on *your* customer service!" He stepped closer.

She brought the walker to her grandparents just as Ralph had just gotten out with Cora's help. Ralph turned to the man and shouted, "Buzz off, ya jerk! Can't ya see we're tryin' ta git ta the doctor?"

Cora shushed him.

Ralph waved her off and continued yelling, this time to Cora. "He's no good. Someone's gotta teach him a lesson!"

Cora snapped at him with a firm but low voice close to his hearing aid, "Stay out of it. You're going to make it worse."

Ralph waved at her as if swatting a fly. "Bah!" Then he took his walker and started to leave with Cora next to him. As she passed Callie, she whispered over her shoulder to Callie, "Let's go."

Callie was thankful for Cora's clear head and she led her grandparents past the irate man. Even though she knew she should probably not say anything else, she felt she had to reprimand him, "*You* give the hospital a *bad name.*"

She was alarmed when he started following them as they walked towards the doctor's office, shouting, "You have no right to talk to me like that!" He turned around, got out a paper and pen.

She looked around and she saw him writing. *He's writing down* my *license plate number?* Gritting her teeth, she looked at his vehicle to make a mental note of his. Just then, an old man got out of the angry man's vehicle and slowly walked with a cane towards the elevator. The look on his face said it all; he was absolutely appalled and scared. Suddenly, she felt very sorry for the passenger, thinking how he had been trapped in a vehicle with this volatile maniac; and that he would need to find another way home. She turned to the irate man, "We're leaving," then headed for the ramp to the doctor's office with Ralph still grumbling.

He shook his fist at her, burst out with several obscenities, and topped it off with, "Good riddance!"

After Ralph and Cora were checked in and sat down in the waiting room, Callie went back to reception to report the man's deplorable behavior. The receptionist took down the information and said someone from the hospital would be contacting her.

"Thank you so much. It just makes me so uncomfortable knowing that someone like that is driving defenseless people around town. I'm especially worried about his passenger. Is there any way you could arrange for another driver to bring him home?"

"Absolutely, I was just thinking the same thing. And thank you for being such a good citizen."

Chapter 3

When he exited the doctor's office, Ralph looked up with a frown. "Here's trouble."

Although Callie normally welcomed his backhanded compliment, she knew he often used it as a distraction. When she saw Cora's expression, she knew this was one of those times. Cora looked distraught.

Callie jumped up from her seat. "Grandma, what's wrong?"

"I'm just mad at myself. I should have insisted on checking him over more regularly. I would've noticed that wound a whole lot earlier. Now it's infected. I don't know if I can keep track of all the stuff I have to do to his foot."

"Is it really bad?"

"It must be. They wanted to admit him to the hospital, but he refused. The hard part is keeping it clean and …" She handed the doctor's instructions to Callie. "Here, look for yourself."

Callie took the four-page set of instructions and did a quick scan. Her shoulders dropped as she bemoaned silently, *this looks serious.*

She drove them home, helped them inside, and then drove to her parents' house to drop off their van and pick up her yellow VW. Her car was economical, but there was no way she could transfer her grandparents in it. It was too low to the ground, and being only a two-door, it was impossible for them to get in and out. When she first got the car, it was perfect and she loved it; but now it was more of an inconvenience. So, every time she had to take one of them for a doctor's visit, she had to borrow her parent's van.

When she started handing the keys to her mom, Sharon pushed them back to her. "I've been thinking about it, and your dad and I want you to keep the van over there. You guys need it more than I do. I can just come borrow it if I ever need it. Besides, I want to get a more eco-friendly compact. We'll drop off your car before tonight."

Sharon was nearing fifty, and with all the trials they'd gone through in the last few years, telltale wrinkles had appeared around her hazel eyes and on her forehead. Her strawberry-blonde hair had started showing gray, making it lighter than it had been in the past.

"That's so nice, Mom! It'll save me so much time, not having to come get it so often!" She hugged her mom fiercely.

Sharon hugged back. "Now, that's not an excuse to not come over, you know," she teased after releasing her daughter.

Callie put her fists on her hips in mock indignation. "Hey. You're the one that offered."

Sharon smacked her shoulder. "Maybe I was testing you?"

"I guess we'll see if I pass the test?" She gave her mom another hug.

"I love you," they said in synchrony. Then they giggled, still loving the strange stereo connection they had.

Callie's automatic smile appeared when she feigned, "Get out of my head."

"Never," was her mom's familiar reply.

Although it was always the same routine; it was more like a confirmation of their connection.

When Callie got back home and walked in the door, Ralph was parked in his recliner with his feet up in front of the TV. She wondered why he avoided her gaze when she came in. Normally when he was in a cranky mood, he'd sit in the rocking chair in front of the fireplace. *Oh, that's right, he has to keep his foot elevated. Is he ashamed of neglecting his foot? Maybe embarrassed for not letting grandma check it? He's certainly annoyed that we have to nurse it. I hope he isn't going to be in a bad mood the rest of the day.*

Cora was washing the breakfast dishes, so she said, "I'm back. Hey, I can do that, Grandma."

"No, I'm almost done. I'll let them air dry." She put the last few pieces of silverware in the drainer, wiped her hands, and sat down.

As Callie poured their coffee, she turned to her grandmother, "I'll take care of Grandpa's foot. So, don't you worry, okay? And mom's going to help out while I'm at school."

Cora smiled sweetly, her eyes letting go of some of the anxiety that had gripped her on the way home. "I'm so glad you're here, dear." She patted Callie's hand.

"That's why I moved in. To help, remember?"

"Have I said thank you?"

"More times than I can count." Callie bent over to kiss her cheek. She put the coffee pot down on the dinette table and sat down. *That wound must look awful to be that infected. I didn't realize it could get this bad. We're going to have to keep a better rein on his eating.* She glanced at Ralph sitting in his rocking chair.

Callie had just added some sugar to her coffee when her phone rang. "Hello?"

"Is this Callie Cooper?" asked the voice on the phone.

"Yes. What can I do for you?"

"This is Corinne with the Patient Transport Liaison Committee. You reported an incident in the hospital parking lot this morning?"

"Oh, right."

"Can you tell me what happened?"

After relating the incident, the woman on other end told her, "We've checked the security footage and we know who the man is. He's already had a couple of warnings; and strangely, he reports minor incidents with other drivers."

"He needs anger management counseling."

"I'm very sorry you had to deal with that. His behavior was certainly not in accordance with company policy and we'll make sure it won't happen again. If we need any more information, is this a good number for us to reach you?"

"Of course. But I also wanted to check and see if his passenger from this morning got a safer driver for his ride home."

"Yes, we dispatched a very reputable driver when we received the report. Thank you for your concern."

Cora got up and put her hand on Callie's when she heard her say good-bye. "That was the hospital transport people, wasn't it?"

Callie nodded. "She said they're taking care of it."

"Well, that man was just plain rude and he deserves any comeuppance he gets."

Ralph frowned. "Ah bet he ain't a happy man." His face pinched with remorse for a few seconds as he looked at Cora. "Ah'm ashamed ta think Ah was like that."

Cora smiled at him. "I know. But you've changed. And you've apologized, so you don't have to be sorry about it anymore." She walked over to him and gave him a kiss.

Callie's shoulders relaxed when he took Cora's hand. Callie was still amazed at the transformation he'd made over the last couple of years. It was a long and difficult challenge for him to quit drinking and gambling, and especially to adjust his attitude. He resisted, but getting him to see the therapist was what helped Ralph to recognize how his actions affected others. She admired Cora for her determined loyalty, especially when Ralph had been so cantankerous for all those many years before his transformation.

When Callie heard the mailman drive by, she went out to the mailbox at the street to collect the day's delivery. She flipped through several bills, catalogues, and flyers. When she saw a hand-addressed letter for Cora, she smiled with curiosity. She remembered the name Donna Turner, but she couldn't help but suck in a gasp when she saw that the return address was from a jailhouse in Newport. *How does grandma know a criminal?* There was a story here, so she hurried into the house.

She placed the mail onto the dinette table in front of Cora, with the letter of concern on top.

When Cora saw who it was from, she smiled instantly. But when she saw where it was from, shock replaced it.

Concerned, Ralph looked at her with a frown and asked, "Whats'a matter?"

Either Cora was so focused that she didn't hear him, or she ignored him. She literally tore the letter open and started to read it. Her hands trembled, a desperate frown gripped her as her mouth gaped, and it seemed as if she'd stopped breathing.

To avoid bursting from the compelling desire to know, Callie wiped down the dinette table while focusing on Cora. The letter obviously had terrible news and she didn't want to have to deal with a medical emergency on Cora's part.

Then she remembered that grandma had received a heavy package from Donna Turner about a month ago. She didn't recall whether it was from a jailhouse or not. After Cora opened it, she insisted that it be put in the attic. Callie wondered if the letter and the package might be related because the package was the first delivery she'd seen from Donna since Callie started living here; and now Cora got this disturbing letter so soon after that. It was torture to hold her tongue, but she waited nonetheless.

Callie jumped when Cora let out an anguished wail.

Cora had finished reading and her hands slowly landed in her lap, still holding the letter. Cora closed her eyes and a tear trickled down her cheek.

"What is it?" Ralph demanded.

Callie couldn't contain herself anymore. "Are you okay?"

Staring at the letter, Cora slowly shook her head. "I can't believe it. It can't be true."

Callie sat down beside her and put her arm around Cora's shoulder. "Grandma, what is it?"

Cora looked at her beseechingly, her voice weak as she asked, "Is Rudy still investigating?"

"Not really. Besides, he and Georgia are on vacation. And even when they get back, he'll be helping Mark to get the children's center ready to open. Why?" Rudy had been an investigator for over 40 years. But when his wife Georgia got cancer, he decided to quit. Thankfully, she was now in remission. But why is Grandma asking about him?

Grumbling, Ralph threw his hands up and crossed his arms. "Dunno why Ah thought anyone would listen ta me anyway."

Cora hung her head. "My cousin Donna needs help. She's been arrested. She needs someone to investigate and clear her name."

"Rudy's been training me, I could do it. And he still helps me when I run into a dead end."

"But your classes. Won't your grades suffer?"

Callie thought about it for a moment. "It's still early in the semester, so I can get a refund. I can always take the classes later. This is more urgent."

"Can you handle something like this? The police think she murdered her husband. But I know it couldn't be. She'd never do that. She couldn't."

Callie stiffened in shock. Her eyes widened as she gasped silently. *Murder?* Her mind whirled with doubts — about her ability, or inability, to help. She wondered; what if Donna is guilty? She didn't want to say it out loud, but the police don't arrest someone unless they have pretty solid evidence. And sometimes people do things they wouldn't ordinarily do when pushed. But she didn't want to alarm Cora, so she decided to take a different tack. "Tell me more."

"We grew up together, over at the coast. Well, not in the same house, but we were always at my house or hers. And we lived near a state park, so we'd always make excursions on our bikes over there. I knew ..." She shuddered before continuing, "I know her like I know myself. She could never kill anyone." Cora looked anxious as she continued, "One time we found an injured squirrel at the side of the road. She didn't hesitate. She brought it home so she could help it. Her tenderness ... I'm ashamed to admit it, but she had more loving-kindness than I did. She never gave up, even when it seemed the squirrel wouldn't survive. It turned out that squirrel became her constant companion, loyal to the end. He knew she was a good person."

She looked down. "I can see why someone might want to kill Russell, though. He was always in some kind of sketchy business deal; nobody ever really knew what he did. He wasn't very pleasant. I think he might have cheated on her too..."

Callie groaned inside. *Perfect motive.*

"... I told her not to marry him, but she wouldn't listen. She had vowed to stay single until, oh, about twelve years ago. She was over fifty when she realized how lonely she was; and she didn't want to be old alone. Then Russell came along and wooed her. I guess she fell in love with the idea of marriage. After they got married, she became convinced she could change him. 'A diamond in the rough,' she always said; but he never changed. I could see how someone could do him in. But not *her*. I just don't believe it." She looked up at Callie, "Please, can you help her?"

Callie closed her eyes when she gave her a squeeze. She couldn't imagine anyone being more kind than Cora. "I'll do what I can." Dread and anxiety hit. *This is big. How am I going to investigate a murder? Especially someone who looks so guilty. I'll have to get Rudy's help. I really hate to interrupt their vacation, but I'm stumped.* There was no other choice. "I'm going to call Rudy right now."

"Oh, thank you, dear."

Callie got up to go to her room. She shut the door so Cora wouldn't hear the doubt in her voice. Rudy had married her mother's aunt Georgia just a few short years ago. Since Callie had excellent Internet searching skills, she had helped him by doing research on a case shortly after the wedding. Since then, he had been training Callie how to be an investigator and Georgia taught her self-defense and body language.

While Rudy's phone was ringing, she paced. She felt guilty about calling him. He was probably having fun, and Georgia was just starting to feel better. And now Callie was going to spring this depressing news on him, and ask him to help.

He finally answered. After explaining what happened, she asked, "So what do I do first? Who do I talk to? What do I look for? Where do I start?"

The moment of silence alarmed her. She hoped he was thinking about where to start, and not how to tell her to buzz off.

"Callie."

"Yeah?"

"First of all, breathe. And get something to write with. You were right to call. Her cousin's in Newport, you say?"

"Yes."

"Perfect, you can use our cabin while you're down there. Get the spare key from your mother. You can stay as long as you need to. But I've got to warn you, the electricity is kind of tricky, sometimes it just doesn't work. I'll have to get that fixed when you're done." He hesitated. "No, I'll arrange for someone to fix it right away. Just use the lanterns and fireplace until it's done. There's a generator, but I wouldn't trust it, it hasn't been started in years.

"As for the investigation, check out the newspapers, there'll be quite a bit since it's a small town and that's big news for them. Contact her lawyer to find out what evidence the police have collected. The police have to disclose all that to the defense, so that's the best place to start. When you find out where it happened, question all the neighbors, nearby businesses like diners, stores, somewhere the locals go to see if anyone saw something. Arrange for a visit at the jailhouse and talk to her. Find out what she knows, how the marriage was, his business, her business if any, financials, background, anything to learn about their relationship, their past, friends, etc. Keep records of what you discover, from whom, and when. Most important, not everyone tells the truth, so keep a good eye on body language. We're planning on returning in a week. Maybe we'll come out there after we get back."

She smiled. "I'd love to see you again. Although, mom might object. You know she loves getting together with Georgia."

"She'll understand." Silence again. "Are you planning on going alone?"

"Oh. I didn't think about that."

"Maybe you should ask Gary to go along?"

Callie hung her head. *Is he trying to push us together? He did know about Gary's feelings before I did. But then, that might be a good idea; we'd be able to see each other in a new light. That might help me to figure out our relationship. Although, I'll be pretty busy and that would be distracting. But then, he'll be a good sounding board; he might be able to help me out with the clues.* "Okay, I'll ask him."

"I was thinking of your safety, you know. No agenda. Okay?"

A self-deprecating laugh escaped before she realized he heard it. "Sorry. That was what I thought – the agenda part." *How does he always know what I'm thinking?*

He came back with a calming, fatherly tone, "I get it. But this situation is more important than that. Here's more advice, though. Don't give yourself away while you're investigating; make it sound like you're a disinterested party. Keep your opinions to yourself, unless you're discussing it with someone you trust. You don't want to give anyone a head's up. You never know if you'll be talking to the real murderer. Okay?"

She shuddered. "I wouldn't have thought of that. Okay." She could tell Rudy changed the subject to get her mind off the seriousness of the situation when he started telling her a little about their vacation. After about ten minutes, she was a little calmer and they said their good-byes.

Her head spinning from the mass of information he gave her, she called Gary.

When she returned to the living room, Cora was crying. She sat down next to Cora on the sofa. "Grandma, I talked to Rudy, and he gave me some great pointers. I'm going to bring Gary with me to see what we can find. We'll figure it out. Okay?"

Cora hugged her and wouldn't let go, saying over and over, "Thank you. Thank you."

Callie wished she had the confidence that Cora had in her.

Chapter 4

For the last two days, Callie methodically went through her list of things to do. First, she cancelled her winter classes for refunds because she would miss the beginning of the term. Then, she made several phone calls for the trip to Newport. To familiarize herself with Donna's case, she also did extensive research looking up the news reports about her arrest. The details of the case didn't look good for her.

Among the phone calls, Callie had arranged for Gary to go with her to meet with Donna at the jailhouse on Saturday, so the officers would be expecting her. She wanted to hear her side of the story. At Rudy's recommendation, she'd also made an appointment for them to meet with Donna's lawyer on Monday morning. Following Callie's instructions, Donna had managed to contact her lawyer to give him permission to discuss the case and give Callie copies of everything. When Callie had called her parents to look after Ralph and Cora while she was gone, her dad insisted she come by and get tire chains for the trip.

Today was Friday, departure day. Callie packed and drove to her parents' house to pick up the tire chains. Although she'd taken a driver safety course, she had no experience driving in snow. With snow still in the Coast Mountain Range, she was nervous about the trip.

Sharon welcomed her daughter with open arms when she walked in the front door. Callie knew by her intense expression that she was anxious and worried.

Jack was right behind Sharon. Although he had retired early, he still kept fit with his new hobby, restoring old cars. His sandy hair had started to thin on top, but because it was a light color, and getting lighter with gray, it wasn't noticeable except for when the light reflected off his head, especially with his buzz cut. His usually easy smile was strained and his shoulders were tense. Seeing him so anxious increased her own tension. Sometimes understanding body language was unnerving. His extra long hug confirmed that he was worried. She swallowed hard.

He put on that worrisome smile again, and pointed to a box by the door. "Those are the chains for your trip. You be sure to put them on even if the road only has a thin layer, okay?"

Callie nodded.

"And take Highway 18. It has a lower elevation, so there'll be less snow."

"Thanks, Dad." Even though she knew the answer, she asked, "How come you aren't at the shop?"

He put his fists on his hips and sighed. "Do I really have to say it?"

She looked down and shook her head. "No. I know you're worried." Looking up with a façade of confidence, she asserted, "I'll be okay. I took that safe driving course, remember? But thanks for the advice about the route; I didn't know that."

"That's what I'm here for, to protect you." He gave her another hug.

Callie needed that reassurance. The outpouring of love from her parents is what sustained her.

"And don't worry about your grandma and grandpa. We'll take care of them," Jack reminded her. "After all, they are my parents."

"I know this is a silly question, but did you bring your phone charger?" Sharon blurted out.

When Callie rolled her eyes, Sharon gave her another hug. "I know, I know. Just chalk it up to being a mom. And please, be careful, Honey. You know how I worry."

"It's okay, Mom. Remember? The driving course?" She smiled.

Sharon's face fell. "I was talking about the investigation."

Callie saw her mother twisting her hair and she felt awful. *Yup. She's anxious.* Nodding, she hugged her mom. "I'll be okay," she whispered. *I hope.*

"Be sure to call us if you need anything. We'll be right there," Jack insisted.

Sharon held her at arm's length. "Now, don't be afraid to ask Gary for help."

"That's why he's going, Mom." Callie looked at her phone, "I have to leave now to pick him up; he'll be off work soon. I can't waste any time. As it is, it'll be dark when we get there."

"And call us if you need anything," Jack added.

"Thanks, I don't know what I'd do without you."

Jack put the chains into the trunk. and Sharon gave her one last, long hug before Callie climbed into the driver's seat. As she drove off waving, Callie smiled seeing her parents standing in the driveway, waving back. *Love you, Mom and Dad.*

Chapter 5

It was just four o'clock when she drove up to the retirement home. Gary's schedule as a physical therapist was pretty lean lately and he was able to take off the entire next week. She only had to wait a minute before he came out with his duffel bag. He was ruggedly handsome with a well-built, six-foot frame. But it was only since he had proclaimed his feelings for her that she looked at him differently, and started to appreciate him with a woman's eye. His mischievous, brown eyes went well with his blonde hair and healthy tan; even though his tan was lightening over the winter, and his sun-streaked hair was growing out and getting a little darker. But that just added to his attractiveness. She caught herself watching him as he stuffed his duffel bag into the back seat, but she quickly turned to face the front when he got in. She didn't want to give him any encouragement. At least not until she made up her mind about him.

He sat down, clipped his seat belt, and gave her a big grin. "Road trip!"

She laughed. She could always count on him to lighten the mood. Heaven knows, she sure needed it. That was one of the positives on her list, that intangible quality that she appreciated about him, that he was always able to put her at ease – or when he was in the mood, to push her buttons. And he seemed to enjoy it way too much. Not that she gave him cause.

He worked near Clackamas Town Center and they had to crawl through rush hour traffic on I205.

"Hey. I'm sorry. I just couldn't take today off. Otherwise we could've gone yesterday morning when you called." The apology on Gary's face made her feel guilty for even asking him.

"Are you going to jeopardize your job for not being there next week?"

"Nah. They have temps and people on-call. That's what they were doing before they hired me."

She wondered, *is that really true, or is he just trying to ease some of my guilt?*

"Hey."

She glanced at him. "Yeah?"

"Don't feel guilty, okay?"

How does he do that?

"Guess what?"

"What?"

"You won't believe the patient I had today. It was her appointment I couldn't miss. Anyway, I'm wheeling her into the therapy room and she says, 'Where are we going?'" He chuckled. "I was pretty sure she had memory issues since we've been doing her therapy for two months now, so that confirmed it. Before I could tell her again, that we're going for therapy, she says, 'Are you taking me home?'" He laughed out loud. "You know what my first thought was?"

Callie smiled and asked, "No, tell me."

"I thought she was asking if I was taking her to my house. She's been flirting with me… and guess what? That's exactly what she thought."

Callie glanced at him, noting the sly look in his eyes. "How'd you know that?"

"'Cause she told me to go back for her toothbrush." He leaned back against the headrest and howled with laughter.

She laughed too. *I can see how she'd be smitten by him.* She stole another look at him. *He is pretty cute.* She smiled again as she made herself focus on the crawling traffic. By the time they made it to I5, it was already dark.

They finally started up the incline on the first mountain, and although snow was on the ground among the trees, the pavement was still clear. When they approached the first summit, snow was sticking to the road. Very few cars were on the road now, one in front of them and two behind. She was glad for the car in front. With the cloudy night sky, everything was black, oppressive, light-swallowing black, except for the headlights that barely revealed the bends in the road. Apparently, the driver in the car behind them didn't appreciate the danger and intermittently honked at them to hurry up.

Gary shook his head. "What's the matter with that guy? Can't he tell its dark and slick out here? Hey! There's a pull-out." Gary pointed ahead. "We can put on the chains and let that guy go past us."

"Good idea." She pulled over, and got the flashlight out of the glove box so Gary could see to work. The car immediately behind them went by, but the last vehicle pulled off the road behind them.

Gary pulled the chains out of the trunk and started to work. "Hey, it looks they're putting on chains, too."

Since the other car left its lights on, it helped illuminate the VW as Gary worked. "At least we got rid of the jerk on the horn."

"Yeah. He made me nervous."

When they pulled out onto the road again, there were no cars to light the way in front of them. Even with their high beams on, it was difficult to see where the road went at the bends. So, they had to drive much slower than before.

"Oh no," she exclaimed.

"What?"

"There's somebody behind us. I hope they don't expect me to speed up."

"There aren't too many roads to the coast, so I guess we have to expect it, especially with us going so slow. Besides, it's probably just the guy that pulled out when we did."

"Really? So slow, huh? I suppose you want to drive."

"That's not what I meant. I was just saying that anyone would have to expect it. It wasn't a dig on you or your driving." He looked at her with a frown. "Are you okay? You seem awfully tense."

"It's the road conditions, okay?"

"Look on the bright side, if there's an accident, we'll have help."

She swung and punched him in the chest.

"Ouch!"

"That's just what I wanted to hear."

"What? That you hurt me?"

"No! Your comment. I could use a positive thought; not that we'll be in an accident. How about saying that we'll be okay?" She shot him a piercing glare.

He shrugged. "We'll be okay." He rubbed the bruise.

"Too late."

He chuckled.

Callie's temper shot like a rocket. "Are you trying to make me mad?"

"No. You don't need any help for that."

She punched him again.

"Ow! You've got to quit working out. That hurts."

She hunched forward and her knuckles turned white as she gripped the steering wheel even more tightly. She stewed for several minutes, the steady vibration from the chains unnerving her even more. Although she'd taken that defensive driving course and knew what to do, she had no experience on these road conditions, especially at night. Portland just doesn't get bad snow. And it was getting to her. She made herself take a cleansing breath. "I'm sorry. I am really uptight. I didn't mean to take it out on you."

He opened his mouth to speak; then he closed it again.

"What were you going to say?"

"Nothing."

"There was something. What is it?"

"You'll just get mad."

She emitted a growling hum. "Maybe." She huffed. "Okay. I'll try not to get mad. What is it?"

"I was going to say that I'm getting used to it."

She saw red, but she held her tongue. "Meaning?"

"Meaning that it seems like you always take it out on me."

Anger flashed again. But remorse quickly replaced it, making her shoulders to drop. "I'm sorry," she apologized. "I don't know why, but … I just can't get out of that brother-sister mode. I feel like you're always jerking my chain, and then I feel the need to battle."

"I get it. I kind of feel that way too. I've heard that we take things out on those in our lives who won't leave us." He paused, and a sly smile flickered across his face. "And I think I like getting your goat."

"I knew it!"

"Just being honest." He moved just in time to avoid her fist again. "Are you going to keep beating me up?"

"Are you going to keep baiting me?" His chuckle irritated her more than anything he might have said. "So you're going to just keep it up?"

"I didn't say that."

"You didn't deny it." She wanted to stare him down, but that wasn't an option. They were on a downhill grade now and she had to keep alert. At least the snow wasn't as thick.

When they passed a couple of stores along the road after getting lower in altitude, Gary suggested, "We should probably pull over at the next place to take off the chains."

"Yeah, I was thinking that, too."

She pulled over at a closed gas station and the car behind them pulled over, too. "I guess they had the same idea," she said when she got out with the flashlight. But she didn't really need it with the other car's lights illuminating their work as it did before.

Gary disconnected the chains and put them into the box in the trunk. "I don't know how he could see what he's doing. I was barely able to get them on and off. And he's not even using a flashlight."

"He must have done it okay."

They got in and drove off.

Finally, she saw the signs for Lincoln City. "Thank goodness. I didn't realize how happy I'd be to see street lights." She looked over at Gary just in time to see him smiling.

She turned south on Highway 101. "Hey, Gary. Would you open the map app on my phone? I have Rudy's address plugged in. I know we're still over a half an hour away, but his cabin isn't on the main drag and I don't want to get lost."

"Sure." He pulled it out of her purse and set it up. "You want the voice turned on yet?"

"At about five minutes from Newport."

"Okay." He looked at the map for a minute. "Why didn't we go over Highway 20? It practically goes right by his place."

"Dad insisted. The altitude is higher on 20, so there'd be more snow."

"Makes sense. Hey, there's a restaurant open on the main drag, let's stop and get some clam chowder in a sourdough bowl. It's almost eight."

"Yes. I'm starving."

She pulled into the lot and parked.

There were more cars on the road in town, so they didn't notice the dark green SUV pull into the lot and park at the far end when they walked into the restaurant. The driver turned off the headlights, pulled out a sandwich, and ate in the car. And watched.

Chapter 6

While they were waiting for the check, Callie said, "Thanks for suggesting we stop. I don't think I could've gone another half hour. And then unload the car and try to fix something to eat besides." She smiled gratefully.

"All I know is that I was hungry. I can't imagine you not wanting to eat."

"Is that supposed to be a jab?"

His face fell. "No. Tension can use up a lot of calories, and the road was awful. So I figured you'd need to eat. That's all."

She lowered her eyes. "I'm sorry. I don't know what it is. I just get in this defensive mode around you."

"I guess it's my fault for giving you good reason. I'll try harder not to poke so much. Sorry."

"According to the map, I think it'll be closer to an hour by the time we get to the cabin. We'd better get moving." She reached for the check.

"No, let me pay." He took the check before she could pick it up.

"Thanks." Although she was an independent woman, she appreciated his gesture. She was in her second year of community college, so money was tight. It would be foolish to let pride push aside need and gratitude.

When they pulled back onto Highway 101, the dark green SUV allowed them to get a block ahead before following them. He kept his distance, but almost lost them in Newport. When Callie turned onto a neighborhood street, he turned off his lights before turning. No need to alert them that he was following. After noting where she parked, he parked a block away.

When Callie finally pulled up in front of Rudy's cabin, it wasn't what she expected. She had envisioned a lonely shack in the middle of nowhere, but this was actually more than a cabin. Yes, it was small, and it was on the edge of a sparsely populated neighborhood. There were even street lights. "I guess we won't be so isolated after all," she said happily as she pulled into the driveway.

"Pop the trunk," Gary said as he hopped out.

She pulled the lever and Gary grabbed her bag from the trunk, then he reached for the rest of their belongings in the back seat. Taking advantage of the dome light, she pulled out the cabin key while she could still see and then got out.

She unlocked the cabin door, and then they piled everything inside. When she flipped the light switch, nothing happened. She tried again. Nothing.

She sighed. "Well, Rudy warned me this could happen. I guess we hunt for the lanterns and candles."

Gary turned on the flashlight on his phone, and they started the search. It wasn't long before they found two oil lanterns. They set one on the kitchen counter and the other on a living room end table.

"It's really cold in here. I'll start a fire," Gary offered. "I'm sure glad Rudy already has some firewood and kindling in here."

"Thanks. I'll scope out the place. She sighed with relief when she found two bedrooms. There was one bathroom, a large storage closet, the stairs to an unfinished attic, and a minimal kitchen with a back door to an enclosed porch. When she stepped back into the living room, she stopped short. The sight of Gary fanning the start of a good fire reminded her of when Roy used to squat in front of her parents' fireplace, eagerly starting a fire. She froze as the memory landed in her gut. Then, she reminded herself that Roy was in the past. She took a cleansing breath, pulled the rocking chair up close, sat down, and stretched out her hands to warm them. "Thanks."

"What'd you find?"

"There are two bedrooms; you can pick the one you want."

"I think I'd rather sleep in here so I can keep the fire going. Besides, the heat won't reach the bedrooms; at least not enough to sleep well."

"Oh, right. By the way, Rudy said the electrician is supposed to be here tomorrow morning."

"Good!" Gary shivered.

She looked around the small living room to see what was here, and she frowned. The only furniture, besides a couple of end tables, was a dusty couch, a worn armchair, and the rocking chair she sat in. "I guess we'll really be roughing it," she said wearily.

"You take the couch; I'll sleep on the chair," Gary offered.

"Are you sure?"

"I wouldn't say it if I didn't mean it."

"Thanks."

"You get warmed up. I'll put our things in the bedrooms; except for what we need for now, of course."

"Thanks, again," she said appreciatively. She sat down on the rug in front of the fireplace and watched him as he juggled his phone and luggage on the way to the back of the house. *He's so sweet.* After he turned the corner, she stared into the fire. She shook her head as she wondered; *I wish I could figure this out. I can't decide this based just on physical attraction; although that is there. But that's not enough for a relationship. Do I feel that special kind of interest in him? To be with him forever? How am I going to decide?* She closed her eyes, trying to think. But the answer eluded her like an obscure figure in a fog bank.

He returned with her overnight bag, his backpack, and an armload of blankets and pillows. He threw the bedding onto the couch, looked down at his belongings, and remarked, "I haven't done much travelling except for trips home from college; and there wasn't much of that. I hope I have everything I need." He handed her overnight bag to her.

She smiled. "Don't worry about it. Sit down and get warm." She set her bag on the floor next to her.

"Well, there were the camping trips when we were kids. But I didn't do the packing." He shrugged and plopped into the overstuffed chair and jumped up again. "Ouch!" Rubbing the back of his jeans, he winced. "I think there's a broken spring in that thing. Guess I won't be sleeping there." He gingerly sat on the couch. "At least the springs on this are okay."

She seemed to melt inside. "Did you just test the couch for me?"

He grinned sheepishly. "Maybe."

"Thanks." She turned toward the fire and felt the sting of emotional tears welling up. *He really is sweet.*

They talked for a while, discussing what they'd do in the next few days. For tomorrow, they decided that he'd stay here until the electrician was done so she could go to the jailhouse to visit her great-aunt Donna. *Or would that be great-cousin? Second-cousin? Whatever.* She shook her head. *I'll just call her Donna.*

"So, when you talk to her, what will you be looking for?" Gary wondered as he took off his shoes and stuck his toes near the fire.

"I'll find out her side of the story, what she knows."

"You do realize she might just tell you what she wants you to hear."

"She's not a professional crook, so her body language should tell me a lot."

"You know, there are pathological liars, too. She could be one."

"Yes, I know. But I'll be talking to other people, too. I have an appointment with her lawyer on Monday. I'll find out from him what evidence the prosecution has, get names of witnesses, details of the crime; whatever he's got. And while we're talking maybe watch his body language to see if I can read how confident he is on the case."

"And?"

"Then I go investigate. Talk to people, look at the scene. You know."

He frowned. "Actually, I don't know. I was with you last year when we snooped around on that case with Vera, but nothing other than that. How will you know if you aren't missing something?"

"Rudy said to use my intuition. I guess it's worked so far." She shrugged. "Maybe I won't know? I still I have a lot to learn."

He looked at his hands as he warmed them in front of the fire. "I'll help if I think of anything."

"I was hoping you'd say so." She really wanted his help but had been afraid to ask, thinking it might make him think she had a romantic motive. Or even worse, that he'd think she was taking advantage of him. "We made a pretty good team."

A wisp of a smile crossed his lips. He looked up, and nodded. "We *are* a good team."

Anxiety hit. She knew that's what he wanted, and she closed her eyes to think. *I need to figure this out.* Trying to change the subject, she said, "Maybe we should get some sleep?"

His face fell as he went to the kitchen to turn off the lantern.

Great. I've hurt his feelings.

"I'm not sleeping in that chair," he proclaimed as he returned and rubbed the back of his thigh again. He stoked the fire, prepared a makeshift bed in front of the fireplace on the rug, and climbed in. "I guess I'll see you in the morning. Good night." He turned to face the fire.

Wrapped up in blankets, Callie got up sadly and lay down on the couch. She felt guilty for hurting him yet again.

After a few moments, he chuckled. "With the wood paneling, it's really dark in here. You know what that reminds me of?"

Relieved that he wasn't holding it against her, she asked cheerfully, "No, what?"

"Remember in the winter, how your parents pulled the blinds to block out the street lights and they'd leave a small light on in the kitchen? Then, we'd all scatter around the house and play hide and seek?"

She smiled at the memory. "That was fun, but you always managed to find everyone. So, when are you going to tell me where your hiding place was? Nobody ever found you."

"Well, I didn't want to give up my secret." He chuckled. "I guess it's okay to tell you now. You know the linen closet?"

"Hey, I looked in there, every time … well, I felt around in there. But you weren't there."

"Oh, but I was."

Even though he was facing away from her, she knew he was smiling. She could hear it in his voice.

"I'd pick up a couple of blankets, curl up on the shelf, and lay the blankets over me. When you felt around, I kept my arms tucked in so you wouldn't feel them. There were a couple times you actually tried to pretend you knew I was in there. Actually, you did that wherever you looked. It was so hard not to laugh at you when you were so clueless."

"Hey! Clueless? Well, maybe. I have to admit, that was pretty sneaky."

He chuckled again. "Yeah, I know."

She smiled as she snuggled under the blankets and stared at the fire. With him directly in front of her, she couldn't help but notice his form silhouetted by the fire. His broad shoulders were apparent, even under several blankets. She'd always known he was attractive, and there were many times when women flirted with him. He was attractive to her, too.

But this wasn't real love — was it? When she shuddered, she wondered if it was from doubt; perhaps lessening doubt? It was certainly more than just being chilled.

She hadn't been able to see him grow from a gangly teenager to an athletic young man. Those four years at college had really changed him. When he graduated from college and came back fully matured, she'd noticed. But at the time, she was still mourning the loss of Roy; so she didn't look at Gary in that way — until recently. With Roy definitely out of the picture, she realized she'd been increasingly seeing Gary as more than just a brother. *But am I ready for a relationship? Could he be the one? I wish I knew how to tell. Am I being overly cautious? Roy really hurt me.* Although the pain had lessened, it was still haunting her. Maybe with time, it wouldn't be the first thing she thought about.

Chapter 7

When Callie first opened her eyes, it took a moment to orient herself. *Oh, yeah. Rudy's cabin.* She pulled the blankets down from her face. There was a hint of dawn outside, but not enough daylight to illuminate the cabin. The only light inside the living room came from the faint reflections of the glowing embers. The cold morning air stung her face and she pulled the blankets back up over her head. She really didn't want to get up.

She could hear Gary's slow, rhythmic breathing. She smiled, thinking how peaceful that sounded. For a moment, she dwelled on it. *I could get used to that.* Just then, she realized that even when she was with Roy, she hadn't thought about that. Yes, she fanaticized about him. But never like this, the day-to-day living with someone. Like a true love. The way mom described it. *Is it possible?*

With the blankets still over her head, she checked the time on her phone, 7:40. *I'd better get up and do my run so I can get back by the time the electricians arrive.* She frowned when she questioned herself, *am I just trying to change the subject so I won't have to face my feelings?*

Gary stirred when she got up to head for the bathroom. "Good morning," he mumbled groggily, rubbing his eyes.

"Mornin'," she said quickly as she shivered to the bathroom using her phone to see the way. It was really cold.

He was putting logs on the embers when she returned. This time she paused to watch him, and she smiled. *I think I like this view of Gary.* She caught herself, wondering what that thought meant. Finally, she broke the silence, "I'm going for a run; I should be back before the electrician gets here." She put on all her warm gear and headed for the door. "See you."

"Okay." He raised his arm and waved without looking. As she thought, there was heavy overcast and patchy fog, but it gave the neighborhood an unexpectedly sinister feel. She felt a chill – not just from the cold, but also from a strangely vulnerable, almost creepy vibe. Hopefully, running would help shake it off.

As usual, each breath created a steam cloud as she ran. The exertion started to ease some of the chill. Even though the cabin was away from the main drag, several cars were parked along the street. There were no sidewalks, so she ran in the street. One of the first cars she passed at the corner was an SUV that had steamed windows and she wondered about that. As she passed it, she glanced in. Nobody was in the front seat and there was a mound in the back seat covered with a blanket.

She quickly realized that most of the streets didn't go through in this neighborhood. As a result, she had to change directions several times; so she was forced to keep a mental map of where she was and how to get back.

Backtracking after twenty minutes, she thought better of this route. Tomorrow, she would head in a different direction. It was light now, so relief hit when she saw Rudy's cabin; she didn't get lost. And with a sigh of relief, she saw the electrician's vehicle parked behind her VW.

When she came in, Gary pointed to the back of the cabin where two of the electricians were working. She rubbed her arms as she went to the porch where the lead electrician was working on the panel, and she asked them about how long it might take.

The lead proclaimed, "This is a complete re-wire. It's gonna take at least a day, maybe two."

Callie sighed. "Okay. Can you start right away?"

"Already on it, ma'am. Mr. Burke told me to get it done as soon as possible. The crew's already here." He sent one of his men out to the truck to collect more tools and supplies.

She came back into the living room to warm up by the fire.

"Hey," Gary said cheerfully. "I'll stay here with the electricians." He looked at his watch. "Did you say you're leaving at nine-thirty? That just over an hour. Just fill me in on what Donna says."

Callie nodded. "I know we planned on you being there, but I don't have your photographic memory. So I'll have to take whatever notes I can to remember everything about the discussion."

Gary shrugged. "Coffee?"

"Sure." She picked up a cup and held it out as he poured some from the percolator he'd brewed at the fireplace while she was out. "And thanks for making it"

"No problem."

"It's a good thing Rudy outfitted this place with the rustic tools."

"He knew the electricity was sketchy, so it's a no-brainer. I'm just glad the pipes didn't freeze."

When he said that, it felt like her heart skipped a beat, and she gasped. "I never thought about the pipes." She wrapped her hands around the mug and took a big sip. She scrunched her nose, wishing they had sugar. At least it was hot.

"Actually, if it's below freezing, we won't really know until we get heat in here." He picked up his phone and did a search. "It looks like the low for the last few days has been only thirty-five. The pipes haven't leaked, so we should be okay."

"And I was able to wash this morning. It was really cold, but the water worked."

He put his phone away. "I'll get the rest of our stuff from the car. Why don't you explore the place?"

"That's a good idea. I think I'll look around outside first." With mug in hand, she followed him out the door, but went to the sidewalk to take a more leisurely look at the neighborhood.

Rudy's cabin was halfway up a slight hill, about half a mile north of the bay, with the front door on the south side. The neighborhood wasn't as unpopulated as she first thought when they arrived. Most of the homes were an insipid gray. She wondered why she hadn't noticed that on her run. Perhaps it was because of the distractions of trying to keep her bearings, the strangeness of a different neighborhood, and the odd vehicle with the steamed windows? Besides, the creepy feeling lingered. *Must be the fog.*

As she looked around, she decided that the wind and sand must have sandblasted the paint off most of the houses over the years, allowing the sun to bleach all color from the exteriors. The cedar roofs had the same gray look, and although you would imagine that lack of maintenance would allow moss to grow up there, she realized that the constant scrubbing from the sand must have kept it off. Being a photographer, she imagined she was looking at a black and white photo from the depression era. The only color in the scene came from two hardy cyclamen plants poking their heads up from among the weeds in Rudy's yard. It was so incongruous that she took a picture.

Taking a closer look at Rudy's cabin, she saw a window for the attic and that reminded her to look up there sometime. She hadn't taken too much notice when they arrived last night, but there was an unattached garage at the end of a gravel driveway to the right of the cabin.

Living in Portland, Rudy just didn't have time to maintain this place, and he'd said that it already needed repairs when he bought it many years ago. She climbed back up the four stairs of the covered porch that extended across the entire front of the house. To the west, there was a retaining wall at the edge of the property where the ground dropped down about two feet because of the hillside. Along the north side, the back, a row of hemlock trees separated the cabin from the cabin on the other side. The siding and ornate gingerbread trim that graced the peaks and all along the underside of the porch roof were in various stages of deterioration, chipping paint, broken edges, and missing pieces. The floorboards on the porch looked well-worn, almost to the point of rotting. *If this place was fixed up, it'd be really cute.* She decided to memorialize the interestingly dismal scene with more pictures.

She paused at the western corner of the porch which gave her a partial view of the bay. The fog was lifting, so she hung onto a post and leaned out far over the rail. She could barely see the south end of the Yaquina Bay Bridge. She smiled at the scene and took another picture. Just then, a board creaked. Thinking it would break, she quickly evened her weight. *I've got to remember, this place might not be safe.*

"Nice view," Gary said, startling her from behind.

"I didn't see you come up."

"Hey, this salt air makes me hungry. You want to go grab something to eat, or do you want me to go get something?"

"Would you mind? I want to keep looking around. Besides, I don't want to leave the electricians alone."

"Sure, what should I get?"

"Mmm, how about something hearty and hot? All that shivering last night made me really hungry."

"I know it's your baby, but I'll be gentle." He held out his hand and cocked an eyebrow.

"Oh, right. The keys." She blushed as she pulled them from her pocket and put them in his hand." She got a tingle when she felt the warmth of his hand.

He smiled.

Did he feel it too? She had to get her mind off the subject.

As Gary drove off, she could hear the electricians working inside, opening walls. She went upstairs to the attic. It was especially cold up there, and it smelled musty. With no heat, it was no wonder. A small window at each end of the peak let in very little light. She was just able to stand up straight at the very center because the roof sloped down almost to the floor at the sides. The flashlight barely pierced the darkness so that she could only see where it touched, revealing a floor of old boards on about two-thirds of the area, and towards the back, only 2x10s with very little insulation between them. *No wonder it's so cold.* A quick look revealed nothing interesting, so she turned around to go back downstairs.

Gary came back within twenty minutes and she met him on the porch.

"I brought you an egg and sausage sandwich and a fruit and yogurt parfait. And hot chocolate."

Eagerly, she helped him carry everything in. "Thanks. Let's eat by the fire. I know the electricians are making a lot of noise, but it's warmer there."

When he held the door for her, she smiled and said, "Thanks. You're a real gentleman."

"Hey, dad taught me well. Besides, I like helping you."

She hoped he didn't see the blush on her face as she sat in front of the fireplace. *Why am I so resistant to him?* She pulled out the sandwich, took a bite, and chewed slowly. "Mmm. This is so good." She ate quietly for a couple minutes. "I think it's cool you still refer to him as 'dad'."

"Well, he was more of a dad than mine was. And I really feel it."

She felt a warm glow.

"Hey," Gary said quietly. "I was thinking. I know you told me what grandma said about her cousin. Do you suppose it's really just a big mistake? Maybe even a frame-up?"

"I don't know. Rudy said never to make up your mind before getting all the facts. So, I guess it's a possibility. Have you thought of any questions to ask?"

He shrugged. "You're the P.I. Have you?"

Her shoulders dropped. "Do you think I'm in over my head?"

"I don't know. But I know that I was absolutely overwhelmed last year when we got tangled with the mob." He stiffened visibly. "Do you think it'll be that bad?"

"I *hope* not. But I worry that if she's innocent, will I be able to do her justice? Her lawyer must have an investigator. How could I expect to do any better? I don't even know the area." She sighed, took another bite, and chewed slowly.

Gary looked at his watch. "How far away is the jailhouse?"

"About twenty minutes."

"Just to let you know, you should leave in about ten minutes."

"I think I'll go wash up now; then I can warm up in front of the fire before I leave. I'll finish breakfast in the car if I have to."

"Don't forget to charge your phone in the car. We won't have electricity for a while."

"Oh, right. Thanks for the reminder."

Washing with ice-cold water in a cold room in the middle of winter was torture. Again. *Thank goodness the pipes weren't frozen. Cold water is better than none at all. I guess.* By the time she was finished, she was shivering. The fireplace was not enough to take off the chill. To top it off, the heater in the car was slow to heat up. *I'm sure going to be glad when that electricity is working.*

Chapter 8

It was just before noon and Gary was putting more wood on the fire when she drove up. With a glint in his eye, he jumped up and hurried to hide behind the hall door where he could watch through the crack it made while it sat ajar.

She hurried in, shut the door behind her, and called out, "I'm back." She looked around, put her tablet on one of the end tables, and tapped her chin.

Gary smiled when he saw that. That's what Rudy did when he was thinking. Callie was still unaware that she'd taken on that same mannerism, and he wasn't going to let her know that's what she does.

Callie looked around the corner into the kitchen.

Gary readied himself when she walked towards the hallway. Just as she passed the door, he jumped out and grabbed her.

She shouted, grabbed and twisted his arm, kneed him in the groin, and threw him to the floor.

He rolled over slowly, groaning.

"Gary?!"

All he could do was croak, "Did you just shout 'hi-yah'?"

"Did you really think that was a good idea for a prank?"

"I did at the time," he whispered. "Oh-h…"

She helped him to the couch. She stood over him with her fists on her hips. "I guess you won't be doing that again."

He slowly shook his head.

She picked up her tablet, sat down next to him, and waited for him to recover.

"I guess I deserved it. Forgot about your training." He took in a shaky breath. "Okay, I'm good, really. How'd it go?" He forced a smile.

They didn't notice the lead electrician going from one bedroom to the next chuckling to himself.

"I put all my impressions and the questions on my tablet. But I had to wait until I got back to the car."

Gary chuckled.

"What?"

"If I'd been there, I could've helped you remember everything."

She huffed and stared. "Well, you weren't, so I did what I could!"

He shook his head. *She's so defensive. I wish she could relax a little.*

She eyed him. "What?"

"You don't want to hear it."

"Hear what? Do you think I'll be insulted?" she challenged.

He shrugged.

"You do, don't you?" She stood up with her hands on her hips again and started to tell him off. "You think …"

"Hey…" He reached out and took her hand. "I was just thinking that … that we make a good team. That's all." He smiled gently. "And you're cute when you're defensive."

Callie's face felt warm as she turned away. She knew he'd seen her embarrassment.

Gary got down on the floor closer to the fire and sat down cross-legged on a blanket. He patted the spot next to him. "Come sit down. Tell me how it went."

Feeling uneasy, she fussed with her tablet. She decided to just get to Donna's interview. "The jailhouse was kind of like when we visited Vera at the Oregon State Hospital last year; really noisy, guards everywhere, we couldn't touch. You know the drill. Only this was more depressing. Even though it was well-lit, it still felt dingy."

"I can't imagine what she feels like. How was she?"

"Depressed. Hopeless. I don't know if I can help her. I want to; I just don't know what my chances are of finding anything the police haven't."

"Just start from the beginning. What did you see when she came in?"

"She wore a rumpled, orange jumpsuit, and she had her gray hair pulled back in a ponytail. It was weird though. She really reminded me of grandma before she made all those changes three years ago. Did you know Donna's the same age as grandma? Their birthdays are only a day apart; of the same year."

Gary stiffened in surprise. "Really? That's a weird coincidence."

"Right? She made me think of how grandma might look in ten years. Only worse. I can think of two reasons why grandma looks better; grandma's more upbeat now, and Donna's going through this awful mess. Mom says that stress can make you look older." Callie paused for a moment to think, and then continued.

"Her eyes are the same brown as grandma, but tense, sad, and red; I'm pretty sure she was crying. That can make you look older, too. Her body type is a plump pear, like grandma was before she lost weight. She had a lot of worry lines; not recent, but deep creases like she's been worried for years. Lots of tension in her shoulders and face. From the way she held herself, kind of slouched, I think she's given up." Callie looked down to her hands as she rubbed one over the other. "I guess I'd look like that too if I was in her position."

She looked up again. "Grandma let Donna know I was coming. She was disappointed that grandma couldn't make it; but she understood because of grandpa's health. Anyway, she wants me to check things out for her. Right after I introduced myself, she said, 'I didn't do it.'"

"Doesn't everyone say that?"

"Yes, but the look on her face; I think I believe her. She just looked so innocent and vulnerable."

"But you don't know her; she could be really good at lying."

"I thought of that too, and I reminded myself that Rudy taught me not to make judgments until I have all the facts. Anyway, when I asked her to tell me what happened, I could see the weariness in her face, I guess from having to recount her story for the umpteenth time.

"She said the first thing she remembered was waking up to a lot of commotion in the middle of the night, around two. She got up, put on her robe, and looked outside. Even though the outbuilding isn't within sight, she could tell it was on fire, from the glow and smoke. The fire department was there."

"Why didn't the sirens wake her?"

"I don't know. I didn't think to ask." Callie's shoulders dropped. "I knew it. You should've been there."

"It's okay. We'll probably go back and we can ask then. So, the fire engines were there. What next?"

"Apparently, one of the neighbors had called them."

"An outbuilding?"

"Yeah. She said it used to be a barn, but Russell fixed it up for his business. She said he must have had his supplies and inventory out there, 'cause he didn't keep anything in the house."

"We'll need to see how big that building was. And find out what was in it."

"I'm planning to go out there to check it out."

"What kind of business was it?"

Callie scratched her head. "You know, when I asked her that, she hesitated like she really had to think about it, and said she didn't know. That made me wonder. I noted my impressions on my tablet. Here." She pulled up the notes and let him read them.

> *About not knowing his business – Bad memory? Concocting a story? Doesn't really know?*
>
> *Looking down a lot. Shy and timid? Or shamed and guilty? Maybe just hopeless?*

"After a moment of looking like she was thinking, she said she never really knew what he did, and he'd change the subject whenever she'd ask. Then she paused again and slouched. She said she gave up trying to be interested. Here's more notes."

> *Was he really secretive? Sounds odd and suspicious. Or is she making up the whole story? Is she hiding something?*

"We should get the police reports; they should have a clue in there about what kind of business he had," Gary suggested.

"That's on the list of things to do." Callie's hands dropped to her lap. "Do you think she really doesn't know?"

Gary seemed to mull that over in his mind. "I've actually heard of cases where the husband was secretive and the wife really didn't know anything. And there are some spouses who want to be in total control."

Callie's face fell. "I guess you're right. I feel really sorry for her."

"Be careful, though. If she's lying, you don't want to get suckered in. But then, if he was secretive, odd, and suspicious… We're going to treat this as if it could be either way."

Callie huffed. "Right. So, back to the interview. She said when she saw the fire, she put on her coat and boots, and by the time she got outside, the whole building was burning and the firemen had two trucks and several hoses spraying on it. She was thankful the building was a ways from the house; it could have caught the house on fire, too. I could see in her face that she had that sick, horror come over her at the thought that if it did, she could've died in her sleep." Callie shook her head slowly. "You can't fake that kind of dread. I can't help but feel it was genuine."

"Do you think you're getting too emotionally involved?" Gary looked worried.

"I can't help it if I'm empathetic. I can't help myself; I believe her. Not necessarily from what she said, but more from her body language."

He looked at her straight on and asked slowly, "Could it also be because she resembles grandma so much?"

Callie stared at him blankly for a moment. "Huh. I don't know." Then, she rested her forehead in her hands with her elbows dug into her knees. "I guess it's possible," she mumbled.

"Two trucks, huh? The fire was that big? I wonder if all his records and inventory were destroyed? And who called it in? We need to find out which neighbor it was, and how close they live. And why they were up in the middle of the night."

"Those are good questions." She made a note on her tablet to check that out. "When she told me they found Russell's burned body, she looked genuinely distressed."

Gary raised an eyebrow. "Could that be from the shock of finding out he was dead, or was she faking it?"

"Another good question." She made another note on the tablet.

"So that's when they called the police. But they didn't arrest her right away. The fire investigation results came back as arson, from a gasoline fire. And murder. He'd been stabbed first. Apparently, five times."

"Five times? Whoa. Sounds like the killer was angry. I've heard that usually happens in domestic violence. That doesn't look good."

She grimaced and added, "At least he was dead before the fire." Sadly, she looked at Gary. "The police found his blood on her butcher knife. It had been washed and put away, but apparently you can't get all the blood off. They did a DNA test. The blood was definitely his. They found his blood on her clothes in a paper bag stashed in her garbage can. The bag also had a rag with chloroform on it. So they've concluded that those were the clothes she wore for the crime, and she used ether to subdue him. And the gas can in the shed only had her prints and his on it. I know, it doesn't mean *that* can was what was used to start the fire, or that she used it recently. But with everything else…"

Gary grimaced. "So, all the evidence points to her, doesn't it?"

"There's more."

"Seriously? How could she look more guilty?"

"The door to the outbuilding was locked with a deadbolt. There was no key on Russell's body or in the building."

"I'm guessing Donna had it."

She nodded. "It was in the junk drawer in the kitchen."

Gary shook his head. "Oh, man."

"She swears she doesn't know how it got there. She said Russell never let her have a copy and he never let her in the building. He kept the only copy on him at all times." Callie rubbed her temples.

"What's your gut feeling?"

"Her body language suggests she's telling the truth. But we're back to the question, is she one of those people that can pull off a lie?"

"Let's think about this." Gary rested his elbows on his knees and put his fingers together like a tent. "There was no key on Russell's body, right?"

"Right."

"That means someone else locked the door. So, why is the key in the kitchen drawer? She says that Russell never gave her a copy, right?"

"Right."

"Let's assume she's guilty, for argument's sake. If he didn't give her a key and she stole it somehow, why would she put it in the kitchen drawer? Logic would dictate that she put it in his pocket before starting the fire, right?"

"Right. Make the story sound valid."

"However, if he did give her a key, why say she didn't have one? That would only arouse suspicion, because lies imply guilt. Why would she do that?"

Callie sat up straight. "And why lock the door? Just leave the door unlocked so it would look like anyone could have done it. This has to mean she didn't lie, she didn't have a key, and someone else put it in the drawer to implicate her. But who?"

Gary looked her in the eye and exclaimed, "The murderer, of course. And that means the murderer knew how to get into her house."

"And they would have planted all that evidence. But how did the murderer get her clothes? And why would they kill him and pin it on her?" She rested her chin on closed fists.

"If we find the motive, then we'll find the answer." He thought for a moment. "Are her fingerprints on the key?"

Callie's mouth opened slightly. "I don't know. We'll have to find out." She deflated. "But she could've worn gloves. You know, I didn't get the impression that she wasn't smart. Intimidated, maybe; but not stupid."

"Okay, let's move on. We have to find out what her lawyer's plan of action is."

"She told me about him. She doesn't have any money, so he's a court appointed lawyer, so she's stuck with him. She said he looks young and inexperienced, and apparently nothing's in it for him because he wants her to plead guilty for a reduced sentence."

"We already figured out she must be innocent. Surely they've thought out the situation. Why aren't they looking for the real murderer?"

"I don't know. It must be one of those cases where they say, 'Don't confuse me with the facts, I've already made up my mind.' Can you believe he's only talked with her two times in the month she's been in jail? The first time was just to introduce himself and take her statement. And the second time, he instructed her to plead guilty. She refused because she insisted she didn't do it. She sounded so scared."

"So, it's a good thing we have an appointment on Monday to see that lawyer."

"Right. We'll be able to get copies of everything. As soon as she found out I was coming, she told him to answer any questions I have about her case." She looked at Gary. "Can you think of any questions I should ask him?"

"Yeah. Find out what he's been doing for her defense. What has his investigator done, and what are the results? And tell him what we've already figured out."

"You're going with me, right?"

"You bet. There seems to be a lot more to this than we thought."

"Oh, and she's given me permission to look around the house and the burnt outbuilding. I have the name and address of the neighbor who has her house key. Her name's Sheila Myers. She's supposed to be checking the incoming mail." Callie paused. "Donna's worried about the overdue bills."

"Well, with her in jail..."

"That was my first thought, but apparently, it's been bad for several years. She said they've been getting calls from collectors for years. She'd tell Russell about a call, and he'd say he'd take care of it; but then they'd just keep calling." Callie sighed. "I don't think I could be in her position. Russell demanding that he control the finances, her not knowing how much he earned, the overdue bills, and she couldn't have seen the tax returns since she didn't know his income."

"Do you suppose he forged her signature on the taxes?" Gary shook his head. "You know that makes her look even more guilty?"

"Oh-h, you mean for a motive. I didn't think of that." She turned to look at the fire in the fireplace. "There's one other thing."

"What's that?"

"Apparently, there's an insurance policy for half a million."

"What? If they're as poor as she says, how can they afford it?"

"She asked him that when he told her about it..."

"Wait. She didn't know?"

"Yup. Anyway, when he told her about it, she asked him why he did that. Where'd the money come from for the premiums? Why'd he get it for so much? His explanation was that he wanted her to be taken care of. He said he felt bad that he couldn't provide for her like she deserved. Blah, blah, blah. Which she thought was weird because he'd never before made sure she was taken care of. She said he never did tell her how he was paying the premiums."

"Whoa," he breathed. "That really makes her look guilty."

"Remember, she said she didn't know about it until after he got the policy. I know, I know. It could be a lie."

"Even if she told the truth, she could be guilty. I mean, it would be a way to get out of debt." He grimaced. "Have you talked to Rudy yet?"

"Not about this. Not since we left Portland. He said that I need to check out their neighbors, their habits, find Russell's financial records, if that's possible, where did they go, who are their friends. That kind of stuff." She leaned forward, placing her forehead into her hands and her elbows on her knees. "What have I gotten into?" She slowly sat up. "Poor grandma. How am I going to tell her?"

Gary put his hand on her shoulder. "We'll get through this." He waited a moment for her to recover. "Is there anything else?"

She rolled her eyes. "Yes. Donna has a sister, Patty. If you think you had a dysfunctional family, wait till you hear about this. Donna said Patty thinks she's guilty and wants to get hold of her house after she gets convicted."

He let out a long whistle. "That's low."

Callie nodded. "Donna said Patty lives hand to mouth, never married, and hasn't had a steady job. Ever. And it gets worse. Grandma told me a little about their past. Their real mother was grandma's cousin, she died when they were little, and the father, maybe two different fathers?, they were nowhere to be found. Their mother's best friend adopted them, but then the adoptive mother got terminal cancer and died when they were in their twenties. She willed the house to Donna, and everything else, well almost everything else, went to Patty. Patty thought that was unfair and has always wanted the house."

Callie faced Gary with a purposefully blank look.

"Okay, what did you leave out?"

"Donna's worried that she'll go to prison and never get out."

"Yeah. I guess that's possible."

"But the thing is that Donna has to find something in the house."

Gary frowned. "What do you mean, find something?"

"There's a secret."

"Seriously?"

She nodded.

"Do you think it has to do with the murder?"

"I'm pretty sure it doesn't. Donna said their adoptive mother told her that she hid a secret for her. Just for her. Donna doesn't know if the secret's among the mementos she left her, or if it's in the house itself. Donna mailed the mementos to grandma before she was arrested because she didn't want Patty to get her hands on them. It was the only way she knew how to protect them in case the secret was hidden among them. Remember, I told you about her getting that heavy package. Grandma looked through it and didn't see anything special, so she asked uncle Dean to put it in the attic since he was over visiting. Anyway, Donna still doesn't know whether the secret is in those items, or somewhere in the house. If it's in the house, she doesn't want Patty to get it before she discovers what it is."

"Did Russell know about it?"

"No, that's why Donna kept the house in her name. She said that if Russell had known there was a secret, he probably would have torn the house apart looking for it in case it had any monetary value."

"Oh, brother." Gary rolled his eyes. "That's really sad."

"For sure."

"So she doesn't know what the secret is?"

Callie shook her head.

"Any clues?"

"Nope."

Gary leaned against the couch to think. "Do you suppose Russell was getting close to the secret? That could be a motive to kill him? Or maybe he did find it and it was worth something? And he was going to sell it?"

"But Donna doesn't know what the secret is."

"That's only what she told you."

"But then why would she send the package to grandma?"

"Good question." He frowned. "Let's say he found it. Could she have sent the package to make it appear unrelated? Or maybe it was a dark secret, like something that could scandalize them, and Donna didn't want it to be exposed?"

Callie's mouth dropped. "I never thought of that. If that was the case, then it would've been evidence she sent to grandma. Common sense means Donna would've destroyed it. Oh-h, this is getting confusing."

"It was just conjecture. So, does Patty know there's a secret?"

"No. But since she wants the house, we can't let her into it. I promised both grandma and Donna."

"I don't get it. Why did the mom tell Donna, but not Patty?" Gary looked genuinely confused.

"Callie slumped in frustration. "I'm really getting curious about what this secret could be."

"When we get back home, we're going to examine that package."

"Right," she said, staring at nothing.

"Are you thinking it might be something like what your mom went through, when you two inventoried Alice's mansion?"

She scrunched her eyes shut, exclaiming, "Oh... that would be awful! Donna's already had so much heartache." Her eyes snapped to attention. "Do you think it could even be worse?"

He shrugged. "From what you said, her husband sounds suspicious, too. But that's probably not related to the secret since it was her mom that told her about it. And that happened long before Russell came into the picture."

She rubbed her temples. "This is so complicated. I'm worried that we're just looking at the tip of the iceberg."

"So what's next?"

"I'll go to Donna's house to look around this afternoon, maybe see if I can find any clues to this secret. But I'll have to work on the most urgent issue and get the feel of the crime scene. While I'm there, that'd probably be a good time to talk to the neighbors, too."

"You want me to go, too?"

"Actually, I would. But the electricians are still here. I feel bad that one of us has to stay here all the time."

He looked towards the kitchen where they were putting in additional outlets. "Yeah." Turning back to her, he added, "You want me to get lunch, or do you want to go?"

She handed him the keys. "I think I'll stay and look around here some more."

"You want anything in particular?"

"Hamburgers? With everything. Maybe fries. And a mocha. Just make sure it's hot."

He chuckled. "My thoughts exactly."

Chapter 9

Anxiety was slowly building. The whirl of emotions and the flood of information were almost too much to deal with. Thinking about the electricians, Donna's case, and the ever-present indecision about whether to dive into a relationship with Gary. Callie hated leaving him hanging like this. If she decided to keep things the way they were with Gary, things would go on being awkward, probably getting worse. That would be too much to ask of him. But she didn't want to make a decision based on *the lesser of two evils* just to make the awkwardness go away. If it was the wrong decision, it would only escalate.

She didn't want to lose Gary from her life. But she just didn't feel that spark, the romantic tingling, the butterflies in the stomach. And that bothered her. Could she be in a relationship with someone, anyone, without those feelings? She didn't want to settle with someone just because she felt comfortable with him, but she felt that's how she was leaning. But this was *Gary*, the guy who was always there for her, always more than just a brother.

She wondered what to do as she wandered around the cabin to see what the electricians had finished and what still had to be done. She approached the head electrician to ask a few questions. "So, how bad was it?"

He stopped what he was doing to face her. "Just be thankful you called us."

"Why?"

"First of all, the breaker box was totally inadequate, and that's not even accounting for adding the extra outlets that Mr. Burke requested. Several wires had been chewed by what looked like rodents, maybe rats or squirrels. And there was no ground wire. You called us just in time. I'm just surprised the house hadn't burned down." His expression was dead serious.

A whiny "Oh-h," escaped, surprising even herself. With more than a little dread, she asked, "So how long do you think until you're done?"

"If you want us to stay until we're done, probably be done by tonight. That'll mean a couple hours overtime, and it'll save us from coming back out tomorrow."

"That would be great." A huge wave of relief swept over her. "And thank you."

He nodded and went back to work.

She felt better knowing the place would be dependable, safe, and more comfortable. Since she'd be in a bed tonight, she decided to unpack their things and put fresh sheets on the beds. She tried to concentrate on Donna's problem while she worked, but she couldn't stop thinking about her indecision about Gary.

She went to the bathroom to put her personal care items away and saw Gary's toothbrush sitting in the holder. She stood there in front of the bathroom mirror and cried. Everything hit her at once: this rickety cabin, Gary's sweetness and unwavering support, and guilt over her indecision about him. And of course, there was the enormity of Donna's situation all sitting on her shoulders. She felt like she was riding a roller coaster. Each issue seemed to be growing and demanding first place for her attention.

She had to distract herself, so she decided to explore the rest of the house while there was still daylight. She washed her face, took a couple steadying breaths, and put her toothbrush next to his.

As she made a mental map of the place, it was disturbing to see how much cleaning it needed. But that was to be expected since it had been vacant for so long. Dwelling on that, she wondered if a week would be enough to get the place clean and organized. But she didn't have that luxury. She sighed with resignation. Of course, Gary will be helping her until he has to return to work. Yes, that was comforting, but next week she'd be on her own. She shuddered at the thought of how overwhelmed she'd be when she has to do this alone.

Soon enough, Gary had returned and he called out, "Lunch is served."

His cheerfulness made her smile. That was a quality that dad had taught him, and she felt more at ease. She came out of the kitchen to find places set at the table with temptingly hot food. "Thanks. You're really a big help."

"Boy, you must really be hungry."

She groaned. "You have no idea."

He walked around the table and gave her a hug. "I understand. It's been stressful. You'll feel better after a hot meal."

She tried to swallow the lump in her throat, but it was stuck. So she just nodded.

After a few bites, she found her voice again and she explained what she'd learned from the electrician.

"That bad?" He looked genuinely shocked.

She nodded. "I guess we were lucky the lights didn't work."

He slowly shook his head. "I hope the furnace works."

She groaned. "I didn't think of that. We just might have to camp out in the living room again."

He smiled enigmatically.

Curious, she wondered out loud, "What?"

"I kind of enjoyed camping out in the living room."

"But, it was so cold!"

"I liked being able to talk about things before going to sleep. And the fire warmed the place up after a while; we'll just have it going earlier tonight." As if to avert her eyes, he looked down at his fries as he smeared some in the dip.

She had to admit that she had liked it, too. Dare she say it out loud?

"So, you leaving for Donna's house next?"

She nodded. "Any ideas for what to look for?"

He shrugged. "You're the detective."

She let out a huge sigh. "You know as well as I do that I'm not really a detective yet. I just thought you might have some thoughts on it." As she said it, she became aware that she valued his opinion more than she'd realized. Did she really just figure that out? And what does it mean?

"Well. Maybe look at how the layout matches with her statement. See how close the neighbors are, and what they might have been able to see. But until you get the details from her lawyer, I'm not sure what you can figure out."

"Yeah. I'll just look things over first. What about tomorrow? It's Sunday, not much we can do."

"Maybe talk to the neighbors? And you mentioned that Donna and her husband frequented a couple of diners, maybe the staff knows something about them?"

Puzzled, she chewed slowly. "What could they know?"

"I don't know. Maybe they overheard a conversation or heard them argue. Or anything out of the ordinary. Or they noticed body language." He shook his head. "Well, maybe not. I wasn't even aware of body language until Georgia gave me the lowdown on it."

Pointing at him, she mused, "I think you might be on to something. Impressions come from body language. Even if you're not aware of it, you still get a read." She smiled. "So, that's what we'll do. We'll visit those diners and talk to the staff. She only mentioned two places, so we could do breakfast at one and then lunch at the other. We can talk about it afterwards."

"Deal." He took an enthusiastic bite of his hamburger.

She felt more relaxed now that they had a plan and the electric was going to be fixed. She hoped. They still didn't know whether the furnace would work.

Gary found the access to the crawl space behind the house just a couple of feet from one of the hemlock trees and both of them investigated. No furnace, but he noted that Callie cringed when they discovered evidence of a rat's nest. He removed it and put it in the garbage can.

The furnace had to be on the main floor since it wasn't in the attic or under the house. After searching for a while, they found a utility closet off the back porch. Gary scratched his head. "Why on earth would they have the only access from the outside? Oh, well. Looks like it's a gas furnace." He slapped his forehead. "The pilot light. I'll bet if I get that going, it'll work."

Callie tensed with anticipation. "Really? Do it."

He fussed with it for twenty minutes and finally got it to start. He threw his arms up in victory. "Yes! We're going to have heat!"

When Callie grabbed him in a bear hug, the surprise made him freeze for an instant. Of course, he hugged her back, reveling in the feeling. He knew it was only from gratitude, but he gladly accepted it for what it was.

It was nice, like a tranquilizer and a stimulant all rolled into one. He really hated to tell her the bad news, but she had to know. And then it'd be over.

"I'm going to have to turn it off."

Callie stepped back and whined, "What! Why?"

"The blower is electric. So we have to wait until that's up and running."

Callie stomped her foot and grumbled.

She was so cute when she was mad.

Chapter 10

It was just before two when Callie left with her new video camera, a gift from Rudy just a couple of months ago. Using it here meant it wouldn't just be an expensive toy; it would be a useful business tool. Since Gary wouldn't be going, he said that if she took pictures he might see something she didn't. Of course, she had planned on recording everything anyway, but she hadn't thought about that point. The fact that she overlooked it made her shake her head. Rudy was right, two heads are better than one.

Her map app was a lifesaver; Donna's property was about five miles from the coast and hard to find. In fact, if she hadn't seen the mailbox at the end of the driveway, she might have missed it altogether. When she pulled up to the long muddy driveway, she stopped to give it a visual once-over. She turned off the engine, got out with her camera, and started examining the deep ruts in the driveway. She started reciting her observations along with the footage. "Looks like a dual axle truck went up the driveway. Correction; looks like different sets. The wider set is probably from the fire truck... it looks like there could've been two of them." She panned the driveway as she added, "The tracks extend across the entire width of the driveway. The driveway isn't that wide, so that's probably why the vegetation's been squashed along the sides." She zoomed in and added, "Vegetation is barely starting to spring back some. The regrowth looks about right for this time of year accounting for the fire about two months ago. Oh. There are tracks from a dually." She harrumphed. "Seems like it's been here recently, though, more recent than the fire truck. Donna doesn't drive, so who's been here? And why?"

She kept recording as she made note of oddities as she walked up the curved driveway towards the house. She was glad the camera had auto-adjust on lighting since very little sunlight reached the ground near the house. The ground was slippery from the rains, and it never really got a chance to dry out between one rain and the next. She walked along the grass and weeds to keep from slipping. Thick bushes and trees stood at the curve of the driveway obscuring the house from the road. Getting close to the top of the driveway, she felt oddly alone and it came out in a nervous whisper, "This feels really isolated. It's like being in a deep, fairytale forest, but a scary one, where ogres or goblins live. Where-they-lie-in-wait-to-gobble-up-intruders kind of forest." The thought gave her a chill and she shuddered which shook the camera.

She had almost gotten to the house when she realized she couldn't see her car anymore, so, she carefully made her way back, and drove it up to the house. She sat there, carefully scanning the area. She looked back down the driveway and saw that the tracks she just made were almost as clear as the ones made by the dually. She recorded it.

She got out, zipped her coat up to her neck, and panned the area. "The trees are so thick, they'll totally obscure any possibility of seeing sunsets from the porch." She shuddered again from the gloom. She couldn't imagine living here being so remote and having to endure that crushing feeling of depression and hopelessness.

"The path to the house is slippery." Then she made a slow pan from left to right of the small, dingy tan house with brown trim. Vines crept up the three wooden steps of the front porch and continued up the aged 4x4s holding up the porch roof. One of the risers on the stairs was missing and the other two looked rotten. The angled roof slanted down towards the right of the house. There were no eaves or gutters, so moisture dripped down the shingles which undoubtedly increased the aging of the exterior. "Not very inviting; unless it's to escape the ogres." Realizing she'd just said that, she shook her head and took a cleansing breath. More pictures.

Standing in front of the house, she noticed that there were multiple rutted, tire tracks where she parked, and recorded it. "The dually must have been parking here. "We know Russell didn't park here that night 'cause he was dead and the truck wasn't here." Then she added as a reminder to herself, "Be sure to ask Donna what she knows about the truck."

She walked up to the garbage can at the corner of the house and took a picture. "And right by the back door."

She shrugged her shoulders and walked slowly around the house, examining the build, condition, and lay of the property and documented it with more pictures. "From the looks of things, Donna and Russell must have had very little money; confirming what Donna said. Almost everything needs attention, repairs, paint, weeding, and a little pride. It looks like this deterioration has been going on for a lot longer than Donna's been in jail." She shook her head trying to avoid the mud as she headed towards the back of the house. Stepping on patches of weeds so as to keep from slipping on the uneven mud, a gentle breeze hit her. "A damp, burned smell just blew by. Must be from the building where Russell's body was found." Checking the direction of the wind, she figured the building must be to the left, so she headed that way.

As she walked, charred vegetation slowly came into view. Blackened trees surrounded the gutted skeleton of a building that remained. She noted, "Looks like the investigators sorted through the remains of the fire and left anything they didn't think was important." She aimed the camera at a blackened and warped file cabinet that stood alone among the debris, like a monument. Continuing, she panned the area.

"Looks like the building was about thirty feet by forty feet, probably a small barn to begin with, but apparently big enough for Russell's business. Just charred studs, the remains of burned furniture and tools. I don't see evidence of any inventory he might have handled. Could it have all burned up? Maybe he didn't sell stuff? But then, the investigators could have removed whatever was left. There's no computer. I guess they confiscated it."

She returned to the file cabinet. "Looks like it's fireproof, but the bottom drawer was left open. Too bad he didn't keep it shut." She decided to look inside the drawer and tried to pull it open farther. She grunted with the effort. "It won't budge. Looks like the heat from the fire warped it. Wait, I think there might be just enough room to reach in. Eww. The papers are water-soaked and the top edges are burned and disintegrating."

Hoping that the centers of the pages might be partially intact, she reached in farther. Still soaked, papers were stuck together. So it was tricky to pull them out, but they hadn't disintegrated as much as she expected. Carefully, she pulled some apart to examine them. "What?" She zoomed in to record what looked like newspapers. "Can these be articles about him or his business? Or maybe Donna? There must be some kind of importance to this, otherwise, why keep them?"

She reached in the drawer to pull out more. This revealed comics and want ads. Several more attempts produced more newspaper remains. "Wait a minute. All these newspaper sheets have been cut to the size of printer paper. That's odd.

"Looks like none of the other drawers will open. I can see why the open drawer would warp, but why won't the others open? Could they be locked? But why lock the cabinet and leave that drawer open?"

She headed back to the car. She had put the camera into its case, carefully put all of the papers she could retrieve from the drawer into a plastic bag. As she was ready to shut the trunk lid, her peripheral vision caught a movement about halfway down the driveway at the curve. She looked just in time to see a small person hurry into the wooded area.

She slammed the trunk closed and rushed to follow. Running up the path, she caught glimpses of someone in jeans, a black coat, and a dark knit cap dodging vegetation. The person had a good head start, but he or she tripped over a root and stumbled before going on. That helped her to close the gap. She was thankful that Rudy had urged her to run, because she gained quickly. Just as they entered a clearing, she grabbed the fleeing person's left arm, and a slim boy in his early teens swung around with horror in his eyes.

Panting, he pled, "I'm sorry! I shouldn't have trespassed. I won't do it again. Honest."

"I'm not mad. I just want to ask you some questions." She realized they were behind a house which sat farther up the hill. She memorized his appearance as they talked, about 5', maybe a hundred pounds, small brown eyes, sunken cheeks, and severe acne.

"I can't do that. Mom will kill me. Please let me go."

"She doesn't have to know you trespassed, or that you even spoke to me."

He shook his head desperately and cringed. "I'll get in trouble. Please."

Callie put on her damsel in distress face. "I'm helping someone in trouble. But I need your help." She nodded towards the house up the hill. "Is that your house?"

He cringed again.

"Come on, let's get out of sight." She pulled him back into the forested area and pointed to Donna's barn. "Remember the fire that burned the building down there?"

His eyes got big and his face became red. "No. No. I have to go. Now." He pulled, but he couldn't get free of her grip.

"Please believe me; I'm not going to hurt you. I just need some answers."

The boy started trembling as if she was going to beat him.

"Can you at least tell me your name?"

"Ethan."

"Your last name?"

"Ethan Myers. Can I go now?"

"What's your mother's name?"

"Sheila. Please, let me go?"

"Sheila? Is she friends with Donna?"

He nodded; still trembling.

"Okay. But if your mom says it's okay, will you talk with me?"

He grimaced. "Please don't tell her."

"I won't tell her you trespassed. So will you talk with me?"

"I guess."

As soon as she loosened her grip, he fled. She watched as he ran towards his house and rushed in the back door. She started back to Donna's house and realized that he had led her on an overgrown path. She wondered if he went this way often. *Since his mom and Donna are friends, maybe he saw something.* She shuddered. *Maybe Donna did do it. He'd certainly be afraid to tell his mom that her friend murdered her husband. If that's what happened, grandma's going to be devastated.*

When she got back to her car, she retrieved the camera, and as she recorded the pathway to Ethan's house, she explained her encounter. Then she added, "Well, it's not likely that Sheila is the neighbor that phoned in the call to 911. There's too much vegetation in the way. She couldn't have seen it. But it doesn't look like any of the neighbors have a good sight line either. Unless they saw smoke or flames above the tree line. We'll have to wait for the information from her lawyer to find out who it was." She turned off the camera.

Chapter 11

Callie was about halfway back to Donna's driveway when she heard a raspy mumbling voice. She quietly followed the sound through the overgrowth which led her to the burned out building, but she stopped short to remain out of sight. She watched a short, skinny woman whose thin lips gripped the stub end of a joint. She had glasses, a knit cap over short brown hair, and a denim jacket over a couple of shirts. She didn't seem to mind that mud was caking on her worn tennis shoes as she walked around the burned out building as if trying to find something. She would occasionally shudder or twitch.

Callie squinted at the sight, thinking the woman was high on something besides marijuana. She decided to just watch for a few moments before confronting her. Then she wondered if that was a good idea. Maybe she should just stay in hiding until this woman leaves.

The woman walked up to a bunch of burned items. She picked up each item, examined it, and then dropped it back to the ground while grumbling, "Never was no good. Probably won't find nothin' outta any of this crap." She stopped and looked down the path towards the house. "Maybe that car has somethin' in it."

That was it. This woman wasn't going to do anything to Callie's car. She came out from the path and called out, "Can I help you?"

The woman jumped, turned around, and glared at Callie. "Who do you think you are?" The woman demanded.

Callie introduced herself. "I'm here because Donna asked me."

The woman snorted in contempt. "I don't believe you. You're just lookin' to steal something."

"Isn't that what you're doing?" Callie asserted. "Now, tell me who you are."

The woman raised her shaky head as if to prove something. "I have a right to be here. I'm her sister." She pointed to her chest when she asserted, "That gives *me* first choice. You need to leave." She pointed to the road with a shaky hand.

Callie was pretty sure who this was, and she summoned the persona she had earned as a child, Calamity Jane. Callie had been such a rascally daredevil that her mother started calling her Callie, and it quickly replaced her given name, Diane. Callie planted her fists on her hips and confidently sauntered towards the jittery woman. Nodding with intimidation and contempt, she taunted slowly, "So, you're Patty."

Callie assumed with satisfaction that when the woman's eyes enlarged, it was because of fear. It seemed as if she couldn't think of a comeback. Finally, she woman muttered, "Yeah. What of it?"

"I know about you."

Patty's demeanor shrunk even more. Her trembling lips belied her attempted bravado. "I just remembered, I have to be somewhere." Patty bluffed, "You better leave when I do. Donna's gonna be mad if she knows you're here." She turned and hurried to the driveway.

Callie followed her to make sure she really left and especially that she didn't touch her car. Patty looked over her shoulder several times in her departure, each time increasing her pace. By the time she reached the street, she was practically running.

When she was out of sight, Callie made a note to herself that she would have to keep an eye out for that woman.

She decided to drive around to Sheila's house to ask for the key. She could feel out the situation while talking to her.

Chapter 12

Sheila's house wasn't in much better condition than Donna's. The paint was peeling and a broken window was boarded over. One gutter was hanging off the roof at the front corner. But at least there wasn't any visible rot.

As she climbed the steps, they seemed sturdy; but the moss and dew made them slippery. There was no handrail, so she stepped carefully.

She knocked.

No answer.

She knocked harder.

Finally, she heard footsteps inside and the door opened.

"Yes?" The woman looked at her suspiciously, and pursed her lips which emphasized smoker's creases. Her bleached blonde hair was pulled back in two pinch clips, but there were several stragglers, and she brushed one behind her ear. Her glasses sat low on her nose, revealing blue hooded eyes. She looked about fifty and a little plump, but with curves in the right places. She was wearing a blue sweater and worn jeans. Her shoulders looked tense, and her arms were folded close to her stomach. Maybe from the cold, or perhaps suspicion.

Callie smiled. It always helped to disarm people. "Hi, my name is Callie Cooper. Are you Sheila Myers?" Callie smiled again.

"What do you want?"

"Donna's cousin is my grandmother."

"Okay." Her voice seemed less tense, but her shoulders did not relax. "Donna told me you were coming, but I had to make sure. Come on in." She led Callie into a small living room with a worn area rug over faded floorboards. Straight ahead must be the kitchen since the stove was in her field of vision. Callie noticed that all the furniture was very worn when Sheila motioned for her to sit on the lumpy couch.

Callie carefully sat down and looked up. "Then you know that she sent me to talk with you to see if we can find out what really happened to Russell." She took off her sunglasses and put them into her bag.

"So you think someone else did it?"

"We want to explore all possibilities." *Does that mean she thinks Donna did it?*

Sheila nodded. "Can I get you some coffee or tea?"

"Coffee would be nice."

"Milk or sugar?"

"A spoon of sugar, please. Thanks."

When Sheila left for the kitchen, Callie noticed a door to the left was slightly open. She wondered if Ethan was listening from the other side.

Sheila returned with the coffee, placed it on the wobbly coffee table, and sat in an overstuffed chair with a floral design and doilies covering visible holes. "What do you want to know?"

"Is it just you and Ethan, or does anyone else live here?"

Sheila stiffened and her eyes narrowed. "How do you know about Ethan?"

Oops.

"Oh. Of course, Donna would have told you about him. My husband left … oh, maybe ten years ago, so it's just the two of us."

"I'm sorry about that."

"Oh, I'm not. We're better off. At least he isn't spending what little we have anymore." Although her words sounded like she was relaxing, her face and shoulders still showed tension.

"So what do you do for a living?"

"Why do you need to know that?"

"I'm just collecting information. One never knows what might lead to something else."

Sheila shrugged.

That's got to be a boob job. How did she afford that?

"I clean houses, do yard work, just odd jobs. At least we get to eat, and we have a roof over our heads."

Callie crossed her legs, hoping it would create a more relaxed image. "I was wondering, did you or Ethan see or hear anything that night of the fire."

Sheila shook her head slowly as if trying to recall something. "We heard the sirens."

"What were you doing? Or did they wake you?"

She hesitated and pursed her lips, which emphasized her smoker's creases. "I got up and looked outside. I wasn't sure what I'd see, it was pitch black, you know. But then I noticed the glow from the fire. I didn't see much with all the trees and whatnot. But, I was worried that the fire could get out of control and come over here."

"Did you see evidence of anyone out there? Or, go outside to investigate?"

"I could see there was a glow of fire over there. But no, I stayed in."

So, why did she repeat that? Nerves? Rehearsed lies? She didn't deny seeing anyone, and she didn't indicate whether she was asleep or not. And if she was worried about the fire coming, why wouldn't she investigate? Hmm. "Is Ethan here?"

"No. He earns money doing odd jobs too."

Liar. "Is there a good time I can talk to him?"

"His jobs are kind of sporadic." She shrugged. "It'd be hard to get a specific time."

Why doesn't she want me to talk with him? This wasn't going anywhere so she decided to try a different approach. "So, how long have you known Donna?"

Sheila put a finger to her lips, thinking. "Let's see, I moved in before Ethan was born, almost fifteen years now."

Callie decided to make her think she was a friend, and smiled again as she cooed, "That long? So, you must know them well."

"Yes. Well, Donna at first; before she married Russell. We hit it off right away. We helped each other out all the time."

"So, what was Russell like?"

"He was a nice enough man. Not like my husband, Paul – uh, my ex-husband. Do I call him an ex? We didn't really get a divorce, he just disappeared. Besides, I didn't have the money to get a divorce; and he was gone, so why bother." Sheila rested her elbows on her knees as she continued. "Let's see, Russell. He was a go-getter, always trying to earn money. Not like Paul. He wasn't home much, you know, working. But he was friendly. And like I said, if I needed a man's help, he was always willing to fix things."

"So, what do you think of Donna?"

She stiffened. "I told you, we were friends."

"Yes, but what do you think of her?"

"She's sweet and kind. Pretty mellow. Trusting." She shrugged. "A little naïve, though."

"What do you mean?"

"She doesn't know anything about business or money management. Russell always had to take care of it."

Yeah, well he didn't do a very good job of it with them so far in debt. "Anything else you remember about them?"

Sheila looked down at her hands and fidgeted.

Okay, what are you hiding?

Sheila looked up again. "Well, they kind of led separate lives. He was out hustling and she was mostly there alone. I felt sorry for her. I drove her to wherever she needed to go. She didn't drive, you know. And he didn't want her working. He was proud like that. And we hung around together, me and Donna." Then, as an afterthought, she added, "When I wasn't working, of course."

"Donna said you have a key to the house, and that you collect the mail for her."

"Yes."

"Has there been any important mail?"

"I've already told her about the important stuff and handled it for her. We arranged for a power of attorney so I could take care of her finances." She seemed to eye Callie suspiciously.

Callie didn't respond. She didn't want to alarm her, or cause distrust. "Donna said I could look around the house and I was wondering if I could borrow the key."

"Of course. But let me warn you," she emphasized with a pointed finger. "Don't let her sister Patty in the place," she added sternly.

"Why's that?" She knew why, but she wanted to hear Sheila's take on it.

"Both Russell and Donna told me, and I've seen her in action. That woman is greedy, and nasty. She's never managed her life well." Sheila looked up at the ceiling. "I guess I can tell you. She's on Medicaid. Claims she's disabled. Mooches off everyone. I'm pretty sure she spends all her money on drugs. So, naturally, she'll never amount to anything. But Donna doesn't see it; or maybe she does and just doesn't admit it. At least Donna's got it right not to let Patty in the house. She's already broken into the shed and taken most of the stuff in there; hand tools, weed whacker, lawn mower."

Callie's mind wandered for a moment. *That would explain a lot about Patty; doing drugs is a strong motive.* Callie came to attention again when she realized Sheila was still talking.

"…has always wanted Donna's house and stuff. Now with Russell gone and Donna in jail, she thinks she's entitled. So, don't let her in."

"Oh, of course not. I promise." Although Donna had warned her not to let Patty in the house, this information had not been part of the discussion. *Is all this true? Has Sheila's imagination gone wild, or could she be stirring up trouble? Or maybe Donna's too ashamed to tell me?*

"Good. I'll go get the key." After standing up, she paused to add, "Maybe I should go with you. If Patty shows up, she can be pretty determined."

When Sheila left the room, Callie made notes on her tablet. *If she's Donna's friend, why did she mention Russell first? Why did she lie and say Ethan wasn't here? Cora's and Donna's description of Russell doesn't match with Sheila's. Why? Donna giving her power of attorney sounds pretty sketchy, and scary. Find out whose idea that was. I'll have to get Donna's written approval to look into the finances to see if there's anything fishy going on. Friend or no friend, it's a huge step to give up control. Find out more about Patty.*

Chapter 13

Callie followed Sheila through the front door into the cold living room of Donna's house.

Sheila let out a groan then said, "Well, looks like Patty's been at it again. This time she got into the house."

Surprised, Callie looked at her. "What do you mean?"

"The TV and DVD player are gone."

"Are you saying she stole them?"

"That's right. I first noticed stuff missing from in the shed about a month ago. That must've been when she heard Donna was arrested. I've told Donna about it. Looks like locking the doors isn't going to keep her out of the house though."

"Why haven't you called the police?"

Sheila huffed. "Don't you think I have? They can't do anything because nobody's caught her in the act. They say it could be anybody. And it's not like they're going to sit and watch the place."

"Do you know anyone with a dog?"

"I guess that's a possibility. But then I'd probably have to be the one to take care of it."

"Yeah, I guess it couldn't just stay here alone. I'm going to take pictures so we'll know if anything else goes missing." Callie got her camera out. By giving that as the excuse to take pictures, Callie felt like she'd ease any suspicion from Sheila.

The inside wasn't much better than the exterior. The floors squeaked as they walked around. The living room was small, but the old, heavy curtains covering the one window in the living room gave it a dark and cramped feel. She guessed the musty smell was a result of the house being empty.

Sheila waved her hand in a grand gesture, but at nothing in particular, as she commented, "I don't know what you expect to find here."

"All I know is that Donna wanted me to look around." *She's starting to get on my nerves. I wonder if she's here to help or to hinder.* "Say, since you're paying the bills, why isn't the heat on? Mold could set in."

Sheila stood in front of the door with her hands behind her as if holding the doorknob. "All I know is that Donna asked me to pay the bills; and there isn't enough for the gas bill."

I'll have to talk to Donna about that. Callie took in the area as Sheila answered her questions. The built-out area next to the front door suggested a coat closet. She opened the door and peeked in. As expected, there were the usual sweaters, coats, boots, a couple umbrellas, and a plastic bag hanging on a nail that contained knit hats and gloves. There was no light inside the closet, and the walls were unpainted shiplap, making it dark in there. She did a double-take; beneath the coats, it looked like there was a picture at the back wall of the closet. She pushed aside the coats to look at it. *That's odd. It's actually painted on the wall.*

Callie almost jumped when Sheila said, "I wondered about that, too, when I saw it. Donna said her mother painted it. Weird place to paint it, huh?"

"I'll say." She took a picture and shut the closet door. Callie looked down at the worn pine floors, no rug. To her right, the furniture was sparse. A set of rabbit ears sat on an end table to the right of a fireplace which was on the south exterior wall. She assumed that must have been where the TV and DVD player were. To the left of the fireplace, a large stack of firewood took up the entire corner of the room. The rest of the small living room was filled with a rocking chair, a faded, overstuffed couch with worn spots, a floor lamp, and a couple of end tables. She glanced at Sheila and asked, "Have you been here very often?"

"Before she was arrested, I was here at least once a week. When I wasn't working, we'd cook, or mend clothes, or just sit and talk over coffee. You know, just to keep each other company. Since she was sent to jail, I've been coming every day to get the mail and check on things."

"That's very helpful. Donna's lucky to have a friend like you." Callie hoped a compliment or two might help Sheila's mood.

Sheila did seem to soften a little.

"Did you have a favorite place to sit? Living room? Kitchen?" Callie wandered to the fireplace to look at the pictures on the mantle as they talked. It looked like they were all framed home photographs, nothing professional.

"Usually the kitchen table." Sheila came up and stood to her right.

Callie picked up the picture on the end.

"We'd been fishing that day. It was pretty rare for everyone to have the time and the money to go. That's a shot of all of us on the dock. Ethan was just ten at the time. We asked some guy to take the picture for us," Sheila volunteered.

Callie studied their faces. Donna was grinning as she held up a fish on a line. Sheila and Ethan stood next to her, and Russell was standing behind all of them, wearing a bored expression. She noted that he was only a couple inches taller than Donna. He had a full head of medium brown hair and sunken eyes. Or was that just shadow from the sun? She looked again at Sheila in the picture. *This was taken before the boob job. Where did the money come from? Her husband was long gone by this time.* "Did Russell change much in the last four years?"

"Not much."

"Go bald? Gain or lose weight?"

"No," she snapped.

What's with her? Callie put the picture back. She strolled over to the end table, and pointed to the 5x7 next to the rabbit ears. "That looks like Donna, probably younger. Is that Russell next to her?"

"Yes."

Definitely sounds irritated. I wonder if I'm getting close to something. I wonder if it's because these two pictures have Russell in them. His eyes were sunken in this picture too. Since this was an indoor shot, it meant that the dark circles weren't from shadows. "Do you know when this was taken?"

"Donna said it was just after they were married. About twelve years ago."

"Are there any other pictures?"

"I thought you were looking for clues?"

"I just want to get a feel for them, for Donna and Russell." *I can't tell her I'm looking for inconsistencies. I don't trust her.* "Do you know if there's a picture album?"

Sheila paused.

Callie had the distinct feeling Sheila was only pretending to think about it. *What is she hiding? I've got to find out what it is.*

"Do you know how long they've had their furniture?"

Sheila straightened in surprise. "Why would you need to know that?"

Callie smiled, hoping it would disarm her. "Just curious. I need to learn everything I can about them, and how they live. So, I'll be taking a lot of pictures as we go," she repeated.

Sheila frowned suspiciously and crossed her arms. "Donna was always telling me how broke they were. Now that I'm in charge of her finances, I can see it for myself. So, I guess it's no surprise about the furniture. She just couldn't replace them."

"So, do you know where their photo album might be?"

"No," she clipped with defiance.

"Okay. Can you show me the kitchen? I'd like to get a feel for where you two hung out."

Turning away from the end table, Sheila led the way across the living room and pushed the kitchen door open which struck the dinette table when about two-thirds open. Standing in the kitchen while holding the door open, she held her left arm out. "This is it."

Instead of trying to hide her irritation, it appeared like she was making sure it was prominently displayed. Callie pretended not to notice. "Thanks. Excuse me." Callie squeezed passed her and pulled the string for the overhead light. She groaned inside when she saw the sparse kitchen.

There were only two small curtained windows, one on the east wall and one on the back door. With the surrounding forest and wood-panel walls, it was very dark. The single bulb fixture on the ceiling barely lit the room, which Callie figured to be about 10x12 feet. The worn, linoleum tiles in a brown and beige checkerboard pattern reminded Callie of a dingy, outdated diner. The small metal dinette table and two chairs sat at the west wall of the room just inside the door that had almost enough room to open. The south wall on the right had a few cabinets and a worn, single-bowl porcelain sink and an apartment-sized electric stove in the corner. A toaster took up half of the counter space between the sink and the stove. She panned the room with her camera.

The window on the east wall was between the stove and the refrigerator which stood by itself in the northeast corner. The back door was on the north wall and it opened to the enclosed back porch. The door inconveniently opened in such a way as to block the refrigerator. On the north wall, to the left of the door, stood a primitive, painted cabinet.

There was an open shelf in the middle with double doors above and another set of doors below the shelf. She walked over to it to see what was inside. The doors on the left side didn't quite open all the way with the table and chairs in the way. It was almost empty, just a few canned goods.

Callie frowned. "There isn't anything in here."

"Since she's been in jail, she told me to take the perishables and toiletries. No point in letting them spoil. I promise, that's all I took. Donna said it was okay. If there's anything else missing, it's because of Patty."

"Okay," she acknowledged, trying to sound pleasant.

The enclosed back porch was apparently an addition and she had to step down onto the floor. The furnace and hot water heater sat to the left, a door straight ahead, also with a window, which led to the back yard, and a washing machine and clothes drying rack to the right. She cringed when she saw that a space heater was the only source of heat in there; probably to keep the pipes from freezing. She took pictures.

When Callie returned to the kitchen, she shuddered from the cold. Perhaps it was from realizing how Donna had to live? She closed the door to the porch and realized Sheila wasn't in the kitchen.

The door to the living room swung open just then and Sheila seemed surprised when she saw Callie watch her enter.

That's weird. I wonder what she's been doing. She extended her hand towards the table. "So you two sat here to chat?"

Sheila nodded, looking impatient.

"Can I see the bedroom?"

Sheila rolled her eyes and spun around to go back out to the living room. She led Callie through the living room, and opened the second door on the left wall. Pointing to the first door, she said flatly, "That one's the bathroom. In case you need to know."

Callie swallowed the urge to growl at her and walked into the bedroom, which had one curtained window opposite the door. The bare floors were in the same condition as the living room, worn. The double bed took up most of the room. It looked like it wasn't properly made, but that the covers had been quickly thrown up to the pillows. There was barely enough room for the two small end tables, each with a small lamp, on either side. An old armoire stood on the opposite wall. If you wanted to call it that. It looked like someone had thrown together some leftover plywood with rusty hinges for the doors. There was barely enough room to open it without hitting the foot of the bed. It squeaked when she opened it, and as expected, it contained clothes and extra bedding.

"If you must know, Russell made that for her. I gather she nagged him for storage."

What? You said Donna was pleasant. Why would you assume she nagged him? "Is that what he told you?"

Sheila crossed her arms. "He may have."

Callie went into the tiny bathroom next. A small tub took up the space at the far end of the bathroom. The toilet was squeezed between it and the small wall-mount sink. A tiny medicine chest was attached to the wall above the sink. She looked behind the door and saw two towel hooks. She cringed when she realized the floor around the toilet and sink seemed spongy and she wondered if it could cave in.

Sheila stood outside the bathroom tapping her foot. Finally, Callie couldn't stand it any longer. She turned around to face her. "Is something wrong?"

"Yes. I have to get ready for a job. If you're done, I've got to go."

"Oh, okay. When's a good time to come back?"

"Call me."

Callie punched the number into her phone. Sheila practically darted for the door.

Chapter 14

Callie drove up to Rudy's cabin just after five and parked just outside the open door to the garage. One of the electricians was busy removing the overhead light fixture with attached pull string. She got out of the car with dinner and approached him to get an update. But before she could say anything, he dropped his flashlight. It landed about an inch from the edge of a grated drain in the center of the garage. But instead of rolling towards the grate, it rolled away and towards the open door.

He called out from the top of the ladder, "Would you get that for me?"

She picked it up, handed it to him, and headed towards the cabin and wondered. She looked back at the grate. *Why did it roll towards the door instead of to the drain? Liquids are supposed to drain down the grate. So, if it goes outside, why have a drain?*

When she entered the back door and walked through the kitchen, she stopped short. Gary was facing away from her, sweeping. A cascade of emotions rushed through her. Walking in the door and seeing him felt so natural. She could get used to this in her life. Then she saw his back muscles flexing with the movement of the broom. She was surprised to feel that level of physical attraction. Again. Maybe more than just attraction. Especially when he bent over to fill the dustpan.

"I brought food!" she announced, as she set dinner on the counter so she could take her mind off other things. She smiled when he turned around. She hoped the smile didn't reveal that she was hiding the lust she just felt. Her throat was tight with emotion as she said, "Thanks." She turned red. Trying to recoup, she added, "When you were out last time and I was looking the place over, I wondered if we'd have time to clean up. Thanks for helping." She could see by the look on his face that he probably suspected she was hiding something. She had mixed feelings about that. She appreciated that he understood her, but it was unnerving knowing he could see right through her.

She picked up dinner and waved for him to join her at the fireplace. "I got clam chowder, fish and chips, chocolate cake, and coffee."

He dropped the broom and rushed over. "Oh, yeah. But let me put another log on the fire. I hope we'll have heat tonight because we're getting low on wood."

"Oh. I have good news about that. I talked with the electrician earlier. He thinks they'll be done tonight."

"Finally, some good news."

She felt a twinge of shame and a lot of gratitude as she opened the sack. "Gary, I want to thank you for being here with me. I don't think I could've handled this alone."

He smiled softly. "Any time."

They unwrapped their food and started to eat.

"Something's bothering me."

Gary was instantly interested.

"When I got here, one of the electricians was working in the garage."

"It's okay; I let him in there to do the work."

"That's not what I meant. I wanted to tell you something else."

Gary's eyes flashed. "What did he do to you?"

"No. That's not it. Just before I came inside, I saw the weirdest thing," Callie mumbled between bites.

"What was it?"

"He dropped his flashlight and it rolled towards the garage door."

"So?"

"It landed right next to the drain in the middle of the garage. But drains are supposed to be lower than the rest of the floor, that way any spilled liquids flow down the drain. Remember when dad set up his workshop? That was one of the issues he had to fix."

"Oh yeah." He frowned with thought. "Do you suppose the momentum of the drop made it roll that way?"

She shook her head. "It was almost at a dead stop, but then it started to roll away, towards the door. Do you think we could check it out?"

"Maybe the ground settled? Did you see any cracks in the cement?"

"I didn't look for that, so I don't know."

"We can look tomorrow."

They sat cross-legged in front of the fire, talking as they ate. "I wanted to show you what I found at Donna's place." She turned on the video camera, and she commented as it played. She told him about Ethan and Sheila, but only giving him the clues as she'd seen and heard them. She wanted to give Gary a chance to voice his impressions, or ask questions without her influence. Or even better, ones she hadn't thought of. "So, what do you think about Ethan?"

He chewed thoughtfully for a while. "Maybe Sheila's really strict? He could've been warned not to take that path. Or not to talk to strangers. Then again, do you think he might've seen something? And admitting it would prove he'd disobeyed?"

"I wondered all of that. Then there's Sheila. Why would she lie about Ethan not being home? He obviously didn't tell her I caught him, or she wouldn't have lied about it."

"Do you think *she's* hiding something?"

"Could be. I felt like she didn't trust me to give me the key to Donna's house, but insisted on being there with me."

"She doesn't know you, so that makes sense."

"That's true."

When Callie explained about Donna's pictures, he thought about it for a moment. Frowning, he asked, "You're sure she didn't have the boob job in the picture?"

"I could tell. In the pictures, Donna was bigger in the chest. But now, Sheila's bigger."

"So, how'd she afford it? You said her husband was already gone by the time the pictures were taken, and they didn't have much."

"That's what I'd like to know." She ate a french fry and said, "I have a hunch, but I'd like to know what you think."

"Well, she obviously has a sugar daddy."

She stabbed a finger at him. "That's what I thought." She leaned back against the overstuffed chair. "I can't ask her about it though, that'd be weird. And she's already standoffish with me. I'll ask Donna the next time I see her." She made a note on her tablet. "Oh, another thing, she seemed kind of antsy in Donna's house."

"How's that?" He sipped some coffee.

"I can't put my finger on it, but she looked uncomfortable. And she even left the room once when she didn't think I'd notice.." She sighed. "I keep wondering, if she didn't trust me to give me the key, then why leave me alone in there? And what was she doing?" Anyway, when I came into the kitchen from the back porch, she was just coming back from wherever she went. She looked like you did when dad had to pick you up after you got caught stealing batteries for your portable radio."

He huffed, and then squinted at her. "You're never going to let me forget that one, are you?"

The devil danced in her eyes. "Not if I can rub it in." She giggled and took a big bite of clam chowder.

He chuckled. "You just wait. You know, you never would have found out if he hadn't brought you with him."

"He wasn't going to leave me at home alone; mom was out shopping."

"Yeah." He huffed. "My dad was home passed out drunk, so I couldn't call him. He probably wouldn't have come anyway. Even if he was awake, I wouldn't have wanted to ride with him driving drunk."

After a moment of empathy for him, she smiled at the thought of reliving their ride home. "Dad sure was mad at you. He really gave you the riot act. And then mom. She wouldn't talk to you for over an hour."

He rolled his eyes. "I remember, okay. I don't need a play-by-play on it. Her silent treatment was worse than dad's scolding."

"I know how you feel. I've gotten it before, too."

"Oh really. What did you do to earn her wrath?"

"Heh, heh. I'm not telling."

He shook his head before continuing, "Okay. Back to Donna's house. So do you think Sheila was hiding something?"

"Probably. But what?"

Hesitantly, he asked, "Do you think Russell was the sugar daddy?"

"No." she stated emphatically. "Donna said they didn't have any money. And by the looks of the house, it shows."

"Not that Donna knew about. He could have had money and didn't tell her about it. Remember, she knew nothing about his business, the finances, not even the taxes. He could easily have hidden money."

She let out a sigh. "I never thought of that. They did all go on vacations together. Well not vacations exactly, but outings. I suppose it's possible."

"You haven't had much experience with cads, so that probably wouldn't occur to you. Let's get back to Sheila. Do you think she was making sure there wasn't any evidence of an affair while you were in the house?"

Callie thought for a moment, and then shook her head. "I don't think so. Why wait until I was there? Donna told her I was coming. She would've had plenty of time to search there before I arrived. Besides, it's been a whole month since Donna was arrested. Russell was long gone by then."

"Right," he said slowly. "I don't suppose it really matters who the sugar daddy is."

"Not for Donna. But I'd be interested."

"You're just too curious."

"Duh. That's why Rudy thinks I'll be a good detective."

"No, that makes you a pest."

She punched his shoulder.

"Hey! That hurt."

"I know." She waggled an eyebrow at him.

"Well, don't pretend you're sorry about it."

"I wasn't planning to. So, no prob."

He slapped her shoulder, and she giggled.

"Just be glad you're a woman, or you'd get yours."

She feigned shock. "Violence? How barbaric."

"Look who's talking! Remember when you slammed me? Right over there?" He pointed at the hall door.

She nodded and laughed.

They stopped their discussion to enjoy the cake. Her feet were still cold, so she propped them closer to the fire.

When they finished eating, they discussed the burned building, finding the newspapers in the file cabinet, and Ethan. "You won't believe what I saw when I was coming back from catching Ethan. I saw a woman snooping around the burned outbuilding, but I hid out of sight to watch her. It didn't take long to see she was high on something. It looked like she was looking for something. You saw the video, there wasn't anything to find. Anyway, when she headed for the car, I had to confront her. There was no way I was going to let her break into it. Turns out it was Patty."

Gary sat up straight with expectation.

"I could see her twitching; and she seemed to have trouble talking. You know, finding the right words. She tried bluffing me into thinking she had a right to be there and *I* was the trespasser. I just put on my tough exterior and I challenged her. She backed off pretty quickly. Couldn't get out of there fast enough." Callie laughed.

"I wish I could've seen it." Gary chuckled.

The electricians finally finished their work just about six-thirty, well after dark. The lead electrician gave them a copy of the work order and payment receipt from Rudy's credit card while the other electricians put away their tools and spare parts. Callie turned on the lights and Gary started the furnace.

As Gary laid out the blankets and pillows in front of the fire, he explained, "It's going to take a while for the house to get warm, so I'm going to sleep here again. How about you?"

"Absolutely. I'm not a glutton for punishment."

"I kind of like it with the only light being from the fire. How about we turn off the lamps?"

They wrapped up in blankets and spent the next few hours talking in front of the fire. Callie laughed more than she thought possible. Since they only planned to visit the diners tomorrow, there was no hurry to fall asleep and get up early.

She didn't want it to end; but it was late, and there was a lot to do tomorrow.

Chapter 15

When Callie blinked her eyes open Sunday morning, she smiled. The room was comfortably warm for the first time since they'd gotten here. Being relaxed, she stared up at the ceiling for the first time. Then, she realized there were no ceiling lights, only lamps in the room. Funny how you notice more things when you're relaxed. She decided she'd have to make sure to be more observant, especially when on the job and stressed.

She looked over her shoulder where Gary was still sleeping in front of the fireplace. His rhythmic breathing almost had a low rumble to it. She sighed contentedly. She rotated from her back so she could face the fireplace – and to watch Gary without straining her neck. He had thrown off his sleeping bag, so she could see his muscles under his draped shirt. She already knew that he worked out and was fit. But just taking the time to observe him evoked a new feeling. Not just lust, more like a yearning.

She decided to relish the moment, letting his rhythmic breathing put her at ease. She smiled as her mind wandered, recalling the hundreds of kind, considerate things he'd done for her through the years; little, thoughtful things. *Funny*, she thought. *Those seem to mean more than big gestures I see in movies.*

Her mind drifted to the myriad discussions she'd had with Mom about men. 'They all have different ways of showing love, depending on their personalities, upbringing, friends, and so many other factors… It doesn't matter if he's the most handsome man in the world if he's selfish, arrogant, or mean.' Mom had told her about a time when she got her head turned by a handsome fellow, but it turned out that he was a lying two-timer. Thankfully, she found out before she committed to a relationship. All the more proof that looks aren't everything.

Thinking about all that put some clarity on how Gary treated her. His actions have shown how he feels; doing favors, understanding, being considerate and helpful, and especially listening. Although he's shyer than a lot of men she's known, he does seem more at ease with her than with other women. He's honest, hard-working, and genuine. And funny. She knew deep down that he loves her. She smiled at the realization that he's comfortable with her. Not that he takes her for granted, but he's able to be himself. She wondered if she shouldn't push his buttons so much. Nah, that wouldn't be as much fun. She needed fun and she knew he enjoyed it too.

Soon enough, she heard him yawn. He stretched, which tensed the muscles in his back. She smiled. *Yes, I'm attracted, but I can't let that distract me.*

He rolled over, saw her looking at him, and mumbled, "What?"

"Nothing. Just enjoying a warm house," she fibbed.

They both got up.

It was wonderful to finally have a hot shower.

Gary opened the door to the diner to let Callie go in first. He wasn't trying to impress her; Jack had taught him to be a gentleman and it had become second nature. Besides, the way Callie filled her tight jeans was nice to look at.

The sign said to wait to be seated.

Gary leaned over to whisper, "They look busy enough."

Callie had already been looking around, so it was no surprise to see her agree so quickly. "I hope that means the food is good."

"Yeah," he agreed. "After yesterday, my gut isn't feeling so good from all the fast food."

The restaurant was bustling, so Callie put her name in for a booth for two. While they were waiting to be called, Callie turned around to see what Gary was looking at. The entire wall of the lobby was covered in oil paintings.

He seemed particularly interested in the unusual depiction of a window. It was as if you were standing inside of an unlit cabin with a fire in the fireplace being reflected on the glass of a window as you looked outside. The interior of the cabin was out of focus as if you were farsighted; just blurry and indistinct. But the scene outside the large window was very clear. You could almost see the rain falling and hitting the window and making rivulets that dribbled down to the sash. The ocean view was dramatic; a stormy sky, crashing waves, and lightning in the distance. Although it was calm in the interior, you felt drawn to the wild and dramatic chaos outside.

Gary whispered, "I feel like the artist was painting you."

"What do you mean?"

"A whirlwind, always reaching out for excitement, danger."

Without batting an eye, she was insulted. But then she caught herself before saying anything. He was right. She had always felt drawn to the wild side. *He knows me better than I do.* Without a comment, she moved to look at the next painting.

This one felt different, almost like looking at Donna's property, but without the house. She could feel the dampness of the forest. Even though there were patches of vibrant colors from some small flowers here and there, it felt ominous, uninviting. She could almost see shadows of something, or somethings, behind the foliage. With a shudder she stepped to the next painting.

Gary smiled. "I like this one."

She had to agree. It was an ocean scene looking at the distant shoreline. Some billowy clouds and whitecaps gave it some brightness. Although you couldn't see the boat you were on, you could almost feel the boat rising and falling with the waves. There was a fishing rod in front of you and a buoy to the left. A striped lighthouse sat on a rocky outcrop just to the right and seagulls floated overhead.

"I like it too."

"Apparently all these paintings are of coastal scenes."

She glanced back at the forest painting. "Yeah," she clipped.

"Well, there are forests here, too."

"True, but I don't like ones that make me feel uneasy."

"Isn't art supposed to make you feel something?"

"Yes, but I wouldn't choose to own them." She moved to the next painting.

It was a sunny beach scene with multiple hot air balloons in various stages of leaving the sand; some off in the distance, some just lifting off, and another still filling. Dozens of people dotted the beach, some busy with the mechanics of getting the balloons ready, a few packing up, and many more spectators. Suddenly, she wanted to float off in one of the gondolas.

The hostess came up and announced, "Callie, table for two?"

"I guess having those paintings is a good way to keep you busy while you wait for your table," Gary joked.

"Did you notice they were all for sale?"

"Yeah. They were pretty pricey, too."

"I wonder if they're local artists," Callie wondered.

"Probably. Never heard of any of them. But that's not saying much."

Soon after being seated, a skinny waitress showed up just behind Gary's side of the booth and put a hand on his shoulder. She kept her eyes on him as she came around the booth to face him, and seemed to shove her bosom towards him, smiling as she purred, "Ooh, you're new to town. What can I do for you?" she chirped between pops of chewing gum.

Callie watched his ears turned red. *So, the red ears aren't only when he's shy with me.* Callie eyed the waitress. She had hot pink bed-head, a dragon tattoo on her left arm down to her wrist, and 5" hoop earrings. Her mini version of the uniforms that the rest of the staff was wearing sported the name tag, "Kiki." It was pinned low on her chest; Callie assumed it was to make room for the two buttons that gaped open at the top. Or to draw attention to what the opening revealed.

Callie narrowed her eyes as she contemplated this scene before her. It didn't take a rocket scientist to see that this woman was openly flirting with Gary. And he looked incredibly uncomfortable. Callie didn't know whether to be jealous or laugh inwardly. She caught herself. *Am I jealous?*

He ordered, "I'll have the number one, but with bacon instead of sausage."

"Sure enough, honey," she cooed.

Callie ordered, "An omelet with everything, and dry toast."

The waitress turned to her with a puzzled look. "Does that mean you want the pancakes, hash browns and sausage with it?"

Callie stopped for a moment to process that. *What?* "No. I want all the fillings that come in an omelet."

"Oh. Sure." She started writing that down. "Anything to drink?"

"Two coffees."

"Wow. You must be thirsty. You know we have free refills."

Callie groaned inside. *Seriously?* "No, I mean one for each of us."

"Oh. Sure," she said between snapping her gum. She wrote it down and swiveled off.

"Hoo boy," Gary breathed.

Callie didn't know whether to be mad or to laugh. "That was like talking to Aunt Bonnie."

He smiled wanly. Then he bent forward, leaning his elbows on the table. "Do you think we'll be able to get anything out of her?"

She shrugged. "She'll probably answer any question you ask her, that's for sure."

They both laughed.

Kiki brought the coffees, one in each hand, and placed them on the table. As she bent over purposefully, her bosom came within six inches of Gary's face.

He leaned back and asked for sugar.

"Sorry, I didn't have enough hands," she said as she pulled a packet from her cleavage. She waggled an eyebrow and asked, "Cream?"

Callie felt a twinge of alarm when Gary's ears turned bright red.

He refused to look at her and shook his head. "No thanks."

Kiki turned to go back to the kitchen, this time with a more serious wiggle.

Callie rolled her eyes. "I don't believe it. She could throw her back out with that much movement." She leaned forward. "Why would Donna and Russell come here?" she wondered.

Gary added sugar to his coffee. "Maybe *he* liked it."

Callie watched with a grimace. "You actually used that sugar?"

He leaned forward again, coming close to her face. "It's not the same one." He tipped his head towards the window as he added, "There's some over here behind the salt and pepper. I dropped the other one on the floor under our table." You want one?"

She giggled. "Yes, please."

He reached for a sugar. "What questions are you going to ask?"

"I don't know. Maybe you should. I don't think I can hold her attention." She gave him a sly grin.

"Hey! That wasn't my fault. I didn't do a thing to encourage her."

"I know. But she seems to like you. She probably thinks you're cute." She snickered.

He raised an eyebrow. "Oh, you think I'm cute, huh?"

"Oh shush it." She turned red. "Just cover the questions we went over at the cabin. And don't tell me you don't remember."

He shrugged. "What can I say? I could always say I got flustered." Turning serious, he whispered, "Here she comes."

Kiki put their plates in front of them, again leaning in to Gary. This time, he put his hand on her wrist.

She smiled as if they were alone on a date. "What can I do for you, darlin'?" she asked huskily.

"I was just thinking, you must know everyone in town."

"How'd you know?"

"You're so friendly, and you're bound to meet everyone."

She perked up. "Yeah, I guess I do."

Callie could see Gary was struggling to look interested in her.

"I was wondering if you know Russell and Donna Turner."

She stood straight and pulled her hand back. "Oh. Yeah. They've been in a few times. Him a whole lot more than her, though."

"Do you serve them?"

"He always sits in my section, so yeah."

"What can you tell us about them?"

She paused to think. "He's a really good tipper."

What? Callie wondered how that meshed with them being poor. Maybe he *was* hiding money?

"Well, he *was* a good tipper. I don't know if you heard, being new in town and all. His wife killed him."

Callie groaned inside. *That must mean everyone must think Donna did it. Not good to hear.*

Gary obviously pretended not to know about that. "Oh. That's too bad. So you must be pretty broken up about it."

Kiki shrugged.

"You said he was a good tipper?"

"Yeah."

Gary leaned in as if to get a bit of juicy gossip. "How much?"

"Don't ask me the percent; I'd never be able to tell you. But on a twenty dollar ticket, he'd always leave me a ten." She leaned forward to whisper, "But he'd wait until his wife was on her way to the door. He didn't want her to know, He said she was stingy. So, I didn't say anything. I didn't want him to get into trouble. He had a nice smile." She turned her back to Callie as she leaned on the table with her chest in his face again.

Callie could see Gary struggling to keep an interested smile on his face.

He cleared his throat and continued, "Do you remember anything else? Like, did they get along, what they talked about, anything?"

"They got along okay. Except for the last time. They argued. *Real* loud. In fact, some of the customers complained and the manager had to come over."

"They argued, huh?"

"Well, *he* was loud, but it sounded like she was the reason for it."

"What do you mean?"

"He was real defensive. Said he couldn't ever please her. He said he even bought that insurance because she insisted. He couldn't believe she was so ungrateful." She frowned, thinking again. "Funny, I don't remember seeing her look mad or upset; just ... kinda like she didn't want to be here."

"Do you mean like she was embarrassed?"

"Yeah, like that. Funny, I didn't think of it like that before."

"I don't suppose you remember when that happened?"

"I sure do. I was bringing a full tray of food to the table next to them when it happened. She jumped out of her seat just as I turned to put the first plate on the table, and she practically knocked me over. The whole tray flew to the floor." She huffed. "Every plate got broke, and there were some real nice breakfast steaks. All of it was ruined and the kitchen had to make everything all over. And of course *I* had to clean it up. Then the manager blamed me for it, and I was put on leave for two days. As if it was my fault! Made me run short on the rent. So, yeah, I couldn't forget that."

"So when was it?" he pressed.

"Oh yeah, you did ask that. Um, let's see." She started to mumble, "The check was short at the end of November, 'cause it was December's rent. That means it happened just before Thanksgiving." She nodded. "No, it happened on Thanksgiving day. Yeah. We were really busy."

Gary looked genuinely sorry for her. "Too bad."

"Tell me about it." She looked back towards the front of the restaurant. "Uh-oh, the manager's gonna get on me if I don't move it." She winked. "Be back soon."

When she walked away, Gary leaned across the table. "What do you think of that?"

Callie finished her bite of omelet with a smirk. "I think she likes you."

His ears turned red again. "No. I mean, what do you think about what she just told us?"

"I can't see Donna creating a scene. Not about the tray debacle, but their conversation. I didn't get that kind of vibe from her. Besides, wouldn't that subject be something you'd talk about in private."

"Exactly. So, why make a scene?"

"Maybe they didn't mean for it to go that far." Her eyes opened wide. "Or maybe they *wanted* everyone to hear?" She frowned. "But then, why would she act embarrassed?"

"We have to consider the possibility that she's guilty and it was an act. If she was into a scam with Russell and was yelling too, it could make her look guilty. They had to know the police would find out about the insurance policy, so she had to act embarrassed to make it look legit."

"I suppose you're right." She sipped her coffee. "So, let's say he set up the argument. Why would he do that? It doesn't make sense."

He took a big bite of pancake and chewed on it for a while. "We have to remember that Russell died within a couple weeks of that outburst." He held his coffee cup with both hands as he thought. "Unless she double-crossed him," he suggested.

She sighed. "I think we need more information."

Chapter 16

"Hurry up, you're going to be late! This is the third time I've told you."

"Okay, okay." Ethan huffed. *She's always on me.* He wasn't happy, but what could he do.

"You can't afford to get fired." Sheila helped him gather his cold weather gear and almost pushed him out the back door.

He was still buttoning his coat when he heard voices while walking down the path. He stopped. He knew the woman's voice and he didn't want her to see him. Not again. So, he waited, hoping she would leave soon.

It was several minutes, but finally the woman and the man walked away from the burned out building towards Donna's house. Keeping out of sight, he went farther down the trail. He had to go that direction anyway to get to work; besides, he was curious. But he made sure to use the underbrush to keep out of sight.

That woman was telling the man about the night Russell died. When they reached the house, she stopped, lifted the lid off the garbage can, and said, "This has to be where the sack with Donna's bloody clothes and the chloroform-soaked rag were found. Apparently the police pulled them out that same night."

Ethan stiffened. *Bloody clothes. No way!* He gasped. *That's the night I saw Junior put something in that can. And that was right before the fire!* He groaned inside. *It must've been Junior that did it!* His breath escaped slowly. *Mom is gonna freak!* He leaned against a tree and covered his mouth. *How am I gonna tell her? Aw, geez. I can't.*

He waited, knowing he'd be late for his job. But he couldn't leave now, that woman would see him. He couldn't let that happen. He didn't hear anything else they said, he was too alarmed by the fact that it must have been Junior who had put those bloody clothes there. He needed to make a run for it.

Gary was about to open the car door for Callie when he heard, "You again!"

They turned around to see Patty coming up the driveway. From the description Callie gave him from her first encounter with Patty, he would have recognized her anywhere. She had a joint in her lips, and she had on the same clothes that Callie had described.

Patty was marching up the driveway, arms waving. "You had to bring reinforcements?" she demanded out of the corner of her mouth.

From what Callie had told him, Gary knew Patty couldn't explain why she was here; and this had to be a bluff. He played it innocently. "Calm down. My name is Gary Rawlins, and this is Callie Cooper. And you are?"

"I don't have to tell you nuthin'. Now, you get outta here before I call the cops."

Callie took over. "Like I told you last time, Donna asked me to look around, and she has given us permission to be here. You, however, aren't supposed to be here."

"How do I know all that? You're just here to rob the place while she can't do nuthin' about it."

Gary pulled his phone out. "Well, I guess I'll just call the police and they can sort this out."

Patty stopped in her tracks. She twitched, looked around, threw the joint stub on the dirt, and ground it out with the heel of her boot. She clamped her mouth shut and her nose flared as she forced out a breath. A shaky finger pointed at them as she growled, "Stay outta here. I mean it." She turned and stomped away.

When she was gone, Callie whispered to Gary, "That's Donna's sister."

"Yeah. I see what you were talking about. But I've got the feeling we haven't seen the last of her."

Ethan darted from tree to tree until finally, the woman and the man left, and he hurried to get to work. Getting a job at his age was difficult and illegal, and he couldn't afford to get fired. He hoped his boss would understand.

After a little window shopping, Gary and Callie had lunch at the second restaurant. Interested as to what they'd discover, Callie took the lead to talk to the waiter because Gary told her she'd get farther with the questions than he would. Surprisingly, They quickly realized that the scenes seemed strangely similar, as if they were scripted; only this interview didn't have the dramatic collision with the tray. Apparently, Donna and Russell had breakfast here, and then they had lunch at the restaurant where they argued in front of Kiki. On the same day. More than a coincidence.

Callie wasn't paying attention, so she didn't see Gary's pensive look.

They started to speak at the same time. Gary let her go first.

"This is too weird. First of all, why would they have the same argument? And on the same day?"

"It sounds like a rehearsed script, doesn't it?"

Callie squinted with suspicion. "Or, they just wanted to make sure somebody noticed what they were saying."

"Then why not make a scene like they did with Kiki?"

"Another thing. If they were so poor, how did they afford to go out to eat twice on the same day?"

Gary shrugged. "It was Thanksgiving."

"Gary, you know what it was like to grow up poor. Could your dad have afforded it?"

"No, he'd spend what he had on alcohol."

"You know what I mean. Even without that, poor families just can't do that."

"I know, you're right."

"So, why then?"

Gary was silent for a moment. "Kinda makes her look guilty of insurance fraud, doesn't it?"

"But we're back to the question, 'why would Russell go along with that?' It doesn't make sense for him to plan his own death."

Gary took Callie's arm as they walked outside. The sun was peeking out from broken clouds and the temperature had actually risen to the high forties.

"What do you say we take in some of the sights?" Gary suggested as they walked to the car.

Although Callie knew that Gary had taken her arm as a gentleman's gesture, it still made her anxious. Hoping that accepting his gesture and liking it didn't give him encouragement before she was ready, she decided to roll with it and enjoy. "That's a good idea. Maybe take in a few of the shops? And we need to stock the kitchen."

"Shop first? For fun? Then groceries? Then when we get back, we can check out the garage."

"Deal. But we'd better move the car."

She knew that the restaurant manager would be upset with her leaving the car there as they walked around town. It would be impolite to say the least. And they might find the car towed when they returned.

So she headed for the tourist traps and the sand. If this was any time between spring and fall, finding a parking space would have been more than difficult. But it was still winter and she found a prime spot right in the middle of the would-be action.

They visited an antique store which had old furniture, books, trinkets, figurines, and artwork. She bought a small glass turtle. They picked up salt-water taffy and fudge at the sweet shop next door. They looked at the shops that sold kites, sand toys, swim suits, cameras, and whatever paraphernalia you might need on the beach.

Apparently, the nice weather rise brought some people out of their cocoons. They saw a couple riding a pedal car on the side streets, and a few kids flew kites at the water's edge. Noisy seagulls floated overhead looking for scraps. They were thankful they weren't here in the thick of tourist season; there was hardly any wait time for service at any of the stores.

They finished shopping around three, and then they headed for Donna's neighborhood to question the neighbors. Most of them knew Russell, but few had met Donna. So nobody could give a character reference for her. However, a couple of neighbors had plenty to say about Russell. Apparently, he had done some odd jobs for them, and neither of them were happy about his work or his attitude. One of them complained about his sloppy work and lack of tact and actually tried to file a complaint; but since Russell didn't have a contractor's license, nothing could legally be done about it.

"So, I think we might have discovered what his business was; unlicensed handyman," Gary offered on the way back to the car.

"That could explain why there were no business records."

"And we have people who didn't like him."

"Which means more people with a motive."

He nodded.

"But is that enough to kill someone?"

"Probably not." Gary stopped in his tracks. "Wait a minute. If he was a handyman, where are his tools?"

"Maybe the police confiscated them?"

Chapter 17

When they got back to the cabin around four, they put away their supplies before heading out to the detached garage.

Gary raised the pull-up door. He was surprised at how empty the garage looked. A bare workbench was built onto the back wall, and an old generator sat below it. On the wall to their right, a ceiling-high shelving unit held a few cans of paint, miscellaneous hardware, and some hand tools. In the far right corner, between the workbench and the shelves was a metal barrel that held a shovel, rake, hoe, and random pieces of wood in varying lengths. The man-door was on the side wall about four feet from the far left corner. Between the workbench and the man-door sat an old washing machine and dryer.

"Not much here," Gary sighed as he took in the sight.

"You didn't see it when you let the electricians in?"

"Didn't really pay attention. In fact, I didn't even really look inside when I unlocked the door." He looked down at the grate. "What should we use to test this out? Got any marbles?"

A devilish look crossed her face. "Maybe just shake your head? Just be careful not to lose too many in the process."

"Ha, ha," he said blandly. "Now, what are we going to use?"

She looked around, turned on the overhead light, which now worked with a switch instead of a string, and walked over to the shelves. "Hey, there's a dead flashlight here. That'll work."

"Perfect."

He started by laying the flashlight on the floor, parallel with the pull-up door, halfway between the grate and the door. It rolled towards the door. Then he placed it about six inches closer to the grate. Same result. He continued this process until finally he placed it one inch from the edge of the grate. Again, it rolled towards the door. Then he placed the flashlight on either side of the grate, testing whether or not it would roll toward the grate. It didn't.

"Well that does it. Nothing's going to drain in here unless it gets spilled over there," he announced, pointing to the back wall. "There aren't any cracks, so the ground probably hasn't settled."

Bending over, Callie started at the grate. She cocked her head and leaned closer. She used the light on her phone to see better. "Gary."

"What?" he asked as he put the dead flashlight back on the shelf.

"Look at this."

He stood next to her and shrugged. "Look at what?"

She got down on her knees and poked her finger between the slots. "This grate is only a couple inches deep."

"What? How can that be?" He got down on his knees too. "That's the weirdest thing I've ever seen. Why would anyone design it that way? Wait. There's no hole for anything to drain away."

"Well, it clearly isn't your average drain." She started moving her phone to examine the space below the grate. She pointed to the edge nearest to him and asked, "What's that?"

He bent low to see. "I don't know. He poked his finger in and felt an inch-wide metallic protrusion. "Wait, I think it moves."

"It moves?"

"Yeah. It's kind of hard to move, but it slides to one side."

She sat back on her feet. "Are you thinking what I am?"

Goosebumps appeared on his arms. "Maybe."

"And?"

"That maybe this is like the bookshelf in Alice's library?"

She nodded slowly. "Does it open?"

He pushed the piece of metal to the side as far as it would go. He took a breath and lifted it an inch by pulling up one of the crossbars. It moved, but before he opened it, he cautioned, "Go pull down the garage door and lock it." He didn't want to alert any neighbors who might be watching.

Callie raised her eyebrows. "Right," she said knowingly as she got up trying to act nonchalantly.

When she locked the door and turned around, he opened the grate.

This is trippy. Nervously, he reached in and pulled a large suitcase out of the cemented hole under the grate.

Her eyes popped open almost as wide as her mouth before she managed to sputter, "What in the world?"

He set it down on the concrete floor and looked up at her. "Let's find out."

She hurried over to squat down next to him. "Okay, I'm ready."

He swallowed, took a breath, and put his finger to the latch. "Here goes." He pushed the latch and it clicked. He looked up again. "Not locked," he said with a nervous grin and pulled it open.

It was no wonder that Callie was speechless; he was too. His heart seemed to race up into his throat, and it seemed like an eternity before he could suck in a breath.

"What?!" she whispered.

"It looks real."

"Whose is it? How'd it get here?"

"I don't know any more than you do." He picked up a bundle to examine it. He fanned the corners with trembling hands.

"How much?" she demanded with unnecessary volume.

"No idea. We'll have to count it to find out." He looked back into the suitcase where there were countless bundles of hundred dollar bills.

He counted his stack as she reached in and started to count the bundles. She set them on the floor next to her as she stacked them in groups of ten. After five minutes, she exclaimed with a pale face, "There's over a thousand of them. How many in a bundle?"

"This stack has a hundred bills." He figured in his head for a moment. "Uh, that's over a million dollars in here."

"Do you think Rudy knows about this? Like, maybe it was hidden here when he bought the place?"

Gary checked the serial numbers on the bills. "Even if he bought the cabin only ten years ago, it wouldn't be possible. See, this one was printed in 2013."

She grimaced. "Do you think this could be counterfeit?"

"No. He wouldn't do that, would he??"

"I don't think so." She winced. "He earned all his money, didn't he? At least that's what he said."

"How do we find out? I mean, if we asked him, and he is a counterfeiter, where would that put us?"

"We can't exactly go to the police and say, 'Hey, would you check this out for us?' If it was fake, we... or Rudy could be arrested. If it's real, then we'd have to tell the police where we got it. We couldn't turn him in, that would... Oh, I think I'm going to be sick."

"So what do we do now?" Gary asked.

"I don't know," Callie moaned.

They had dinner in front of the fireplace and discussed the day's events, especially on their ground shaking find. They still hadn't come to a decision about what to do, but in the meantime, the suitcase would stay hidden in the fake grate. It seemed the safest place for it. Since they couldn't do anything about it for now, they decided to continue with their original plans. However, concentrating was now a lot more difficult.

The evening went by quickly after that as they both went to their rooms to unpack.

Callie was grateful that Gary took the smaller bedroom. He had explained that since he'd lived in a dorm for four years, anything was an improvement. Not that this room was spacious. Even though it wasn't as cramped as his, it was still tiny. The door barely swung by the edge of the bed, so that she had to push it almost closed to get past it. A mirror was attached to the back of the door, probably to give yourself a once over before leaving. Faded wallpaper with stripes alternating with columns of flowers had started to peel at the edges. The vertical lines gave her the claustrophobic feeling of being in a prison. The visit with Donna at the jailhouse undoubtedly added to the closed-in feeling. Was that just yesterday?

One small window on the north side had no view except for the trunks and branches of the hemlock trees just outside. A bedside lamp with a 40 watt bulb provided the only light in the room. The paint on the pine floors was wearing off from decades of scuffling footfalls. An armoire, if you wanted to call it that, took the place of a closet at the foot of the bed. This room reminded her of the bedroom in Donna's house. Only Donna's bedroom probably had more space than this.

Callie couldn't focus. Not only did she have Donna's case on her mind, but also that suitcase now demanded her attention, like a belligerent toddler having a tantrum. She had to call Rudy. She pulled her phone out of her pocket and took a deep breath.

He answered with a cheerful voice, "Hey there, Callie, what did you find out?"

"Um, a lot more than I expected. But it's not about Donna. Well, I did find out a lot about the case, but that's not why I called you."

"Ooo-kay, can you explain a bit more?"

"Well, I kinda found your fake drain in the garage."

"Ah."

"Ah? What in the world, Rudy?! Where did you get all that money?! I know I don't really have any place to be asking, but actually I kinda do. You're family. And if you're putting Georgia at risk, it is my business!"

"Take a deep breath, Callie. It's nothing like that. No one is in any danger, but we can't talk about it over the phone."

"But you will tell me?" She paused, "And are you sure I'm not in any danger being around it?" she asked cautiously.

"I promise to tell you everything about it. And I assure you that it being there won't put you in any danger."

After hanging up, she tried to let go of the anxiety, but the questions kept bombarding her. *Is he minimizing the situation just to calm me down? What if it is counterfeit? Could he have gotten it illegally?* She cringed at the next thought. *Maybe he blackmailed someone? He does find out a lot of information about people.*

Wait! I have to stop speculating. Think about… how am I going to concentrate on anything else? She pressed her hands to the sides of her head, as if to shut out the suitcase screaming like a toddler. She took another deep breath and reached for her backpack, which she had plopped onto the bed. An unexpected sadness came over her.

She stopped to figure out why. Yes, the room felt oppressive. Yes, she had just discovered a huge secret about someone she loves. But neither of those reasons were the cause. It took awhile to admit that tonight she really wanted to be near her best friend again. The door was ajar, and she stood looking at herself in front of the mirror on it. *Who are you trying to fool? Just face it. You like him. A lot. He's more than just a friend.* She slumped. The same old conundrum faced her. *But what if being with Gary doesn't work out? Then, I'd lose my best friend.* No matter what she considered, whatever reasons pro or con, she didn't want to lose him as her friend. Would diving in be worth the gamble?

She was about to cry, and her throat started to close up when Gary called out, "Do you want to use the bathroom first? Or should I?"

"You go ahead," she squeaked.

He poked his head around the door. "You okay?"

She forced a smile and cleared her throat. "Sure. Just a frog," she lied.

He squinted at her in suspicion and she knew he could tell she was struggling. "Okay. Sure you don't want to talk about it? I know you were convinced Donna was innocent, but what we learned from the restaurants probably shook your opinion. Or is it about the money?"

"Yeah. That's it. I'll be okay. You go first in the bathroom." She knew he didn't believe her, but she didn't know how to convince him otherwise. She sure couldn't tell him the truth, so she shooed him out.

When he closed the bathroom door, she plopped onto the edge of the bed and moaned, "What am I going to do?"

She finally decided. She was going to sleep in the living room. She knew that she'd spend the night tossing and turning if she tried to sleep in here. She picked up her bag and squeezed past the door. Just as she stepped into the hallway, Gary came out of the bathroom which was just across the hall. She gasped as they almost collided. They stood face to face for the longest moment.

Finally, she smiled knowingly. "Yes. I'm going to sleep in the living room." She pointed behind her as she explained, "I was getting claustrophobic just standing in there."

He chuckled. "My room is just as bad." He looked at the door to his room and rephrased it, "No, it's worse. I'll join you."

After settling down and talking for a couple of hours, Callie was finally relaxed. She had almost forgotten about the money. Almost.

Chapter 18

It was early Monday morning and Gary had reluctantly joined Callie on her run. Although he worked out, he wasn't a seasoned runner. If he hadn't gotten so winded, he would have been able to give back some of the teasing she gave him over it. But he took it well. What choice did he have?

They got back just in time to miss the incoming storm. The wind had started, and soon afterwards, dark clouds took over with patters of rain tapping at the windows. It quickly became a torrent.

Today, they were going to meet with Donna's lawyer, Phillip Evans, but the appointment wasn't until ten, so they decided to make an elaborate breakfast. They had the time to kill, and they'd need the fuel for going out in the bad weather. But it was the fun of actually being able to cook together was special.

The German pancake was in the oven and still had ten minutes to go. Gary fried bacon while she cleaned the mess from preparation.

"Gary?"

He looked up with a smile. "Yeah?"

"I'm sorry I gave you such a bad time earlier."

He squinted at her. "You're apologizing for that?"

She sighed. "Don't make this any harder, okay?" She checked the timer. "I know you're really trying. I guess I just fell into my old habits. I'm not really insensitive you know." She collected the silverware from the drawer.

He rested his hand on her forearm. "I know you better than you do."

She looked at him. His face was an open book. The compassion, empathy, and…. she had to admit it; she saw his love for her too. That special love she'd seen on her dad's face when he looked at her mother. She put down the silverware and covered her face as if to hide the tears.

He pulled her into a consoling hug. "Hey, I didn't mean to make you cry," he soothed as he stroked her hair.

His tender words and comforting embrace made the tears flow. Too mute to say anything, she nodded quickly.

Afraid that his tenderness would push her into an emotional decision, she mumbled, "I think the bacon is almost done."

He looked over his shoulder at the bacon, let go, and placed the bacon onto paper towels. She took in an unsteady breath as she set the table.

As she suspected, breakfast was uncomfortable. They didn't talk about their moment.

"When we meet with Mr. Evans, we've got to tell him about what we've found." When he paused, she couldn't pinpoint the expression on his face. Was he angry? Sad? Disappointed? "Don't be surprised if he already knows."

"Then why wouldn't he talk to Donna about it?" she asked

"I don't know."

After cleaning up from breakfast, they still had an hour before they had to leave. They both decided that they'd use the time to do some cleaning. Since Gary had already swept, they methodically scrubbed the living room floor. Although it was difficult to remove the years of stuck-on grime, she enjoyed the teamwork and camaraderie as they worked. They had barely finished the one room before it was time to leave. Of course, they had worked in some play with a water fight near the end. Because they were still a bit damp when they got ready to go, it didn't matter much that it was raining.

Callie's tablet and phone were charged and ready to go. They locked the front door and steeled themselves. The rain came down hard as they dashed for the car. They were in for a soaking, much worse than the sprinkles they gave each other a few minutes ago. When the car doors shut, Gary and Callie were unavoidably drenched.

Gary shook water from his hands. "I say we park in the garage from now on."

"Agreed." She wiped her hands onto a semi-dry spot on her jeans and put on her seat belt.

Gary pulled up the address on his phone app. "It's just across Hwy 101."

They had hoped for a covered parking structure, but that thought had been wishful thinking. If they were in downtown Portland, they might have scored one. Another dash to get into the building exposed them to further dousing. Leaving a trail of raindrops inside the entrance, they decided to visit the bathrooms first to towel off.

When they walked up to the male receptionist, he was furiously typing something. He looked up from his monitor and asked with a forced smile, "How can I help you?"

"We have a ten o'clock appointment with Mr. Evans. Callie Cooper and Gary Rawlins."

"Oh, yes. Mr. Evans is expecting you. Down the hall, third door on the right." The receptionist pointed to his left and smiled politely, obviously anxious to return to his task.

When they approached the open door, Gary whispered, "Do we just walk in?"

She shrugged. Just to be safe, she knocked lightly on the door frame to get Mr. Evans' attention.

He looked up and waved them in. "Come in and sit, please." He stood up and held out his hand.

After the obligatory handshakes and introductions, they sat in the two wooden chairs in front of his desk. The small interior office had no windows and Mr. Evans' certificates and diplomas were displayed on the wall behind him. Callie knew the public needed to know his qualifications, but the display still felt a little pretentious, as if he were bragging. She did notice that the most recent date on one of them was just two years ago. The wall of books on the right extended to the ceiling. A narrow table behind them held stacks of files and several file boxes with lids.

Mr. Evans was dressed modestly, a navy-blue suit with a cream-colored shirt and blue, paisley tie. No wedding ring. Although it was mid-morning, he looked tired. His near-black eyes seemed puffy. She wasn't sure if they were naturally like that, or if he just didn't get enough rest.

Maybe allergies? She hoped he wasn't coming down with something; the sallow skin color added to that effect. Even for a young man, his auburn hair was already starting to recede. At least, he hadn't resorted to a comb over. His small, thin lips stretched into a narrow smile when he asked, "What can I do for you?"

When Callie explained how Donna had requested her help to look into the case, Mr. Evans' countenance changed. Dropping all congeniality, his eyes and mouth narrowed and fell like a stone. He folded his hands on the desk and sat rigidly. The only response that could be considered polite was his silence.

She ignored the attempt at intimidation and continued. "Mr. Evans, I'd like to learn what the police have gathered as evidence. And I'd like to talk with you about Mrs. Turner's defense strategy."

He didn't move and said nothing, not even a grunt.

Steeling herself, she gave her best shot to present a genuine smile. "I know you're busy, and I apologize for taking some of your time. I really appreciate you meeting with us." She regretted not starting this way at the introduction, and she let her regrets show. So much for a poker face.

He seemed to soften a little and nodded.

"I know that you have records of the prosecutor's information. I understand that Mrs. Turner has contacted you to release that information to me." Remembering Georgia's lessons on body language, she used them all to present a cooperative and friendly demeanor. She wanted and needed Mr. Evans' cooperation. She smiled demurely.

Mr. Evans leaned back in his chair. "I'm wondering why she think it's necessary to ask for your interference."

Ouch. She would need to handle this discussion with kid gloves. "I spoke with her, and she mentioned that she's only seen you two times, so she's feeling vulnerable and desperate. And on the second time, you advised her to tell the DA she was guilty and to make a deal with them. Have you considered the fact that she's innocent?"

"First of all, I cannot assume anything. Nothing has been proven yet. More to the point, there is an abundance of evidence in the prosecutor's case. I advised her to plead guilty to obtain a deal because I'm looking out for her best interest." He leaned forward. "With no deal, she'll go to prison for a long time."

"Didn't your investigator talk to the waitresses?" From his response, she realized that was not the way to approach this. He had flushed clenched jaw, and his folded fingers gripped each other.

"Of course he has," Mr. Evans enunciated.

The damage was done, so she just went with it. "So, about the arguments in the restaurants. Don't you think it's odd that she'd run out of there so quickly? As if to escape? In embarrassment?"

"You are assuming she's innocent. She could easily have goaded Mr. Turner into that argument and then pretend to be embarrassed. That would show premeditation. And that's what the prosecutor will argue."

This wasn't going anywhere, so she turned the conversation. "What about the key to the outbuilding?"

"What about it?"

"Let's assume she's guilty. She said she never had a key to the outbuilding. If Russell didn't give her a key, and she stole it somehow, why would she put it in the kitchen drawer? Logic would dictate that she put it in his pocket before starting the fire, right? However, if he did give her a key, why say she didn't have one? That would only arouse suspicion because lies imply guilt. Why would she do that? And why lock the door? Just leave the door unlocked so it would look like anyone could have done murdered him. These facts have to mean she didn't lie, she didn't have a key, and someone else put it in the drawer to set her up."

"People don't think about details when under emotional pressure."

"But if the murder was premeditated, as you suggest is possible, she would have planned it out, right?"

"People also drop the ball. I'm not saying that's what I believe; I'm saying that's how the prosecutor will present his case."

Frustrated, Callie beseeched, "So, you're not even going to argue the case?"

It was clear she had said the wrong thing when he stood up and held his hand out towards the door. Callie was sure he was dismissing them, but then he led them out to the hallway. "My assistant has put copies of everything in here." He opened the door next to his office. A conference table with numerous chairs seemed to be the only furniture in there. Two cardboard boxes sat on the corner of the table nearest the door.

"Thank you, Mr. Evans," Callie said as her face burned.

He gave each of them an obligatory handshake and waited with folded arms for them to collect the boxes and leave.

The rain was almost horizontal now, and by the time they got the boxes into the car, the cardboard was dangerously wet. Shutting the doors after scrambling in behind the steering wheel, Callie put her hands to her face to wipe off some of the rain. Her cap was wet and dripping. Although she had tucked her hair into her coat, the rain had managed to soak through and run down her back.

She hung her head, moaning, "I didn't handle that well at all."

"It's okay," Gary comforted. Although he was still trying to shake off the water, he took her hand with warm fingers. "I don't think anyone or anything was going to change his mind. At least, we have something to look at."

She looked at him appreciatively and then laughed. "You look like a drowned rat!"

"You'd better look in the mirror."

"Right," she conceded. As an afterthought, she giggled as she shook her head to spray him.

Chapter 19

The storm howled around him, and Craig had to wipe the condensation from the windshield several times just to be able to see. His left leg jiggled from agitation. Again, he pulled a gloved hand from under his armpit to look at his watch. "When is she getting back?" he grumbled. His irritation went on for over an hour until finally he saw her car return. He sat up in anticipation. He wanted to enjoy every moment. "Yes!" His grin dropped when, instead of parking in front like usual, that horrible woman passed the front of the cabin and entered the driveway. When the man got out and opened the garage door, he pounded the steering wheel in frustration. "No!" Shaking with rage and hunger, he decided to get lunch at a restaurant so he could warm up and think. "At the very least, tomorrow," he reassured himself.

Gary opened the garage door and Callie drove in. They hoped that parking in the garage would expose them to less time in the rain. It didn't work out as well as they planned. Yes, getting the boxes out of the trunk saved about a minute of standing in the rain, but going from the garage to the back door was about the same distance as if they had parked in front and gone in the front door. And the front door had an awning which would have protected them as they unlocked the door.

When they burst in the back door, they were saturated. Just getting to the table to put the boxes down left a watery mess that they had to wipe up. After they both put on dry clothes, Gary built a fire while Callie toweled her hair.

Opening the file boxes, they realized that just to read all of the information in them would take hours, if not days. They made sandwiches so they could work as they ate.

They rifled through the files for a few minutes and found everything; police reports, interviews, autopsy report, lab reports, and evidence collection.

Starting with the police reports, Donna's position looked bleak. There didn't appear to be any oversights or negligence. But what did they know? Neither Callie nor Gary had any experience with the police or the law.

She sighed. "Do you think Rudy might see something if we showed him these reports?"

"I'm sure he would. He's been an investigator for about forty years, hasn't he? He knows what to look for."

"Yeah. I really can't just call him. I wouldn't even know whether anything here is complete or not. And they won't be back from their trip for several days."

"Since we're going home on Saturday, let's just bring everything with us. We can ask him when he returns."

"Good idea." Callie felt hopeful again.

"I'm curious what the autopsy shows, if you want to check out something different."

"That's pretty gruesome. Why?"

Gary shrugged. "Just wondering what the body looks like on the inside."

"Is that somehow related to you being a physical therapist?"

He chuckled. "I don't know. Maybe?" He reached for the envelope with the autopsy report. "Hey, there's a disk here, too. And photos."

She scrunched her nose. "Photos?"

"Yeah. Lots of 'em."

With one corner of her upper lip raised in disgust, Callie said, "I think I'll pass on the pictures."

With a queasy look, he started to look at them and quickly put them face down on the table.

"Do we have something to play that disk on?"

"I don't think so. Do you suppose there's a transcription of it?"

"I guess we'll find out." She grimaced. "Do you think the descriptions are graphic? You know, all the gross stuff?"

"I don't know. I've never been involved with an autopsy before. Why? Do you want me to read it?"

She nodded.

He chuckled as he looked through the papers. "Here's the report. And there's a transcription. Which one do you want me to read?"

"First the report. Not too sure I want to hear the details in the transcription."

Gary started to read. "They took x-rays first, and except for the scrapes where the knife entered, there was no evidence of any broken bones, past or present. Next is the visual. Looks like there wasn't much skin left, mostly charred." He shuddered.

Callie took in a shaky breath at the thought. She appreciated the fact that he was affected too, genuinely grossed out. Not that she wanted to see him cringe, but his reaction just showed that he had feelings and wasn't afraid to show them.

"The fire damage was pretty extensive." He grimaced, took a breath, and continued. "The report explains the remains of his clothing: jeans, socks and tennis shoes, probably a polo shirt because of the button placement, no jewelry, and the remains of a knit hat. Huh. Apparently, he was laying on his left side, so that part of his face didn't burn as much; there was about three days' growth of beard. A couple missing teeth and the rest had varying degrees of decay and staining.

"Since he was lying on his left side, his left arm and hand were also kind of protected and didn't burn as much." He looked up. "The fingernails were long and dirty, and the first and second fingernails had some tissue under them. Apparently, he scratched someone."

"What? Do you think it was Donna?"

"I don't know. Wouldn't it show up in the lab report?" He shook his head. "If it matches her, she's sunk."

"Okay." She motioned for him to keep reading.

"Next, the internal exam. There was a three-inch wide, six-inch deep stab wound to the heart, plus four more stabs in the chest, same dimensions." He grimaced." He looked at Callie and said, "I'm guessing Donna's butcher knife matches the wound."

"Unfortunately, at least, she told me that's what they said."

He shook his head and continued. "Samples were taken from the blood, organs, stomach, and the tissue under the fingernails. Everything was sent to the lab."

"I'll find the reports. You keep reading."

"The stomach was empty, and it looks like there was evidence of an ulcer. And he had pre-cancerous lung disease, and early signs of pneumonia." Gary seemed to flinch. "Now this is weird. He had signs of malnutrition, too."

"Donna said they didn't have money." She looked up quickly. "Wait. How can she be overweight and he be malnourished?" she queried.

"One can be malnourished and still be overweight." He frowned. "Wait. Says here he was underweight. If they were eating the same foods, why wouldn't they manifest their malnutrition the same way?"

"I don't know. You're the health expert."

"I'm not an expert. I know a little, but I'm no expert."

Callie curled her lip. "He sounds like he was in pretty poor shape. I suppose he could have eaten less to leave more for her?"

"That would make sense. Well that's it for the autopsy. You want to read the lab reports next?"

"Sure. I can read that." She picked up the report that she had set aside. "Blood work. No traces of drugs, but there was nicotine present." She rested her hands in her lap and looked up. "He must've been a smoker. Smoking however, is pretty expensive, so that could be where some of their money went."

"It's sad when people have no money, yet they spend what they can get on addictive behaviors." Gary frowned.

"Thinking of your dad again?"

He nodded. "Sorry, keep reading."

"Oh. Here's the part the DA is using to press for premeditation. There was evidence of chloroform in the lungs." Callie looked up. "Do you think a woman could overpower a man using chloroform? I've trained in self-defense, but I don't think I could hold a saturated wad of cloth or tissue over a man's mouth for long enough to do the trick."

Gary thought for a moment. "Maybe his malnourishment and pneumonia weakened him?"

"Think about it. Isn't he going to struggle? Fight for his life?" she asked. "When your adrenaline's pumping, you can be pretty strong. How long does it take for the chloroform to put someone to sleep? It doesn't make sense."

"That's a point her attorney is responsible to make. Let's make a list of questions and go back to him."

"Good. We'll do that." She handed him her tablet so he could start the entries. "Next, the liver. Says here, he had a fatty liver and the early stages of cirrhosis. He was a drinker?"

"More wasted money," Gary stated flatly.

"I'm really not liking this guy." Callie held up the report to continue. "Oh, here's the report on the tissue under his fingernails. Dermal skin, a few hair follicles included ..." She scanned the report. "What? No DNA test?" She sat up rigid, disbelief flaring in her wide eyes. "Why wouldn't they do a DNA test on that tissue?"

"Probably because it wouldn't prove anything even if it matched her. Besides, he could've scrapped anyone and not necessarily when he died."

"But don't they have to get all the information and then figure it out? Who decided not to do the test?" she growled.

"All questions we can ask the DA tomorrow. That's where we're going, isn't it?"

"Yes. And you can be sure we're going to ask. And, we're going to address the interview with Kiki and how Donna dashed out." Callie raised an eyebrow as she added, "Also, about the chloroform and how much of a chance a woman would have to be able to hold it on a man's face long enough for it to put him out. And the key in the drawer. Does that cover everything?"

"Not getting the DNA test. And find out if they checked Donna for any scratches." He typed the questions into the tablet as he said it. "Do you want to go over the witness list?" He was already looking for it among the stacks of papers when she said," Yes."

"Here it is." He read the names, stopped, and looked up when he read Sheila Myers' name. "Why is her name on the witness list for the DA? I thought she was Donna's friend. Wouldn't she be a character witness for her?"

"Maybe the DA snagged her as a hostile witness?" Callie suggested. "She has to know why she was summoned. I wonder why she played innocent and didn't tell me anything."

"I don't suppose the DA will tell us why."

"Probably not."

Gary raised the witness list to continue, but stopped again. "Didn't you say Donna's sister is Patty?"

"Yeah. Are you saying her name is there?"

"There's a Patricia Mortenson listed. Is that her?"

"I don't know. We'll have to ask Donna." Callie turned her head in confusion. "Why would she be a witness for the prosecution?"

Gary sighed. "We have to be ready for the possibility that Donna's guilty. Patty must know something for the prosecution to put her on as a witness. After all, they are sisters. Don't sisters confide in each other?"

"Usually, but I got the distinct feeling that Donna wasn't close with her. And then there's Donna's neighbor, Sheila. She pretty much said the same thing."

"Okay. But let's be objective. If Donna's guilty, she could be just making up everything. Sheila is her friend, so she would naturally back her up about Patty."

"But you saw Patty, she isn't a nice person."

"That could be because she perceived you as an interloper. There's always an explanation for a bad attitude. Even if Patty's a terrible person, that doesn't mean Donna is innocent."

"Even so, we need to talk to that lawyer again. We have a lot of questions to be answered."

They spent the rest of the day looking at the investigative reports and the list of evidence to be presented. They drank a lot of coffee.

Chapter 20

Callie checked the forecast for the day. It would be overcast, in the forties most of the day, and, thankfully, no rain. They put on their cold weather running gear and went out for their run. Gary locked the front door as Callie bounded down the porch steps. When she landed on the middle step, it broke, throwing her to the ground.

When Gary heard the crack, he jerked around just in time to see her fall. He hurried to her side to help. "Don't move. Let me check for anything broken." Her arms were okay, right leg okay, but her left ankle was in a lot of pain, and she yelped when he tested it. "It isn't broken, probably a sprain. Let me help you back into the house." He lifted her up and carried her inside while avoiding the broken step.

After setting her carefully on the couch, he did a closer examination. Besides, a sprained ankle, she had bruised her elbow and scraped her shin where her jeans had ripped when she landed on a rock, and there was some imbedded gravel in her left palm. "Looks like you won't be going for a run anytime soon. At least, we have time to clean-up and bandage your battle scars."

"Yes!" Craig hissed in triumph. "It worked! Now to plan my next move," He chuckled and rubbed his hands together.

Leaving Callie behind with a bag of frozen peas on her ankle, Gary made the trip to a drugstore to buy what was needed: ibuprofen, an ice pack, and an ace bandage for her ankle. When he returned, he put the ice pack into the freezer to get it cold, and then he wrapped her ankle. He insisted she take the ibuprofen right then. He pulled the chair close so he could sit down beside her.

"You're really good at this. Thank you for being there." She squeezed his hand.

A surge of joy overwhelmed him. Although he knew her gesture was only an expression of appreciation, it was still a step forward. A very small step, but progress, nonetheless. He squeezed back. "Glad to do it." He studied her carefully. "So, when I go back to work, how do you think you'll do?"

She looked down at her hands. "I've been questioning myself, thinking about that very issue. I guess I'll just have to dig deep and figure things out."

"Any time you need my help, I'm just a phone call away."

When she looked at him, he saw a glimmer of what he hoped was love. And when she smiled, it was definitely not a sisterly look.

She broke the silence. "There's another storm forecast for tomorrow afternoon. Supposed to last for a couple of days."

"How bad?"

"Gale forces. So we either go back tonight, or we're stuck here until after the storm."

He really wanted to stay, but the call was up to her in addition to whatever came of their visit with the DA.

She fidgeted for a moment. "Do you think we'll really be able to convince the DA of Donna's innocence?"

He shrugged. "I don't know. Even though we have the list of witnesses, we don't know what they're going to say. And about the evidence, we don't know his arguments. As for the interviews, we don't know how he will interpret them."

"I suppose we could talk to Mr. Evans again. He might give us some insight."

Raising his fingers with each point, he said, "I really don't think (a) he will tell us anything or (b) have anything new to tell us. My impression is that he only wants to get the trial over with, regardless of what happens to Donna."

Callie slumped down. "That's how I feel too." She seemed shocked at the words she'd just said. "Wait. That's not what I meant. I meant... I meant I feel useless. Like nothing I do or say will make a difference in the case. I wish Rudy was here. I'll bet he'd have something to say."

"Don't you dare call him," Gary warned. "Georgia needs this vacation. We both know that. Besides, he might not have anything to add."

"I wouldn't say that. But you're right; we can't interrupt their vacation."

Gary made lunch, and they left with enough time to make their appointment with the DA.

Chapter 21

Thankfully, it wasn't raining, so Callie and Gary didn't have to rush to enter the building. Callie hung onto Gary's arm to relieve some of pressure on her ankle as they walked. He had offered, but she'd refused to let him carry her. They had to wait almost half an hour before they were called to Drake Furman's office.

When they came through the doorway, Drake Furman stood erect beside his desk. Although he was short, at least two inches shorter than Callie, his presence was imposing. He had intelligent, black eyes and firm, thin lips. She wasn't sure if he actually had broad shoulders or if his suit was enhanced to give that impression. In either case, looking at the man made her know he meant business.

After the introductions and handshakes, they were directed to sit in the two chairs in front of his desk. He sat down and crossed his arms. "So, what can I do for you?"

Callie sensed irritation. She wondered if he was taking time from something urgent, so she decided to keep the visit short. "Donna Turner asked for my help…"

Instantly, Furman's face changed imperceptibly. Was it irritation? Pity, perhaps?

She continued. "We've gotten the disclosures from her attorney, Mr. Evans, and we would like to address a couple of issues."

He nodded in acknowledgment. "Go ahead."

She outlined the issue of the key to the outbuilding and how it didn't add up.

His condescending look made her feel uninformed and inexperienced.

"You do understand that no matter how well a person can plan out a crime, something is always overlooked. Crimes of passion dramatically increase the chances of that happening."

"But since you claim she planned it out, how can you say it's a crime of passion? Aren't those usually in the spur of the moment?"

This time, the look on his face was patronizing and demeaning, and she felt stupid.

"There's always emotion involved, especially in domestic crime." He seemed to look down his nose at her. "Anything else?"

"Yes. When you interviewed the waitresses, there was no record of something that we discovered when talking with them." He seemed to take notice, and her self-confidence increased. "Kiki, the waitress at The Chowder House, said that Donna jumped from her seat and ran out just as they were loudly discussing the insurance money."

"She did say that during our investigation."

"But the point that I'm making is that Kiki heard them earlier, and Donna had asked Russell why he got the insurance. Donna never knew he was going to get it."

Again, the look. "Mrs. Turner could have staged the scene at the restaurant. But even if it was true, that doesn't change the motive. Whether they planned it together or not, she murdered him to keep all the insurance money for herself."

"But at the restaurant, she jumped up because she was embarrassed…"

"Like I said," Furman interrupted. "The argument only proves she knew about the money. So, instead of that implying innocence, it's just another nail in her coffin." He leaned back and eyed her. "Is there anything else?" He pressed those thin lips even tighter.

Callie's phone vibrated. She glanced at it quickly and saw Gary's text, *We're only showing the defense's hand. Let's go.*

He was right, they needed to leave. She smiled at Mr. Furman. "Sorry to take your time. Thank you for meeting with us." Gary helped her exit the office.

Gary helped her get into the car. When he got into the driver's seat, he looked at her defeatedly. "We should've talked over our arguments before coming here."

"You're right. Donna's lawyer isn't going to be able to use those arguments now. Furman will certainly strengthen his rebuttal on those points. Thanks for stopping me before I listed all of them."

"Any time." He couldn't help himself. He's the DA, and it's his job. "So, did that hurt?"

"My ankle?"

He looked at her tauntingly. "No. Saying I was right. Did it hurt?"

Almost instantaneously, she punched his shoulder. But he grabbed her wrist just as she was a fraction of an inch from a second punch. "Ah, ah. Don't bite the hand that feeds you."

"Then don't poke the bear," she countered with a growl.

He chuckled, and in a moment, they were both laughing.

After Callie's final laugh, she looked somber. "Thanks for the heads up. I don't know what I thought we'd accomplish by meeting with him. You're right. We probably gave him more ammunition for his case." She hung her head. "I'm so stupid."

"We're both new at this. It didn't occur to me until that moment. We know better, now."

She looked up sadly. "Thanks. I don't deserve your support, but thanks. I just hope we didn't ruin her case."

After dinner, Gary went outside to fix the porch step. He went to the garage to find a tape measure to see how long a board he would need. Since there wasn't much in there, it didn't take long. But while he was there, his gaze kept returning to that grate. Where did it come from, all that money? Callie had filled him in on the phone call she had with Rudy, but they still didn't have any answers. It had been difficult thinking about the case with this elephant in the room. He put the tape measure into his pocket and went to the front porch.

That's funny. I didn't notice that before. The break is pretty clean. Rotten wood doesn't do that. He strong-armed both pieces of the board from the riser and held the broken parts together. His heart sank.

He brought the two pieces into the cabin. He didn't really want to tell her, but she had to know. "Callie?"

She looked up from reading a report. "Yeah?"

"You have to see this." He held the two pieces in front of her.

After a moment, her mouth dropped open. She looked up and moaned, "I can't believe it. Someone deliberately did this?"

"That's right. Somebody cut the board from underneath almost all the way through. There's no way this was an accident."

"But why? Who would do that?"

"I don't know. Do you think whoever did this is trying to stop our investigation?"

"If that's the case, then Donna's definitely innocent." She gasped. "Remember, Donna said Patty wants the house. Do you think she believes that if Donna gets sentenced, then she could get it? Maybe she thinks if she stops us, then Donna's certain to be sentenced? Do you think that might be it?"

"That's pretty low. But if what Donna and Sheila says is true, then maybe." A surge of rage flared in his nostrils when he realized this case was putting Callie in danger. "I'm gonna go fix that step." *Maybe hammering that new board in place will vent some of my anger.*

Chapter 22

It was hard to believe it was already Wednesday morning. Another storm was headed for the coast, and it was going to be a "big blow," as the newsman called it. They figured they'd barely squeeze in a visit with Donna, but they'd just have time to get back to the cabin to ride out the storm before they could head back to Portland. Gary had to go back to work on Monday, and Callie had to bone up on all the paperwork they had received from Donna's lawyer. She had allowed herself the weekend to do that before Rudy and Georgia returned from their trip next Tuesday.

Callie wanted to ask Rudy to help her with some of the legal issues, but she had to get every detail firmly etched in her head and sorted out so she'd know what she was talking about. She wanted to be able to ask intelligent questions to see if she was overlooking anything.

This case made her realize now how much time an investigation takes, and she was only getting started. Not only was investigating time consuming, but also it required a lot of analyzing. With all the times she had helped Rudy, he had done most of that. Now, she was responsible for it.

After the fiasco with the DA yesterday, they had missed visiting hours at the jailhouse, but today, they were looking forward to taking everything they had found so far to Donna. The hope was that she might notice a discrepancy. Or, better yet, some fact might jog her memory of something that may have previously seemed unimportant. Because her lawyer hadn't talked with her much, a lot of information was probably overlooked.

Although Callie's ankle was better than yesterday, it was still very tender. Gary had made sure to wrap it properly, and it really did make it feel more secure. They were both grateful for today's weather; Callie wouldn't feel rushed having to hobble around in the rain. Although she was protective of her car, she was thankful Gary would be the designated driver, at least, until the storm was over.

Because visiting hours started at one, they decided to get breakfast out, but when they got to the curb, they saw that her tires had been slashed. Callie was furious as they went back inside. She arranged for roadside service to get towed to a shop for new tires. The procedure took up the whole morning, almost making them miss the start time for visiting hours.

On the way to the jailhouse, Gary broached the subject. "There've been too many weird things happening, but this one takes the cake. I don't think you're paranoid anymore."

"I know. After we leave Donna, let's call the police."

"I agree."

They arrived about ten minutes before visiting hours started, and the papers they brought for Donna to look at were approved. They hoped she might see something to strengthen her case. Her lawyer, Mr. Evans, certainly hadn't tried very hard so far.

Callie and Gary had talked about his lack of interest last night. By the certificates and diplomas on his wall, he had just recently earned his degree. You would think that getting in that office meant that he was very good, but he was probably overwhelmed being a recently-hired Public Defender. They guessed that the demands of his position probably meant he didn't have much time to devote to each case. Donna definitely needed all the help she could get, and they were determined to provide all they could.

Callie turned on the recorder when the door opened. They had decided that Gary would ask the questions while Callie would enter in her tablet any new information that needed to be discussed.

Donna looked surprised to see Gary sitting there when she walked into the room. When she saw the file box on the floor, she looked puzzled.

"Donna, this is Gary Rawlins, a friend of mine. He's helping me with your case. Before we start, has your lawyer talked with you about the evidence against you?"

"A little. He said it was pretty strong."

"But did he go over each piece with you to get your take on any of it?"

"Not really."

Callie sighed. "Okay. Gary will ask you questions and tell you about what we've discovered so far, and I'll take notes."

Gary started off with the incident at the restaurant where the tray of food was dumped onto the floor.

"I was really sorry that happened. But I couldn't believe what Russell was saying. To buy that large amount of insurance... I was so scared about how we'd pay for it. Then when he said *I* had insisted he buy it, I couldn't believe what I was hearing, 'cause I had no idea he was even thinking about it."

Donna hesitated. "He had done the same thing at the diner where we had breakfast. I almost thought he was *trying* to embarrass me. Then, at lunch, he said I didn't appreciate what he did for me. Well, that was the final straw. I couldn't stay there and be maligned and embarrassed any longer. That's why I had to leave."

Donna lowered her head and sighed. "It was really weird. He's always been the one that walks out when he got uncomfortable. He always avoided a confrontation. He'd rather leave than talk about something negative. Lately, though, it seemed like no matter what I said, he'd get offended, like I was attacking him." She looked up. "I'd never start an argument like that. At first, I avoided confrontations because I loved him and didn't want to hurt his feelings. But after a while, it was because I didn't want him to accuse me or get upset, but he always found a way to be offended."

Her frown lines deepened. "It was so unlike him, to start an argument like that, especially in public." Her voice seemed to become a whimper when she added, "And he was so loud. It was like I was with a stranger. I didn't know how to handle what he said, how he said it, and then laying the guilt on me." She looked aside to hide the tears welling up.

"The waitress said he was a good tipper. Did you know that?" As Gary asked the question, he could hear Callie typing notes on her tablet.

Donna's eyebrows shot up. "What? I didn't even know he went out. When we went to those two restaurants, that was the first time in over a year that we had eaten out." She seemed confused. "Where'd he get the money?"

"I don't know. That's what the waitress told us." Gary shifted in his seat. "Did Russell change much after you married him?"

Donna nodded. "He was very attentive and interested before. But after we got married…" She shrugged. "…he was gone most of the time. I just assumed it was work, but he never took a company job. He said he had to hustle. Whatever that means."

"We found out that Russell had been doing odd jobs for people around town."

"I wouldn't know. He never told me."

"Did anyone ever call the house to talk to him?"

"Yeah, but nobody ever left a message." She paused. "No, there was this one guy. He was really mad. He said if he ever caught up to him…" She grimaced. "I don't think I can repeat what he said." Then she gasped. "Do you think *he* might have killed him?"

"Did you tell Mr. Evans about that phone call?"

"I never thought about it, and he never asked."

Callie typed as fast as she could.

"How long ago was that?'

"Mmm, probably two months, maybe three. A couple weeks before… before he was killed."

"We'll make sure to get his phone records, but we'll need Russell's number."

She slumped and moaned. "I don't know it. It's programmed in my cell phone."

Gary saw Callie nod her head as she typed. To keep going, he stated, "So, we saw evidence of tracks from a dually in your driveway."

"That would be Russell's truck."

"Do you know where it is? The police don't have it."

Donna seemed to get lost in thought. She rubbed her forehead as if trying to bring up a memory. "Funny. I don't remember seeing it that night. You know, the night of the fire." She relaxed and added, "Junior must have it."

"Junior? Who's he?"

"That's Russell's son from a previous marriage. They work together."

"Oh." Gary looked at Callie. "Did you know about Junior?"

"No," Callie said in surprise. "This is the first I've heard anything. Donna, do you know how we can contact him?"

"He just got a new number not long ago. It's programmed in Russell's phone. I didn't get it from him before I was thrown in here."

Gary squinted. "Do you know where it is?"

"Russell's phone? He never let it out of his sight. It was always in his pocket. Don't the police have it?"

"We have a list of everything they found in the building. No phone and no remains of a phone."

"Well, that's just not right." She looked genuinely confused. "Where'd it go?"

Gary looked at his notes. "Okay, let's continue. We want to talk about the autopsy report. It's kind of gruesome, so if you're not okay with hearing it, we can skip the details."

Donna shrugged. "I had a job working for an undertaker when I was in my thirties. I helped him pick up the bodies and bring them to the funeral home. I saw some pretty gross stuff, so I can handle it."

As Gary listed the external details, body size, burn damage, long fingernails, two missing teeth, Donna looked increasingly skeptical, but especially so when he listed the teeth.

Callie interrupted, "Is something wrong?"

"He always kept his nails short. But two missing teeth? That's impossible."

"Why do you say that?"

"He wore dentures. He said he got them when he was in the army. He even showed me the tattoo of his ID on them once."

Gary and Callie looked at each other.

"Okay, let's see what else it says. He had no wedding ring, no wallet, no phone on his person. And they weren't found in the building."

"Well, he regularly took off his ring. Said he didn't want it to get caught while he was working. Sometimes I wondered if he was having an affair. But no wallet? Besides the missing phone? That's hard to believe."

Gary's suspicions were growing, but he continued. "Most of his clothing was burned off, but they were able to determine that he was wearing jeans, polo shirt, and tennis shoes."

Donna shook her head quickly. "No. That's not possible. He always wore button down cotton shirts, never a polo. And he never wore tennis shoes. Didn't even own any. He had a hammertoe on his left pinkie toe, and the tennis shoes didn't give enough room for the toes. They made his toes hurt. So that's not possible."

Gary was pretty certain that either the autopsy report had gotten mixed up with another, or the body wasn't Russell's. He decided to just finish. "Okay. There's more. The internal exam." She listened with a frown as he listed 'empty stomach, malnutrition, ulcer, pneumonia, lung disease, fatty liver, cirrhosis, no evidence of broken bones, new or old…'"

Donna interrupted. "That can't be Russell. He broke his arm five years ago. He couldn't work for over a month. So either that medical examiner is way off, or it's another body." She paused a moment and added, "If he had pneumonia, I'd have known it. He wasn't coughing, no fever, and no other signs. As for that other stuff, there weren't any signs of them, either. And he didn't smoke."

Gary's mind whirled with this new information. Donna's right. The dead body couldn't possibly be Russell's. After all, how many badly burned bodies would the medical examiner have to work on? It's not like they were located in Multnomah County where there were far more bodies to examine and a greater chance of a mix-up. Even so, not another body like this one. Because Callie was adding notes the whole time, Gary knew they'd have a lot to talk about when they left. As eager as he was to discuss this with Callie, he had to finish the interview with Donna to get all the facts first. "You said he had a hammertoe?"

Donna nodded.

Tapping the autopsy report, Gary declared, "There's nothing in here about a hammertoe. It would certainly have been listed if the examiner found it. And he couldn't have missed it. We should go over any other identifying marks he has that might help us. We're going to meet with your lawyer to give him this information. His investigator needs to be the one to prove it."

"Well, like I said, he had dentures and the hammertoe. I think the broken arm was the only bone he ever broke. I can't think of anything else."

Callie looked up. "Tell us about Junior."

"His name is actually Russell, but we always called him Junior so I could keep them straight. His mom died when he was about ten." She looked down. "Russell actually told me he resented having to raise him by himself. It's 'cause Junior has Asperger's Syndrome. He's high-functioning, but he really can't live independently. They couldn't live together either, but they needed each other." She winced. "I'm pretty sure Russell has it too, just not as severe." Catching herself, she whispered,

"Had it." She sighed. "I just can't get used to the fact that he's gone." She took a cleansing breath. "He would get so irritated with Junior. Russell would have to tell him over and over about some task. Junior couldn't help it, with the Asperger's and all. And Russell's frustration level was much more fragile than most. Have you ever seen two temperamental kids together? They'd get on each other's nerves all the time. I couldn't handle seeing them fighting, and I couldn't reason with either of them."

"So, why do they need each other?"

"Junior depends on Russell to handle his finances because he can't do it on his own. And Junior helps Russell in his work, the physical part."

"What does he look like?"

"He's thirty-five years old, about 5'8", blonde hair, brown eyes. He has a pug nose, jowls, and a husky build. Most of the time, he forgets to shave or put on deodorant or shower, even. And he limps." She looked embarrassed. "He confided in me that Russell pushed him once, and he fell down a flight of stairs. Broke his left leg. The break never healed properly; that's why he limps."

Callie grimaced. "Why would he do that? Push him, I mean."

Donna sighed. "Like I said, I think he has Asperger's too. Russell was never diagnosed, but I found his discharge papers from the Army. The code for his release was because of an attitude problem. When I saw those papers, that's when I suspected he has Asperger's too. He has a lot of the signs. He never really shows or recognizes emotion, except for anger. That's how he reacts to just about anything that doesn't go his way, with anger."

"Why did you marry him?" Callie beseeched.

"He seemed attentive. He picked wildflowers for me. Always wanted to be with me. I don't know. I guess I didn't see what he was really like then." She sighed. "When I was young, I had decided I didn't want to get married. Then when I was older, I started to think, 'what have I done?' But by then, eligible men were hard to find, especially at my age. Marrying Russell seemed like a way to not be alone."

"So, he was never officially diagnosed with Asperger's or anything similar?"

"Not unless there's something in the Army's records. But I doubt it. Asperger's wasn't recognized until the last couple of decades."

"Why did you stay with him?"

"I don't know. It wasn't a horrible marriage. I'd seen so many wives with way worse husbands, so I counted my blessings."

Gary got the discussion back on track. "Do you know how to get hold of Junior?"

"No. Russell rented an apartment for him. It could even be somebody's extra room or garage. It came out of whatever they earned." She paused. "I don't know where he's living, but it's got to be close. When Russell would call, he'd be there within ten minutes. That might help in figuring out where he is because he had to walk. Russell wouldn't let him have the truck."

She suddenly looked stricken. "He's driving the truck!" she exclaimed with a horrified expression on her face. "Russell would let him drive on country roads, but he never got a license."

Callie added to her notes.

"We couldn't have Junior live with us. There just wasn't enough room. And Russell couldn't live with him anyway. Besides, I couldn't have handled the two of them together."

"Why?"

"They… uh, when they argued, they'd get physical. It was like watching two ten-year-olds, I tell you. I told Russell that if he wanted Junior here, then he'd have to leave." Donna bowed her head. "I own the house. I guess Russell didn't want to be kicked out, so he didn't have to think about it."

Gary saw in Callie's face that she wanted to reach out and hold Donna's hand, but that wasn't allowed.

"I'm sorry you had to live that way," Callie said sympathetically.

"Where would I go? Besides, it was my house. My sister was no help. The only way I kept my sanity was by corresponding with Cora."

Gary asked, "So, you think Junior has the truck?"

"He has to."

"Do you know the license plate number?"

"I know the letters, DAC. I remembered that part because when I saw it, I thought, oh, Donna and Cora. I can't remember the numbers, though."

"That's good enough. What make was the truck? Color, Year?"

"I'm sorry, I don't know. But it has a double cab, and it's beige. Oh, there was an accident a few months ago. I don't think they reported it though. I'm pretty sure they settled it privately. They picked up a fender at a wrecking yard. It's dark blue. The chrome doesn't match. I guess it wasn't the exact model or something. Russell didn't care. He never paid attention to how something looked."

Gary saw that Callie noted the information with a smile. He knew that description should help the police find Junior. Then he saw her groan inwardly. *I'll bet she's wondering if Junior might know something. And not having a license, he'd probably get pulled over.*

He couldn't hold it in any longer. "We all know that body was probably not Russell."

Sadness came over Donna as she asked, "Then who was it? And where's Russell?"

"We don't know, but we have to prove that it wasn't Russell. Is there anything at your house that has his DNA on it?"

She frowned in thought. "His toothbrush and hairbrush?" She tisked. "But it's been so long, over two months, and he wasn't diligent about using them."

"Is it okay if we have Mr. Evans' investigator meet us at your house so he can get a DNA comparison?"

"Of course."

"I just hope the samples are still viable."

The guard walked in to announce that visiting hours were over.

Callie said goodbye to Donna as Gary packed up the box of papers. He waved as Donna got up to leave.

The wind was starting up as they went out to the car.

"Looks like the storm is coming in," Gary said as he put the box into the car.

"At least, we were able to see Donna before it started." She pulled out her phone to call Mr. Evans to arrange for his investigator to meet them at Donna's house on Friday. Hopefully, the storm would be over by then.

It was just after five when they got back to the cabin, and the drops of rain were beginning to fall. Gary immediately secured all of the shutters; he didn't want any flying debris to break the windows. They had enough problems with whoever was harassing them.

When he finished, he hung his wet coat in front of the fireplace and lit a fire. As Callie sat by the flames, he stood by the front door window to watch the storm for a few minutes. Out over the ocean, darker clouds were moving in. Debris occasionally blew by. The sound of the wind gusting along with the shaking of the trees made him nervous. He couldn't remember ever being in a storm that was going to exceed 80 mph.

Callie chided, "See any flying monkeys?"

He turned around and grinned. "Only the one sitting in front of the fireplace."

She stuck her tongue out at him.

Being trapped here for more than a day is going to be difficult, having her so close and off limits. On the other hand, it would also be really nice, marooned together and able to bond even more. So he did what he always did, he pointed out the positive. "It's a good thing we have enough food."

"Well, we did stock up for the storm." She smiled. "We might as well eat dinner and have our Monopoly rematch."

"I'm going to wipe the floor with you. Again," he announced.

"Oh, no." She cackled wickedly. "*You're* going down."

Because the storm was supposed to last a day and a half, they had prepared themselves for a possible blackout. The firewood was piled high for at least a week's worth of heat, the makeshift beds were put in place with extra blankets, lanterns and flashlights were within reach, and the phones were charged.

Gary didn't want her standing on her sprained ankle, so she set up the board while he made the nachos. He actually piled the food onto a platter that he found in the cupboard. When he brought it out, she had to laugh.

"You must be pretty hungry."

"Well, yeah. Besides, what else is there to do but stuff ourselves?" He set it down on the floor next to the Monopoly board. Then he went back for the hot chocolate.

"Ooh. Yum. You read my mind," she purred when he handed the cup to her.

The game went on longer than they expected, with Callie finally foreclosing on the last of Gary's properties after eleven o'clock. The wind had increased to over forty miles per hour according to the weather report on the radio.

Gary put more wood on the fire and they snuggled down into their respective blankets in their usual spots. They talked for a while discussing everything they wanted to tell Mr. Evans' investigator when they met with him on Friday. Callie had already called Sheila to make sure she could let them into Donna's house.

He could tell she was getting tired. Her voice had slowed down, and she took longer to respond to his questions, so he said good night. He could hear the smile in her voice when she also said, "Goodnight." It wasn't long before he heard her rhythmic breathing. With the fairly steady wind, he was lulled to sleep too.

Chapter 23

Callie stood next to Gary in front of the storm-proof picture window to watch the tide come in. Just outside, was a small grassy yard with a stone wall at the top of a ten-foot drop-off to the beach. An array of rocks stood as a barrier between the sand and the growing waves that washed over them. A paved road gave access to the beach just beyond the second house to the right. She looked up and down the coast and noticed that the lighthouse was lit.

Two sea gulls had perched on the stone wall, which was only a few feet from the window. One of the sea gulls looked at her and cocked its head. Quickly, it looked away and then back again. She smiled, wondering what it was thinking as she watched it leap off the wall's edge and sail off with the wind. The second sea gull eyed her too, but instead of looking away, it stared at her for several seconds. Just as she started getting a creepy vibe, it left too. How strange, she thought, that they would stare at her like that, as if they were planning something evil. She shook off the uneasiness with a shudder.

The wind was picking up, with dark clouds appearing on the horizon. It was mid-afternoon, but the darkening sky made it feel more like dusk. The ocean started to look angry, hurling the waves high into the air as they crashed over the rocks onto the sand. Even for high tide, the water's edge surged closer than normal. The horizon became hazy, blurred by the rain beyond. The forecast was right; a storm was quickly approaching.

Although the house had survived many storms before, blowing wind created noises that unnerved her. The house creaked and groaned, and she felt goose bumps pop up as the windowpane shuddered with each gust. She began to wonder if it would hold. *No, it's safe*, she tried to convince herself. She looked at Gary to see if the storm was affecting him like it was her. *Apparently not, he looks totally fascinated by the frenzy. Am I crazy to feel this much anxiety?*

She suddenly felt chilled and put on a sweater. Not that it was cold, but watching the weather close in had unnerved her. *Time to take my mind off the what-ifs.* "I'm pretty sure we'll be staying in for dinner. I don't think it would be a good idea to go out. I'll start dinner," she announced as she turned towards the kitchen.

"You need me to help?" he asked.

"No. I've got it."

"Okay." He turned back to the window. "This is fascinating," he said as he pressed closer to the window.

"You've never seen a storm before?"

"Well, yeah. But not at the beach, and not like this. Fact is, we never went anywhere, even before Mom died." He turned around to face her. "If it wasn't for your parents letting me tag along when we were kids, I wouldn't have seen anything." He put his hands into his pockets and turned back to the window.

She suddenly felt sorry for him, almost pitying him. What a shame he had to grow up the way he did. Then she reminded herself that he turned out to be a pretty nice guy. She sighed and said a silent thank you for her parents. They always said that attitude is everything, that it doesn't matter where you come from, that it matters what you do after that, and to make sure you count your blessings and become better.

She pulled out everything she needed and started to chop vegetables at the counter.

The flash of light made her jump. Boom! At first, she thought maybe the lights had flickered, but the thunder was proof that lightning was close. She looked over her shoulder and saw another flash outside, followed by another boom, this time closer together.

Standing directly in front of window, Gary called out, "Wow! Did you see that? That one was close. Looks like this storm's going to be a doozy."

The wind started to howl, and the rain became horizontal. Although it wasn't even four yet, the clouds had darkened the sky prematurely, which for some odd reason made her feel uneasy.

He seemed fascinated by the storm. "Hey, those waves are coming up pretty high. At least halfway up the beach already."

"That's because the storm hit at high tide."

"Whoa! You won't believe this!"

Startled, she tensed. "What is it?"

"Some moron just drove out onto the beach. You think they're storm watchers?"

"Probably. They do some pretty stupid things." She hurried to the window to see. "They better hope they don't get stuck. The rescue teams charge a lot to extract those dopes."

The sound of breaking glass made both of them jump. It came from the back of the house.

"What was that?" Callie's nerves just edged up a notch.

"I'll check all the windows. There's a lot of stuff blowing around pretty hard."

"When you're done, maybe you should double-check all the shutters too. Just to be safe?"

"Will do." He started checking the rattling windows, running from room to room. "Hey, the bathroom window is broken."

He hurried to the door, threw on his coat, and ran outside. She went to the bathroom to see what she could do to prevent any more rain from coming through the broken window. She grabbed a towel to try to hold over the opening, but it was useless with all the wind. Gary came up to it and fastened the shutters. She wiped up water from the floor, walls, and everything else as he went to the next window. She fretted as she worked, refusing to think about the fact that the wind could blow him over the precipice when he got closer to the edge.

When she came out to the living room, she saw him working on the shutters for the picture window. He struggled as the wind fought against him, making his hair whip around. Now, the thought of him getting thrown over the edge became a distinct possibility.

Surely, the lights would go out any minute, so she looked for the lantern. *We should have done this right away. We knew the storm was coming. I was so stupid.*

Finally, after ten minutes, the door burst open, and he was blown inside with the rain. She ran over to help him strong arm the door to shut it, but the floor was slippery from the rain, and the wind gusted just before the door latched. With poor footing, they both went down when the door flung open again. Working together, she leaned against the coat closet door while pushing Gary from behind as he forced the door closed and locked it.

He just stood there, drenched. His hair was pasted to his head and water cascaded off him. Panting from the effort, he took off the coat, but he was just as wet underneath. "I need a hot shower." He headed for the bathroom.

After wringing out what water she could into the sink, she put his coat into the dryer and mopped the floor. She lit a fire in the fireplace and was relieved that the wind made a good draw of air. It didn't take long for the dancing flames to put out some heat.

She had just put the skillet on the stove and added some oil, when he came out of the bathroom. He went straight to the fire to warm himself. "Thanks for the fire." He was still shivering a little.

"Your coat is in the dryer. Will you check the forecast to see how long the storm's going to last?"

He patted his pockets and suddenly yelled, "My phone! It was in my coat!" He started running.

"It's okay. I pulled it out, and it's on the counter. I think we should put it in rice to dry it out first. Here, use mine."

He let out a huge breath. "Oh, man! Thank you." He suddenly looked glum. "Then you found it?"

"Yeah. Why'd you take a hammer out there?"

"I didn't. I found it on the ground outside the broken window. It wasn't there earlier."

She squinted. "What are you saying?"

"I think somebody might have broken the window on purpose."

Her face fell. "Do you think it has anything to do with all the weird stuff that's been happening?"

"I'll admit it's a possibility. I think you may be on to something and not just being paranoid."

"Okay. That gives me the creeps." She swallowed hard.

"I'll get the forecast."

She knew he was trying to take her mind off the subject, but his effort didn't help.

After a few taps, he announced, "Looks like the worst will hit around two in the morning. I don't know how much sleep I'll get with the rattling windows and that eerie wind." His expression seemed morbid.

"Are you sure it's the storm that's getting to you? I hope you aren't thinking about catching the guy that's doing all this stuff?"

He shrugged.

"Why would he endanger his life by being out in this weather?"

"I don't know. But the storm's getting worse, so he's got to be taking shelter."

"What about when the storm lets up?"

"Don't worry. I'll be here."

Although he smiled, she could see it was strained.

"So what about dinner?" he asked.

"If we'll have enough electricity to make dinner."

"What do you mean?"

"Well, the lights were flickering when you …." The lights flickered again. "… when you were outside. Just like that." She threw the chopped chicken and vegetables into the hot skillet before she went to the pantry to find the rice.

They ate dinner on the shag rug in front of the fireplace. The wind was gusting close to seventy miles per hour already, but the roaring fire and warm quilts around them made them feel relatively peaceful and secure.

Quiet conversation and a full belly added to the contentment as they leaned back against the sofa with their feet sticking out towards the lively flames. It wasn't long before Callie slipped into a light sleep.

Hearing a bump, she opened her heavy eyelids and looked up. She became alert when she saw a shadow coming out from the doorway to the basement. Incredibly, it looked like Bigfoot. She blinked. Maybe the shape was just her imagination. She crouched down to avoid being seen. *What next? Why didn't we look in the basement? I can't believe we forgot to do that.* She shuddered, wondering when the creature would find her.

Hearing another bump, she opened her eyes. Now, the fire was merely embers casting an eerie shadow into the room. Sitting up, Callie looked around in the dim light. For a moment, she was disoriented. No Bigfoot. And the basement door is closed. She sighed in relief. *Just a nightmare. How could I think that was real?* She reached over to where Gary had been, but he wasn't there.

Just then, he came out of the kitchen with a bottle in his hand. "Want some water?"

She nodded, and he tossed one at her.

When he put more logs onto the embers, she realized the lights were out. "Did you turn off the lights?"

"No. They went out while you were sleeping. Do you happen to know if there's a lantern around somewhere?"

"When you were outside, I found one. I put it in the closet."

"I'll start it up." As he was busy with lighting the lantern, she realized the wind was still at gale force. The house was still creaking and the shutters were still rattling.

Gary set the lantern on the kitchen island so it would light as much area as possible. As he came into the living room, the light from the lantern cast a long eerie shadow on the wall. In fact, there was a shadow from everything between it and the wall in front of Callie, and as the lantern flickered, the shadows seemed to dance. He sat down next to her in front of the fire.

Callie looked at her phone to see what time it was. Not even past midnight. It was going to be a long night.

"How much charge does your phone have?" Gary asked.

"It's pretty low, it'll probably die before morning."

"With mine in the rice bowl, it won't be working either." He reached over to the land line. "No dial tone. I guess the wind took out the phone lines, too."

"So, when mine goes, we won't have any contact to the outside?"

"'Fraid so. The shutters are all secured, and the storm won't be over for a while. We're safe for now, so we might as well get some sleep."

Gary stoked the fire. They decided to sleep in front of the fireplace since there was no other heat, but Callie couldn't sleep. The howling wind, creaking house, and the flickering lantern casting those crazy shadows were all distracting and unnerving.

But the most distracting thing was right in front of her. They had wrapped up in their sleeping bags, facing each other on the rug in front of the fireplace. She studied his face in the dim light. Funny, how she hadn't noticed little details before. That little mole just below the outer corner of his left eye seemed to fit him well. He had really long, dark eyelashes. She marveled at how strange that a man with light brown hair can have dark eyelashes. She smiled.

His eyes were closed as his regular breathing pushed light puffs of air in her face. Normally, that alone would be enough to keep her awake, in an unsettling sort of way, but now, it seemed reassuring. And who could have guessed that even with the fire, she could feel his warmth. The storm didn't seem so bad. She felt safe.

Just when Callie started feeling drowsy, she was alerted by unexplained noises. They seemed to come from the basement. Again. Then she chided herself. It was probably another dream and relaxed. But the doorknob turned and her heart leapt. She leaned up one elbow to look that way. She thought she saw a glint, like a reflection off a long tool, and a shadow moving. She looked back to wake Gary, but he was nowhere to be seen. She screamed. The stalker was in the house after all! Where was Gary?

A masked man rushed at her and grabbed her. She screamed all the louder and tried to fight him off, but she was pinned against him.

"Callie!" the voice yelled. He was shaking her, and she screamed again. She wrenched an arm free and swung.

"Wake up! You're having another nightmare."

Her eyes flew open to see Gary gripping her wrists. It took a moment to realize what he had said. She had to give herself permission to breathe again.

"Are you okay?" He let go of her wrists. "It was just a bad dream. It's okay." He looked genuinely worried.

Finally, she regained some composure. "I'm sorry." She took a deep breath and exhaled slowly. "Wait a minute? What time is it? How'd I get on the couch?"

Gary sat back. "Don't you remember? We played Monopoly and then talked? You fell asleep."

She frowned. "No broken window?"

He shook his head and frowned. "No," he replied skeptically.

She sat up. "But we were in a house right on the beach."

He shook it again. "Um. Nope."

"No Bigfoot?"

His forehead wrinkled in confusion. "What?" He smiled. "Did you say Bigfoot? That must've been some dream. I think this guy, or whoever it is that's been harassing us … I think he's getting to you." He held her again, gently this time.

Callie looked around. Yes, she was still in Rudy's cabin. And she'd had the most frightening dream ever. "I'm not so tough after all, am I?" Her insides seemed to wilt.

"You're plenty tough. You almost gave me a black eye with that left hook when I was trying to wake you."

"I'm sorry." Callie couldn't help herself. She snuggled in his arms, and being there felt good, reassuring, and safe. Like home.

He rubbed her back and calmed her, "It's okay."

As expected, the storm was still in full force the next morning. Also as expected, the electricity had gone out in the neighborhood as far as they could see.

Because they'd be stuck here for at least another day, they made their surroundings as comfortable as possible. They had gathered enough firewood to last until they left Newport. The cooler was stocked, and they could cook in the fireplace. Blankets, lanterns, flashlights, and new batteries were all set where they could find them. It was almost like that first night here, only not as worrisome. They spent a leisurely day playing cards, playing a tie-breaker Monopoly game, which Gary won, and going over the papers from Mr. Evans once more.

After calculating when Rudy and Georgia would safely be awake, Callie called to give him an update. When she told him about the harassment, he stated that they would find a way to get there as soon as possible, but she insisted that they stay on their cruise. She didn't want to ruin their vacation. She avoided mentioning the grate in the garage. Although it would deflect the conversation, she didn't want to add more fuel to Rudy's anxiety.

The day passed peacefully with discussions, games, cooking, and planning what to do when they returned to Portland.

Hopefully, the storm would be over tomorrow. Before they left, they still had to meet with Donna's investigator to collect Russell's DNA from Donna's house.

They almost forgot about the stalker.

Chapter 24

Callie washed the breakfast dishes, and Gary dried them and put them away.

As Gary put away the silverware, he stated, "Too bad we had to stay in yesterday, but that storm was just too dangerous to be out in it," He looked up as if to see her reaction. "At least, we'll finally get to meet Mr. Evan's investigator at ten. Ready?"

"Do you think we should call him with a reminder?"

"I doubt they'll forget. The DNA's going to be a pretty important piece of evidence."

"I don't want to take a chance. We're leaving for home tomorrow."

He put a hand onto her shoulder. "Calm down. We don't leave for over an hour."

She sighed. "I guess you're right."

"Cheer up. We had fun."

"It's a good thing Rudy had some games here." Callie turned around with a wicked smile. "I really creamed you at Rummy."

"Only because I let you."

"Hah! Then, what about Monopoly? You just couldn't get a good roll! That was not you letting me win."

"I'll give you that one. But I get a rematch," he demanded.

"Since we leave tomorrow, I'll see that challenge tonight."

"You're on."

Callie was still limping, but the pain was now tolerable. Gary rewrapped the ace bandage and helped her with her boots. "I can do it," she protested.

"I know. Just being helpful. I don't want you to make the injury any worse." He looked up as he knelt on the floor. "Are you sure you're up to driving?"

"It's an automatic, so I won't be using my left foot. I should be okay."

"Okay. But if it bothers you, just say so, and I'll take over."

"Aha! So, you're really asking because you want to drive."

He chuckled. "That may be a contributing factor." But his smile quickly changed to concern. "But I'm actually worried for you."

"Okay, boss."

The twinkle in her eye was a clue that she was baiting him. He knew he had to take the bite. "Boss, huh. You haven't seen bossy."

"Oh really?"

Just then, he ran his thumb across the arch of her good foot.

Giggling, she cried, "Don't do that!" She jerked her foot out of his grip and pushed him at the shoulder. "You know I'm ticklish."

Laughing, he toppled backwards. "That's why I did it. And I should've expected you'd knock me down." He nodded teasingly.

She put the boot on her good foot. She knew she'd have to be on the alert for a comeback.

Craig's watch alarm went off. He had to force himself to sit up. It had been another miserably cold night, and to top it off, it was still raining. At least, the worst of the storm was over. His breath made steam puffs, and he shivered as he climbed into the front seat. He grabbed the sleeping bag and tried to wrap it around himself. He knew she wouldn't be running this morning because she was still limping yesterday. He'd thought about parking somewhere else, but that would only make her suspicious.

Two hours passed, and anxiety made him check his watch regularly. *Did I miss something? Her car is still there, so she must still be around.* He was sure she hadn't left before he got up. He impatiently drummed his gloved fingers on the steering wheel.

The damp air and the draft of blowing rain chilled him. Shivering, waiting, and impatience had whipped his anger into full-blown rage. His eyebrows pressed down hard, almost obscuring his ice-blue eyes. He started cursing under his breath. "It's all her fault, and she's gonna pay. I can't believe she reported *me*. *She's* the one who started it! If she hadn't gotten all Nazi, nothing would've happened, and I wouldn't have to do this. *She* was wrong, and *I* get fired. And then that old man complained. Now, I can't get a job anywhere. Who do those high and mighty hospital people think they are to blackball me?"

He fumed some more before adding, "I'll show you, you spawn of the devil." He was glad he'd thought to write down her license number in the parking structure. Even before finding the house where the van was registered, he'd made his decision. It wasn't long before she showed up, and he was prepared.

Following her over those mountains was pretty tricky. Pretending to put chains on almost did him in. With his headlights shining in their faces, he knew they wouldn't see him watching them. They'd just assume he was doing what they had done, putting on chains. Not putting them on was a gamble, but he couldn't take the chance of losing them if he was too slow. It was worth the danger to keep them in sight. Slipping in the snow on the mountains at night was not an experience he wanted to try again.

Although it was mighty miserable here, he was thankful they were here in Newport instead of Portland. It was easier to follow without as much traffic here. He was pretty certain that he'd followed her to all the places she was going to visit. It didn't matter that he didn't know why she was here. He made up his mind last night; it had to be today.

"As soon as she comes out of that blasted house! When *is* she coming out?" he cursed under his steaming breath. "What is she waiting for?" The more impatient he became, the more anger was generated.

Finally, she came out just after ten. He cursed out loud when he saw that man with her again. "Doesn't matter. He'll have to go, too." He smiled, thinking about what he did last night and patted the sack next to him. Considering what the outcome would be, it was worth doing it, even in the storm.

He started the car, turned on the defroster, and furiously wiped at the windshield so he could see to follow her. He was glad her car was bright yellow; he could spot it from several car-lengths behind. The flower decals on her taillights made following her all the easier.

Standing on the porch Callie and Gary looked at the rain. Even though this was the tail end of the storm, they would be expecting diminishing rain for at least another couple of hours. It was a good twenty feet to the car, and the ground was saturated and littered with debris.

He helped her get to the driver's side by holding her around the waist to ease the weight of hurrying. She slipped a little as they rounded the front bumper, and she grabbed his arm for stability. She grimaced as her ankle tweaked, and she almost went down. Gary helped her in before heading around to the passenger side. She wiped rain off her face and shook the water off her hands, and Gary did the same. She giggled.

"What?" he asked.

"It's as if we're two marionettes hung from the same strings."

They both laughed, but she stopped abruptly to look around inside the car. "Did you leave my window open?"

He checked to see if his window was slightly open. "I might've, but you're the one that likes to drive with it slightly open."

Sure enough, she'd forgotten to shut it. She pushed all the buttons for all the other windows to make sure they were all closed tight. "Wait a minute. You're the one that drove last."

"Remember, you insisted on fresh air. I normally don't do that, so I didn't think to close it when we got here."

She grimaced. "Sorry about that. Looks like we have to dry it out when we get back." She frowned when she turned on the key. The airbag light went on. "Gary, what does this mean," she asked, pointing to the light.

He shrugged. "Could be there's a bad connection, maybe a faulty switch. You'll have to have a technician look at it."

"This thing is barely a year old." She slumped. "You couldn't do it?"

"I haven't worked on any newer cars. Besides, I don't have any tools, and I wouldn't even know what to look for."

She sighed. "Would you look up some local dealers and make an appointment for me?"

"Sure." He did a search on his phone as she started the car and turned on the wipers.

On the way down the hill, she was focused on the road. She also kept an eye on the dash to see if the light went out or if any other lights came on. When she pulled up to the stop sign, she said, "Let's grab coffee on our way to Sheila's place."

"Sure," Gary agreed. "Do you think she'll complain about letting you in again?"

"I don't know, but when I explain why, she shouldn't, especially, since we're having the investigator meet us there."

"I'd sure like to see the expression on her lawyer's face when the test comes back." He became somber. "Do you think he'll say it doesn't matter? That the evidence still points to her as the murderer?"

"Could be. However, the motive is gone."

"That's the thing. Why would she want to? And whose body is it?"

When Callie turned the corner, she noticed the concerned look on Gary's face. "What's wrong?"

"I can't help feeling like I'm missing something. What's with all the weird accidents?"

"I don't know. I can't help but wonder if they're all related. But I can't for the life of me figure out what it could be." She turned North onto Highway 101. "Gary?"

"Yeah?"

"See that SUV behind us? I've seen it several times since we've been in Newport."

Gary turned around to look at it. "It's raining. Are you sure it's the same one? There are an awful lot of SUVs around." He paused. "Do you suppose maybe all the strange things happening are making you paranoid?"

"I don't know. Here's the drive thru."

When they entered the drive-thru, Craig pulled over and grabbed his sandwich. Even though the coffee was in a thermos, it was cold from being in the SUV overnight. He grumbled as he poured the cold brew. "Won't be long and I can get a decent hot meal." He huffed. "Then I can go home."

When Callie exited the drive-thru, he allowed a couple of cars to get between them as he followed. "Looks like they're going to that burned out building again. Maybe not. She's been all over the place." He chuckled. "If that's where she's going, I know the perfect spot."

Callie drove for ten minutes before she left the main road. "Do you think we'll find anything else?" She glanced into the rearview mirror. "Uh, Gary, this isn't a coincidence."

"What?"

"That SUV is still behind us."

Gary used the visor mirror to look behind them and frowned. "That's weird. Come to think of it, I think it's the same one I saw parked down the road from Rudy's cabin."

She moaned. "I saw it too. And when I go on my morning run, the windows are always steamed."

"That's weird." He turned back to her with a worried look and said, "I think I got the plate number. With the rain and the bumpy road, I can't be sure. But I'll make sure as soon as I can."

The road had turned to switchbacks, and Callie had to slow down. The storm had turned the dirt to mud, and foliage littered the road. To brace herself, she pressed her left foot to the floorboard, and it hurt, making her lose concentration for a moment. She gasped, turned quickly, and barely stayed on the road.

Gary flinched. "What's wrong?"

"My ankle."

Gary looked worried. "I knew I should've driven."

"Too late now."

The SUV bumped into them just as she turned a corner, causing her to lose what little traction she had, and she just missed going into the ditch. "What's *wrong* with that guy?"

Again and again, the SUV either bumped them or tried to pass. It stayed too close for Gary to see the license plate again.

They had passed the turnoff for Sheila's house by now, and Callie was unfamiliar with the road this far out. She was genuinely worried. Out of desperation, she made a decision. "I don't like this. I'm going to try to lose him."

She took the next street to the right, but the other driver managed to follow. Just then, the SUV sped up and rammed them just as she was nearing a turn to the left. They slid towards the ditch, hit a patch of grass which gave her some traction, and she managed to make the turn, and the next sharp right. By now, her heart was pounding in her chest. The adrenalin made her forget about her ankle.

Just as they approached another turn to the left, the SUV raced beside them and connected on Callie's side. With the muddy road, she had no traction. The SUV literally steered them towards the ditch.

Gary turned to look at the other driver as Callie tried to keep them on the road. "What?! He's wearing a ski mask!"

"Hang on!" she called out. There was a large boulder ahead, so the only choice she had was to steer to the right into the ditch. As the passenger wheels left the road, the car leaned towards Gary's side just before impact. When the car slammed into the tree in front of them on her side, she was thrown forward and her head hit the steering wheel.

Everything went black.

Chapter 25

When Callie regained consciousness, she blinked a few times and realized she was leaning to the right, suspended in her seatbelt. The car was in the ditch and wedged against a tree. It wasn't completely on its side, but there was enough of a tilt to make sitting upright impossible. She had a throbbing headache.

She put her hand to her forehead. "Ow." She reached up to turn the mirror and saw a bloody goose-egg on her forehead. An inch-long gash had dripped blood down her forehead past her right ear.

When she reached to unbuckle her seatbelt, she realized Gary wasn't moving. She turned to look at him and saw him slumped over against the door. The window was shattered under him, and wet underbrush was poking in around him. She groaned with relief when she saw that a tree was holding the car up just behind the passenger seat, missing his head, but the frame over the window was pushed in. "Gary? Are you okay?" She grabbed his hand and gave it a little squeeze. "Gary?!"

His eyes were closed, and he didn't move. Alarmed, she reached out with a shaky hand to see if he had a pulse. She cried with relief; he was alive. She struggled to get her phone out of her pocket to call 911. Thankfully, it was charged. It being dead was only in her nightmare.

Just then, she realized water was dripping on her from her open window. She was already cold, and now she was wet, too. The shivering made her head hurt even more.

During the wait for the ambulance, she decided to focus on Gary instead. She tried to wake him with no success. She felt helpless, remembering that she shouldn't try to move him. As she checked herself for other injuries, she kept talking to him, remembering that even when someone appears unconscious, they can sometimes still hear.

"Gary, don't worry, I've called for help. They'll be able to find us. I gave them our coordinates." Her lip quivered. "I'm sorry I brought you here. I wasted all that time wondering if I should risk our friendship." She'd said that to herself dozens of times, but now it was clear that she cared for him much more than she had been willing to admit. "Now, the thought of losing you is tearing me apart inside." She started to cry again. *What have I done? What if he doesn't make it? What if I can never tell him how much I love him?*

She thought again about removing her seat belt, but reminded herself that she'd probably fall on top of him, hurting him even more. She tried to open her door, but it wouldn't budge. Apparently, the entire frame was bent from the impact. Impacts? She grimaced when she looked forward and saw that the front end was crumpled halfway to the windshield. Apparently, they first hit the tree in front, which she saw coming and blacked out from the impact. The car, however, must have ricocheted to the side and smashed into the tree now located behind Gary.

Panicky, she jerked to look at the passenger door to see how badly it was damaged, but a sharp pain seized her neck when she did. She held her hand against the pain and started sobbing. Along with the neck pain, trying to keep upright made her realize other muscles were aching, too.

Wait! she warned herself. *Don't panic.* She concentrated on Gary. "I'm sorry to get you in this. At least, you got the license plate, or part of it anyway. Hopefully. Do you think he's responsible for all the harassment?" She paused a moment and gasped. "I just realized something. That's why the airbag light was on. They didn't work. Do you think he stole the airbags? She gripped the steering wheel as the gravity of the situation sunk in. "I can't believe it. Why would anyone do that?"

Wait a minute, why am I saying all that out loud? If he can hear me, I don't want him to become more anxious. I have to stay strong for him. She collected herself, determined not to stress him any more than necessary. Another tear ran down her cheek as she unsteadily tried to comfort him, "The paramedics should be here any minute."

Finally, the sirens announced the arrival of the ambulance and police.

"Please help Gary first; he's unconscious," she begged as they cranked her door open with the Jaws of Life.

The paramedics had to cut her seatbelt to extricate her, and then they worked at getting Gary out.

Her heart seemed to stop when she saw them strap him to a spine board.

Chapter 26

Callie heard muffled voices from the next emergency bay where they were working on Gary. As the doctor was examining her, she could only think about the worst possibilities. *What if he's paralyzed? What if he never wakes up? What if ...?* She grimaced at the thought.

The doctor stopped, "Am I hurting you?"

She refocused. "What? No. I was thinking about my friend."

He continued the examination. Eventually, she had four stitches on her forehead, at the hairline just right of center. She also had a concussion, a few bruises, whiplash, and some muscle strain.

But what was the verdict for Gary? Waiting only brought on more worry.

When the doctor walked out, a police officer entered with a pen and notebook in hand and introduced himself. He asked the usual questions about the accident. She hadn't seen the driver; she was too busy trying to keep the car on the road. She'd heard Gary say he saw the other driver. And the vehicle, and he had got the license number – maybe, but he was still being treated. The officer assured her that forensics would handle the accident site, including getting paint scrapings from her car. Then, she mentioned that she suspected seeing an SUV following them around town. Then, she remembered to tell them that it looked like the vehicle parked down the street from the cabin where they were staying.

Spotting her personal effects hanging in a bag on a hook, she asked the officer to hand it to her so she could call her parents.

When she finished the call, she explained to him about how they were looking into Donna Turner's upcoming case. She begged him to have someone retrieve the hairbrush at Donna's house and do a comparative

DNA test to see if it matched the burned body. "Can you please call her attorney to let him know why we didn't meet his investigator?"

After getting the details and the lawyer's name and phone number, the officer assured her that he would take care of the call.

By the time he left, Gary was being brought back from x-ray. She sat up too quickly, and her head felt like it was going to explode. She carefully lay down again to wait out the dizziness, nausea, and hopefully the pain. She put her hand to her forehead, but thought better of it when her hand landed on the stitches. She realized her left shoulder was aching. She turned her head to look at it and was rewarded with instant neck pain. She stopped with gritted teeth. She took some cleansing breaths, but they didn't help.

Determined to find out if Gary was okay, she slowly moved her legs over the edge of the gurney and carefully sat upright. At least, sitting up didn't make her feel any worse, but she still had to pause for her bearings.

The ER nurse came in, and she instantly made Callie lie down again.

"But I have to find out how Gary's doing!" Raising her voice was not a good choice.

"We haven't determined all of your injuries yet, and we don't want you to fall. You can't do anything for him. Now that the shock has subsided some, do you feel any new symptoms?"

"My neck hurts. And my shoulder."

The nurse made a notation on her chart. "Stay put. I'm getting the doctor." After paging the doctor, the nurse pulled the sleeve up on Callie's left arm to look at her shoulder and made another notation. "There may be more going on than we first determined. Stay put. Understand?"

Callie started to nod, but the pain stopped her. Instead she whispered, "Okay."

The nurse left and the doctor returned within a few minutes.

She listened as doctors, nurses, and aides came in and out of Gary's bay. She caught a few words here and there and finally determined that they were setting and casting a broken arm.

It was already six o'clock. She tried to figure out how long it would take her parents to get to here, but concentrating was too difficult. She had just closed her eyes to shut out the light when she felt a hand on her arm. She looked up and saw the nurse.

"With that concussion, we can't let you sleep yet."

Callie was about to object that she was only trying to think, but she noticed the time was after six-thirty. Confused, she just stared at the clock on the wall. *How can that be?* she wondered. Then, she realized she must have fallen asleep.

The nurse smiled, "Your husband is awake."

Husband? "Oh, you mean Gary. Oh, we're not married." Then, the worry was back. "Is he okay? Can I go see him?"

"Not until the doctor says okay. I'll go get him."

The doctor came in with a half smile.

"How's Gary? Can I go see him?"

"He'll be okay. He has a concussion, too, and his right humerus was broken about here," he said as he pointed to his own arm. "About halfway between the elbow and shoulder. He won't be able to work for at least six weeks. We're keeping the both of you overnight for observation. And yes, you can see him. But you'll need a nurse to escort you in a wheelchair. Just for safety sake. We're just about ready to assign you to a room."

When the nurse helped her sit up, her headache increased again. She decided to ignore it. She didn't want to take the chance that they'd make her lie back down if she complained. The nurse offered her left hand to help Callie to the floor. Callie put her right hand in the nurse's, her left hand on the edge of the gurney, and started to ease down to the floor. She had to stand in place for a few moments to stop the room from spinning.

The nurse held her and cautioned, "You don't look good. Perhaps you should wait until you aren't so dizzy."

"I have to see him," Callie asserted.

"We'll take it slowly, but if I decide we have to stop, then back you go." She carefully helped Callie into the wheelchair.

When Callie saw the bandage on his head and the cast on his arm, she couldn't stop the tears. "I'm so sorry. If I'd only known."

He looked over at her with a tired smile. "You couldn't have known. I'm just glad you're okay."

Callie sobbed, "I could've lost you." She stood up and leaned over him, which dizzied her, put both hands on his cheeks, and gave him a long kiss. She forgot about the dizziness.

At first, Gary was stunned, but the tiredness quickly dissipated, and he put his left arm around her and kissed her in return. He was not aware of the nurse watching them with a smile.

When they finally parted, Callie started babbling. "I didn't realize how much you mean to me. Are you okay? I don't know what I'd do if anything happened to you. How long have you been awake?" She went on and on as she clung to his side, holding his hand next to her cheek.

He chuckled at her. Although he could see she was terribly distressed, he felt a blanket of calm come over him. If being slammed around in a car was what it took to help her come around, he'd gladly do it again. Heck, he'd break both legs if he had to. He squeezed her hand and calmly reassured her, "Hey there. We're going to be okay. You can relax now." He knew the moment was now, and he whispered, "I love you."

She fell over him again. This time the impact jarred his broken arm, and the pain shot straight from the break to top of his head. Thankfully, she couldn't see him grit his teeth in pain. He held her tightly to control the urge to cry out.

She managed to say between sobs, "I love you, too."

Totally worth it.

Chapter 27

It was almost nine o'clock when they were finally settled in their rooms. Callie was disappointed that they had to have separate rooms, but at least their conditions weren't serious. After thinking about how poorly she felt, she was grateful that the doctors insisted they stay overnight for observation. She had almost finished the light meal they gave her. Gotta count your blessings. Thankfully, the pain meds had taken care of her headache. Then, she thought about Gary. Not only did he have a concussion, but his arm was broken too. She regretted feeling sorry for herself when he must certainly feel even worse, and he didn't even complain.

She was rubbing her sore shoulder and neck when she heard a commotion down the hall, probably at the nurses' station. She became alert when she recognized her dad's voice demanding to see her. She was contemplating getting up when she heard the voices of her parents and brother, Mark, approaching. Although she was tired from everything that had happened, she scooted up on her pillow so she'd see them clearly when they came in.

Sharon was the first in, and she hurried to give her daughter a thankful hug. "Are you okay? I couldn't stop worrying. When the police officer called, he said they had to use the Jaws of Life to get you guys out. I was so scared." She croaked, "I thought we might lose you." She stood there, twisting her hair.

"I'm okay. It's just a slight concussion. So don't worry." Callie felt awful putting her mother through this worry, if it were her fault.

"Are you sure it's only slight?"

"That's what the doctor said." She may have minimized the diagnosis, just a little. Maybe more than a little. "Gary's the one that is going to be laid up for a while. He's got a concussion too, and his right arm is broken. He won't be able to work for six weeks." Her eyes turned to her dad. "Hey. I hope you didn't break any speed limits."

He shrugged with a knowing smile.

She shook her finger at him. "Now, how sad would it be if we were all patients in here, together? Only because you were speeding on a snowy mountain and crashed."

"I had to appease your mother."

Sharon smacked his arm with the back of her hand. "Don't you lay it all on me. You know you were determined to get here quickly, even more than me."

"Well, maybe just a little."

Callie smiled and let out a contented sigh. "Thanks for being here."

"We wouldn't have it any other way." Jack stepped up, took her hand, and squeezed it.

Mark walked around to the side by the window. He wasn't a tall man, a couple inches short of six feet, but he manifested a presence, and from Callie's vantage point lying in the hospital bed, he looked much taller. She was always impressed by his self-confidence and perfect posture. His light brown hair was always perfectly styled, and although he wasn't dressed to the nines, he had excellent taste. He looked professional just wearing a polo shirt and slacks.

He looked down at her, his hazel eyes sparkling as he needled her. "I knew you'd be okay. You're too ornery to check out. Only the good die young, you know." He winked a misty eye.

"How did I know you'd say something like that?"

"Creature of habit, I guess. I'm going to Gary's room. See how he is." He waved.

"Thanks for coming." She knew he had to leave the room quickly. He wouldn't want her to see him cry.

Jack pulled up a chair for Sharon as he said, "I called Rudy and Georgia. They're going to cut their trip short and get off the cruise ship at their next stop. Then, they'll fly home. I told them we're taking you home when you're released from the hospital. So we'll see them at home in a day or two, depending on what flight they can get."

"I wish you hadn't worried them. I'll be okay. I feel bad they're getting all this stress, especially since Georgia's just over that cancer last year."

Jack gave her the look. "You know how they'd feel if nobody told them. And Georgia was the one who insisted they head home."

She started to nod, but stopped. Reacting to the pain, she grimaced and grabbed her neck.

Sharon struggled to hold back the tears. "Oh, honey. I wish it was me instead."

With a sad smile, Callie responded, "I don't think you'd like it."

For the next hour, Callie's family members alternated rooms to visit her and Gary, getting the low-down about all the strange things that happened, the broken board, the flat tires, the accident, and how they figured out how they knew who the culprit was. Everyone expressed relief in knowing the police would catch him soon.

The family finally left around midnight to stay at Rudy's cabin until they could pick up Callie and Gary when they were released the next morning. That way they'd be able to sleep in a real bed and be able to collect Callie's and Gary's belongings.

Mark unlocked the door to let his parents go in first.

Sharon went in a few feet and stopped in her tracks, staring forward, in the direction of the fireplace.

He shut the door and looked to see what she'd seen. He knew immediately what she was thinking. He quickly surveyed the room, spotted the kitchen, and said, "I'll make coffee."

"You know nothing happened, right?" Jack reasoned.

She looked over to him and nodded half-heartedly, as if she was trying to convince herself.

"You know the electricity was out when they came...."

"But that was, what? Two days at the most?" she interrupted. "So, why would they still be sleeping in here?"

"Nothing happened."

"I want to believe that."

"First, by the placement of the blankets, one of them slept on the couch, and the other on the floor by the fireplace. Totally innocent. And second, you know them."

Mark listened, knowing his mother wanted to trust Callie and Gary. It's those 'what ifs' that get folks. He knew everything was okay. Gary had told him in the hospital room – just a couple hours ago – that it was in the ER when Callie first declared her feelings for him. Thing is, although it would alleviate Mom's anxiety, he couldn't exactly tell her about what Gary said. It would betray a confidence. As he started some coffee, he recalled Gary's enthusiastic announcement.

As soon as Mark had entered Gary's room in the ER, Gary's eyes lit up. "You aren't going to believe this!" Gary blurted out in a joyous whisper. He described the whole scene, including the pain of jarring of his broken arm.

"See. I told you to tell her how you felt. I figured it would take her awhile to adjust, but wasn't the wait worth it?"

"You were right. I was beginning to wonder if she'd ever come around. Thanks for the push."

Mark came out of his reverie when Jack came up behind him. "You're deep in thought. Anything I should know?"

"Huh? Uh. No. Just thinking."

His dad gave him one of those looks that said, 'I know you're not willing to share right now, but that's okay.'

They packed up Gary's and Callie's belongings and went to bed.

Just after two in the morning, everyone awoke with a *Crash!* A light thudding sound quickly followed.

Jack sat up with a start.

Sharon turned over and whispered, "What was that?"

"I'm going to find out."

He climbed out of bed, and when he opened the bedroom door, Mark was tiptoeing out of his room. Jack put his finger to his lips with a "shh."

They crept to the drafty living room. Then, they heard the sound of a vehicle leaving the neighborhood. When Jack turned on the light, they saw the broken window with glass shards on the floor.

"What?" Mark blurted out. "Hey, there's a rock, and there's paper tied around it." He picked it up.

"Wait!" Jack called out just as Mark picked it up. "The police could've gotten prints off it." He sighed. "Too late now. We might as well look at it."

Mark groaned. "I didn't think." He untied the string to open the folded paper.

Sharon tiptoed in. "What happened?"

After explaining, Jack nodded to Mark. "He was about to read the note."

She gasped quietly when she saw the rock in Mark's hand.

Mark looked up, "It says, 'back off.' That's it."

"When Callie told us about the harassment, I didn't realize it was so bad," Sharon fretted. "This has to be the same guy, doesn't it? Do you think he's after us now?"

Jack took her in his arms, and Mark called 911.

"Can we close off that window?" she asked. "It's getting cold in here."

Jack and Mark spent the next fifteen minutes finding enough wood from the garage and nailing it over the window. Sharon had swept up the broken glass by the time the police arrived.

Chapter 28

Callie kept looking at the clock. They were late. She and Gary were due to be released in thirty minutes, and her parents were supposed to take them home. She was just beginning to wonder if the man who ran them off the road had gone after her family when she heard their voices coming down the hall. She let out a sigh of relief.

When they walked into Callie's room, she smiled. "I was starting to worry about you." Even though she wasn't functioning well, she could see that they looked tired. "Bad night?" As she spoke, she realized her parents were more than just tired; they seemed distraught, and Mark's smile was forced.

When Callie insisted they tell her what was wrong Jack explained about the rock, the police coming out to investigate, and finally getting back to bed at just before four AM. "So we haven't had much sleep."

When the nurse came in with the release papers, Mark and Jack went to Gary's room.

Callie was tying her shoes when someone knocked on the door.

Sharon opened the door to the same State Police Officer who had taken their statement last night.

"Miss Cooper, I wanted to let you know that we've apprehended the man who rammed your car. You're lucky. He thought you were dead."

Sharon gasped. "What do you mean?"

"When he found out you were here in the hospital, he went ballistic. Said you deserved to die."

Callie cringed in horror. "Why?"

"Claims you were responsible for him losing his job. And yes, he said all that *after* we read him his rights. We're keeping him in custody here in Newport since the crime was committed in Lincoln County. Because you gave us a license number, we looked up the registration and started looking for him at his residence. Sure enough, we caught him at his home just after midnight. So, with your description and his confession, he's definitely the culprit. He's facing felony hit and run. When this goes to trial, we'll need you in court here in Newport if you want to stick him with harassment too. That won't be for a while, so you should be recuperated by then."

Sharon frowned. "Did you just say you arrested him just after midnight?"

"That's right, ma'am."

She looked at Callie. "Then who threw the rock?"

Chapter 29

The trip back from the coast took longer than expected because of heavy rain and more snow in the mountains. Callie and Gary took turns telling her mom, dad, and Mark what they had discovered and what had happened to them during their stay in Newport. She was grateful that Gary had a lot of input although he was probably just as miserable as she was. On second thought, he must feel worse; not just physically, but likely blaming himself for not being able to protect her.

When they finally arrived home, Callie saw her Uncle Dean's truck on the street. He and other family members had taken turns staying with Cora and Ralph when Jack, Sharon, and Mark dashed off to Newport. Because Ralph needed constant supervision, and Callie and Gary would also be needing medical care, it was decided that they would both recuperate at Grandma and Grandpa's house so that all the care giving could be done under one roof. Sharon and Jack had decided to stay in one of the spare bedrooms so they could take care of everyone.

The drippy parade into the house ended with Cora giving Callie a long hug. "I was so worried. I'm so glad you're going to be okay." She held Callie's face in her hands and gave her a kiss.

"Thanks, Grandma. I love you, too. Right now, I'm going to sit down. I'm still a little rocky." Sharon helped her to the easy chair.

Dean put on his coat. "I've got to go to work. See you. Glad everyone is okay."

Jack gave his older brother a bro hug. "Thanks for being here while we were out of town."

"No problem. They're my parents too. Gotta go." He turned around to wave as he headed for the door.

Everyone waved and hollered, "Goodbye."

As Callie watched him leave, she always wondered how Uncle Dean and her dad could be related. They looked and acted so differently. Dean had a stocky build and brown eyes and hair, whereas her dad was lean with sandy colored hair and blue eyes. Dean was kind of timid, but Dad had fire and sass in him. She understood genetics, but the difference still seemed odd. She smiled at remembering what Grandma had said so many times, "They all come from one belly, but they're all so different."

Then she watched Gary as he aimed for the nearest seat, a dinette chair. She wasn't sure if he was in denial over his injuries or if he just bounced back more quickly than she. A careful look at his face told her that he was in more pain than he was letting on, perhaps exhibiting more bravado than was healthy.

Cora announced, "I made coffee if anyone's interested."

Jack and Mark both went to the kitchen to get a cup.

Cora called out, "Ralph, you want some?"

"Nah." He shook his head, nursing a sour look as he rocked slowly in front of the fireplace.

Callie hadn't seen that look since he'd quit drinking. She wondered if he might have started again since she hadn't been here to supervise.

The stomping of feet on the porch and a knock on the door announced Rudy and Georgia's arrival. When Jack let them in, they shook the rain from their coats. They gave everyone a big hug, and Rudy said, "We came as soon as we could get off the ship and came here right from the airport. Sorry it couldn't be sooner."

Jack put his hand on Rudy's shoulder, "You're here. That's what's important."

Everyone else chimed in with agreement.

When Rudy helped Georgia to the couch, Callie smiled. She loved seeing him dote on her, and his affection was never for show. Georgia had told her numerous times how he helped around the house, fetched things for her, and plied her with dozens of little acts of endearment. His attentions weren't just because she had been sick; he'd been doing it ever since their whirlwind romance started. Deep in her heart, Callie knew that Gary would treat her in the same way. She just wished she had figured it out sooner. She yearned for Gary to feel better.

Then her thoughts turned to herself and how helpless she felt. She felt a tear forming, so she pretended to rub her forehead to wipe it away.

She was feeling sorry for herself. She had willingly taken the role of caregiver for her grandparents, and she enjoyed it. But now she and Gary were the patients, and everyone else was helping them. She desperately hoped that Cora wouldn't feel like she had to wait on her.

Mark brought the dinette chairs into the living room for seating. Then he added logs to the fire. Callie watched as he added the logs and wondered, *why do guys like fire so much?*

Rudy helped Gary move from a dinette chair to the couch.

Georgia was already settled into the spot next to him and arranged a wool blanket around him, and Rudy made sure the arm of the couch wasn't putting any pressure on Gary's cast.

He smiled wanly. "You didn't have to do that. I would've been okay on the chair."

Georgia gave him a stern look. "You didn't look okay."

Rudy chuckled. "Don't argue with her. You won't win."

Georgia pointed at her husband. "Now don't you go giving away our secrets."

Rudy shrugged. "By the way, are you going to be okay financially since you won't be able to work?"

Gary hesitated for a moment. "I haven't thought about that. I don't know."

"Whatever you need, we'll help you out. So don't worry about it."

Callie was already emotional, and she teared up seeing Rudy offering help. Then, she remembered the suitcase and thought, *he can afford it. As long as it isn't counterfeit.*

"Thanks. You're a lifesaver," Gary responded weakly. He looked too fragile to argue.

Rudy chuckled. "That was a close one. I almost slapped you on your bad shoulder." He patted Gary on the top of the head instead.

Gary winced. "I don't know what's worse, you patting me on the head or on the shoulder."

Rudy looked horrified. "Oh! Your concussion. I'm so sorry."

"No. It's the embarrassment. Mostly."

Mark turned around to quip, "He's not so bad off that he can't make a joke." He grinned.

Rudy reprimanded Mark with an accusing finger.

Callie's voice trembled as she said, "I'm sorry, guys. I didn't mean for you to stop your vacation like that. I…"

Georgia interrupted, "You have nothing to be sorry about. It's not like you did it on purpose. Besides, we only had a couple of days left anyway." She got up, walked up to Callie, and gave her a big hug.

Callie took the time to look closely at Georgia. Her hair had almost grown back, only much curlier than before but not as thick. Before the cancer, Georgia had auburn hair, from a bottle, cut in a shoulder-length bob. She looked so young then, but now she also looked so tired. She was a little heavier because of the medications she continued to take to ward off a relapse. Regardless of her health issues, she hadn't lost her best qualities: her zest for life, her spunky personality, and the most treasured one, her infectious smile. "I love you, Georgia."

Sharon had joined Cora in the kitchen to help prepare a big pot of stew for everyone, and Jack had just brought Callie a cup of hot cider.

Jack's eyebrows pinched in worry when Callie rubbed her temples. "Are you sure you're okay?"

"Yes, Dad. The headache's almost gone, and the doctor said I'll be fine in a few days. I just need to take it easy until I have my bearings again." She really did appreciate the concern. It was just more proof of his love and protectiveness. Still, she was uncomfortable with all the attention.

She looked over at Gary and smiled. He seemed to love the attention, but he just didn't look right. "Gary, when did you take your pain pill?" She thought, *that must've been what the look on his face was for, pain.* She chastised herself for not realizing it before.

"What time is it?" Gary asked.

Mark looked at his phone. "Just after two."

"No wonder. Rudy, would you mind getting me some water?" He looked at Callie and asked, "How about you? Aren't you due for one, too?"

"Yeah, I guess you're right. Rudy, could you bring me some water, too?" Callie watched Rudy head for the kitchen. He seemed to move slower nowadays, and the sparkle in his black eyes had diminished a little. When the family first met him, he was vital and energetic. Everyone wondered about his heritage. By his appearance, it was impossible to tell. When asked about it, he never disclosed it and referred to himself as a mutt. His butch-cut, black hair had turned to salt and pepper, mostly at the temples. Although he had come into their lives only a handful of years ago, he looked older now. She wondered if dealing with Georgia's cancer had drained him. On the other hand, he was getting older. She hoped he would bounce back soon.

Callie looked at Grandpa sitting in the rocking chair. He hadn't moved or talked since everyone got there, and he had stopped rocking. Could the tense look on his face mean he was worried about them? He never vocalized his concerns, unless the subject was something that affected him directly. He was certainly better than before he quit drinking. Her insides seemed to sink when that worry occurred to her again. Is he craving alcohol again? Or worse, back to it?

Gary pulled the pill bottle from his pocket, but having only one hand working, he fumbled with the lid. Georgia took the bottle and opened it for him.

Gary sighed furtively. "I'm pretty helpless aren't I?"

Georgia scolded him with her intense blue eyes — intensity from emotion, not color. "Gary? I don't want to hear it. How do you expect to open that thing with one hand?"

He smiled grimly.

Just then, Rudy returned with the water. He had heard what Georgia said and laughed. "You tell 'em, girl."

She gave a quick nod and handed Gary his pill.

Callie smiled and took her own pill. *I'm so glad she's still sassy.*

After Cora turned the burner down to simmer, Sharon walked with her to the living room.

Sharon sat down next to Callie. "On the way here, you filled us in on what you found over there, but what I want to know is why did that stalker harassed you?"

Gary nodded to Callie for her to explain. Apparently, it would be awhile for his pain pill to take effect.

"The police are still looking into it, so we don't know. The officer that came to the hospital did say the man was angry because he believed I made him lose his job. They're going to let us know as soon as they get all the facts from him."

"He actually followed you to Newport? Then stalked you *and* tried to kill you? Just over a handicap parking placard?" Her mother looked horrified.

Jack shook his head with disgust. "You never know how many wackos there are out there."

Concerned, Rudy looked at Callie. "Wait, what happened?"

"It happened just after you left for your cruise..." Callie explained every detail, including her conversation with the hospital liaison lady.

Cora nodded. "He was totally out of control." She sighed. "Callie, I tried to get you to ignore him, but you wouldn't listen. You just kept talking. You can't reason with those kinds of people."

Ralph harrumphed. "Shoulda gave 'im a piece o' mah mind. Can't let 'em get away with that kinda stuff." He folded his arms, closed his eyes, and set his jaw.

Rudy shook his head. "No, Cora's right. Telling him off would only have made him even angrier. It could've pushed him to get physical to boot. Just be thankful that didn't happen." His shoulders dropped. "Well, actually it did, just later. You never know what will set off a person."

Sharon rubbed Callie's shoulder. "I'm just glad you guys are going to be okay."

Rudy put his fingers together like a tent. "So, to change the subject, what I want to know is, what did you find out on the investigation?"

Callie would have to tell the story again. Besides, she could count on Gary to fill in anything she left out. Perhaps, his input would bring more points to mind, or better yet, Rudy could have some suggestions. "I, sorry, *we* have a strong feeling that Donna is innocent." Callie paused with a wave of nausea and leaned forward. It passed quickly, but she was aware of several concerned looks. "We don't have anything concrete, but there were some inconsistencies in the evidence. We were just surprised the police never saw them."

"What kind of inconsistencies?" Georgia asked.

She explained the business about the key to the building. Everyone agreed that her being innocent was the only explanation. "Russell wasn't wearing his wedding ring, and nobody found it. Yes, he could've taken it off, lots of men do. But, we wondered, where did it go?" She paused to lean back and rub her neck. The pill wasn't working yet.

Gary, although pale, picked up where Callie left off. "His phone was missing. We can't think of any reason why he wouldn't have his phone."

Georgia chuckled. "You young people can't understand because you're practically glued to them. But he's an older man. Sorry, was an older man. Us old codgers don't have that same need to always be in touch."

When Callie saw Gary pause, she sensed it was to say something tactfully.

"I'll give you that one," Gary acknowledged, "but nobody seems to know where it is, especially after Donna said he was never without it"

I was right, Callie thought. *He's tactful*. She smiled, knowing he was a gem that she was never going to let go.

Rudy rubbed his chin. "Do the police know about what you've found?"

"Not yet. We on our way to do one more thing when the accident happened. Or should I say the attack?"

Rudy tapped his finger to his chin. "As soon as you're well enough, you have to take all of what you've discovered to them. And about that phone, they can check to see if anyone's been using it. If nobody is, then it's probably lost. In any case, the police can contact the server and get a record of all calls made and received. If someone found it and uses it, they can track down whoever has it, and that somebody might know something."

"There's one other thing. It's pretty big. We're pretty sure the body isn't Russell's."

Everyone stopped what they were doing and stared at Gary.

Gary explained the discussion with Donna. "We were on our way to Donna's house to get Russell's hairbrush so Donna's attorney could get a DNA test to compare with the body."

"Does her attorney know about all that?"

"Yeah, we were on our way to meet the investigator there."

Rudy's eyes popped. "What's the number? I'll call."

Callie raised her hand. "I'll do it. He knows me. No point in making him think all of Portland is involved."

Rudy begrudgingly conceded. "You're right. But do it first thing Monday morning." Rudy rubbed his chin for a moment. "So, what makes you think the body isn't Russell?"

"Donna said Russell broke his arm five years ago, but the autopsy shows no evidence of a break. And... she said Russell wears dentures. The body had two teeth missing, so no match. And there were a few things about the body that didn't match Russell's habits."

Rudy butted in, "Why didn't you say so from the beginning?"

"Saving the best for last." Gary wore a satisfied smile.

"Well, that puts a whole new light on the case. Since the dead man is not Russell, then Donna could be guilty."

"What? What do you mean?" Callie looked dumbfounded.

"It could be an insurance scam." Rudy was practically on his feet. "They could be in it together, make it look like Russell's dead, Donna comes off innocent and voila! They have the insurance money."

Gary sat there dumbfounded.

Callie held her head in her hands.

Cora sat horrified. "No! That couldn't happen. She wouldn't do that. I know her."

Rudy pulled back. "Hey, just a possibility, and that's what the police would think. You have to look at all scenarios."

Georgia waved her hand as if to pat down the tension. "What other bits of information did you discover?"

Gary cleared his throat. "At first, we realized a dually truck had been parking on the property, but we didn't know who it belonged to or where it was. Finally, Callie asked Donna about it, and apparently it's Russell's truck, and Russell's son is driving it. He's been going to Donna's house, even after Donna was arrested, but Donna doesn't know why."

Jack frowned. "That sounds suspicious."

"I agree," Rudy concurred. "Where is he now, Russell's son?"

"Nobody knows," Callie replied.

"Do you suppose Russell's alive and living in the house and his son is taking him food?" Mark suggested.

Gary waited a moment before he continued. "Donna didn't know about the fire until the firemen were on the property fighting the blaze. A neighbor had phoned it in. According to the records, it was Donna's friend who lives nearby. There's no line of visibility between the properties, too many trees and underbrush. Since the fire was just before 2 A.M., she had to be awake. And she wasn't forthcoming about the 911 call. She admitted it only when presented with the phone records."

Rudy frowned, tapping his finger on his chin.

Callie wondered what bit of enlightenment he would come up with.

Ralph's chin quivered. "Yer all fussin' over nothin'. Let the police do their job."

Cora huffed. "You may not care about her, but I do. And I want to hear all of it. So butt out!"

Ralph closed his eyes tightly as if to shut everyone out.

Callie tensed. She hadn't ever heard Cora speak so sharply with him. Never. *She has to be frustrated or angry or hurt. Probably all of the above.* The pain pill had just started to ease the aches and pains so she added, "There's one other thing. It probably doesn't mean much, but we couldn't find any evidence of his business or records. There wasn't anything in what the police collected for evidence either."

Puzzled, Sharon wondered, "How do you run a business with no records? Don't you have to keep track of bills, banking, customers, everything?"

Rudy waved his index finger. "I wonder if he was into something illegal. That could explain it."

Gary grimaced when he sat up. "That would explain why he refused to tell Donna about his business or income. She never saw tax papers, so he was probably working under the table. We did find out he was doing odd jobs, and a lot of the customers were unhappy with his work."

Cora's face wrenched into horror. "Oh, poor Donna."

"Do you think Russell could've done something so bad that a client might've had a motive to kill him?"

"That's a possibility," Rudy offered half-heartedly. "But you said you don't think he's dead."

"There's something else," Callie added. "The file cabinet that was in his office was locked, but the bottom drawer had been left open. The only papers in it were sheets of newspaper cut to letter size. They weren't articles, just random clippings, even comics and want ads. The drawer was warped and stuck open, less than three inches. I had a hard time getting the papers out 'cause they were charred and wet."

"Hmm." Rudy tapped his chin. "It almost sounds like a decoy. To make it *look* like company records had been in there."

"We wondered about that too," Gary said.

Rudy crossed his arms. "Did the police confiscate the cabinet?"

"No. It was still on-site."

"Not to make accusations, but that sounds like shoddy detective work."

Chapter 30

Grimacing, Ralph got up and went into the bathroom.

Callie watched him leave. "What's with him?"

Cora waved her hand as if swatting a fly. "Don't mind him. I told you, he's been grumpy."

Callie scratched her head. "Can I ask you something? Something's been bothering me. Did Donna ever tell you about a secret in her house?"

Cora nodded. "Yes. She wrote to me about it." Her faced dropped. "Oh-h-h!" She sat up with worry. "But I don't think it has anything to do with the murder."

"What do you mean?" Rudy blurted out.

"I got a letter just before she was arrested, and then another letter afterwards, just before a package."

"She mailed you a package?" Jack leaned forward.

"Yes!"

Jack blanched. "What package? Where is it?"

"It's in the attic."

Mark stood up. "I'll get it."

Jack joined him.

They pulled down the folding ladder to the attic, and Mark climbed up. "Hey, Grandma, where in the attic is this package? There are an awful lot of boxes up here."

"It's on the right when you get up there. And the letters are in a shoebox next to it."

"Letters. As in a lot?"

"Well all the ones I've ever gotten. The most recent are on top."

First, Mark handed down the shoe box to his dad and then hoisted the package onto his shoulder and struggled down the steps. "What's in here, rocks?"

"No." Cora giggled. "I don't know why she sent all that stuff."

Everyone looked at her curiously.

They took both boxes to the living room.

Cora looked anxious. "Do you think we should read the letters first? You know, just the two?"

Everyone conceded that would be the best way to start. Then they could hear Donna's words, not just Cora's memory of them. Maybe the reason for the package was in the letters.

When Jack handed the shoebox to Cora, she pulled out the first letter and read it:

Cora,

You aren't going to believe this. The police suspect me in Russell's murder. There are so many things about this that I don't understand how they could be true. I'm worried they could arrest me.

I'm going to send you a package in the mail. Keep it safe. Don't worry, it isn't about the murder. Remember, years ago, when I told you Mom said there was a secret in the house? I've looked all over the house and looked at everything she gave me, hoping there was a clue. But I still haven't figured it out, so I'm sending you everything she gave me hoping there might be a clue to help you figure it out. I sure can't see it.

If anyone asks, please don't tell them about the package. I know the police would just think it was evidence against me and impound it, and then I'd never find out what the secret is.

Please know that I'm innocent and have no idea why Russell is dead or who killed him. You know I could never harm anyone.

Sharon frowned. "She was more worried about this secret than she was about getting arrested? That must be some secret." She turned to Cora. "What did she tell you about the secret all those years ago?"

Cora took a deep breath. "It was right after her mom died. We never understood why she'd hid this secret instead of just telling her what the secret was. We talked about it several times, but we never had a clue what it could be or where it was. The strange thing is that her mom insisted that Patty not ever be told there was a secret."

Everyone exchanged puzzled glances.

Cora wiped a tear and put her hands into her lap. Her lip quivered when she whispered, "I really believe her. I know in my heart that she's innocent." She cleared her throat and added, "Then, this next letter arrived, you know, the one that came just before I asked Callie to help." She reached into the shoebox, pulled it out, and started to read:

> *Dear Cora,*
>
> *I'm writing to let you know the worst has happened. I've been arrested. I've talked to a court appointed lawyer but it doesn't look good. The courts are backed up, so I'll be here awhile. It looks like at least three months till the arraignment. And then more time until the trial.*
>
> *There haven't been any visitors, but don't you come rushing out here. I know Ralph needs your help. Don't be worried; I'm innocent, so I should be okay.*
>
> *I feel like the swing is about to break.*
>
> *Love, Donna*

"What does that mean?" Sharon blurted out. "What swing?"

Cora smiled sadly. "When we were kids, our neighbor had a rope swing. You know, two ropes tied to a tree limb and knotted to a board at the bottom. We'd meet over there at least once a week and swing. She'd sit on the board and I'd stand on the seat with one foot on either side of her. I'd hang onto the ropes, and we'd pump as high as we could. One day one of the ropes broke, and she flew off into a bush. I think the bush broke her fall 'cause if it wasn't there, she probably would've gotten hurt pretty bad. I saw her fly off, but all I could think of was to hold on for dear life. I held onto one rope and swung there until it was safe enough to let go." Cora swallowed. "So, I think she means that this is going to get pretty ugly before it gets better."

Callie frowned. "I have a question about the letter too. She said she'd already talked to the lawyer when she wrote this. She knew he wanted her to plead guilty. Why didn't she tell you?"

Cora winced. "She probably didn't want me to worry. She'd know I would've freaked out."

"Actually, it was the second time they talked that he wanted her to plead guilty. So she probably didn't know that when she wrote the letter," Gary corrected.

Rudy pointed to the opened package. "Let's see what's in there, okay?"

Mark picked up the package and placed it onto the coffee table. Then, he set his chair next to the coffee table, sat down, and reached into the box. He pulled out a paper-clipped set of documents.

"Well, what are they?" Rudy blurted out.

"They look like adoption papers, and the deed to the house."

Cora reached for them. "Let me see those." She looked at the papers and nodded. "Donna and Patty were adopted when they were little. That's what these are about. Their real mom, my aunt, died..." Her head bent down. "...from a drug overdose."

Callie put her hand to her mouth and mumbled, "That's awful."

"Donna was two and a half and Patty was only six months old. We all knew about the circumstances of the adoption, so this can't be the secret," Cora said. "When I first saw these, I wondered why she sent them."

"Here are their birth certificates." Mark handed them to Cora.

Cora looked at Donna's certificate for several seconds and then started to tear up. "That's funny. I never realized this before. I knew Donna was born the day before me and we always joked about it, saying we could be sisters. But I never realized how close. Look, she was born just before midnight, but I was born just after." She held the document in front of Sharon and pointed to the line. Then, she started to cry.

Sharon put her arm around her shoulder and motioned for Mark to retrieve something else from the package.

"It's an envelope full of photographs." He handed it to Cora.

She wiped her tears with the sleeve of her sweater. She took another deep breath to collect herself. She pulled out the pictures, looked at a few, and smiled. "These are from our childhood, wedding pictures, vacations. Oh, this one's when we remodeled my parents' house. I was getting ready to move out, and they wanted to convert my bedroom to a sewing room for my mom. Donna was painting." She laughed. "Donna was goofing around and tapped her brush in my hair. It was an accident, but I smeared paint on her arm to get her back." She laughed again. "Of course, it escalated." She stared at the picture for a minute. "Our punishment was that we had to paint the floor. There was no fixing the mess we'd made." She held the picture to her chest and started to cry again.

After she recuperated, she looked at more photos of kids playing in the yard, her mom cooking at the stove, repairs being done on the house, etc. Most had dates written on them with the names of the people photographed. Two pictures caught Sharon's attention, one showed Donna modeling a prom dress at the front door. The other was her mom setting the table in the kitchen with Patty coming in the door from the living room with a scowl on her face.

When Sharon looked at the backs, she turned her head with confusion. "Why do these two pictures have an 'x' on the back?"

Cora frowned. "I don't know. Maybe they're special?"

Callie took them and pictured herself in the house as if she was standing in one of those spaces.

Mark reached in the package and pulled out a box. "Oof," he grunted. "This is what's so heavy." He opened it and the strangest puzzlement came over his face. "What? What are these?"

Cora gave a sad laugh. "Donna's mother made those. It's a set of jewelry made with stones that she'd found over the years. She had them polished and made them into a set."

Mark set the box on the coffee table in front of Cora. "Careful, don't let that drop on your foot."

Callie laughed unexpectedly. "Sorry." She stifled a giggle.

Sharon reached inside and pulled out a necklace. Trying to be polite, she said, "Interesting." Each square stone was the same size, but in different colors and patterns. They hung from their corners from dual strands. The moss agates were in combinations of grays, greens, browns, and blues. The patterns ranged from striated or blotchy to speckled. She passed it down the line so everyone could look at it. When she pulled out the rest of the set, earrings, broach, tiara, and a ring, she grimaced.

Cora shook her head. "Gaudy aren't they? And some of the stones are manufactured, not natural."

"They're, uh, not very practical are they? I'd get a neck ache wearing this." Sharon curled her lip at them.

"I know when I first saw them years ago, I was glad they weren't for me." Cora grimaced.

Callie snickered. Thankfully, the pain pill was working.

Cora covered her eyes with her left hand as her right hand dropped down to her lap. "Like I said, I don't know why she sent them. She must've paid a fortune just for postage. And I don't see why they're so important." She shrugged. "Must be because her mom made them."

As Gary was examining the necklace, he mumbled, "Huh. What in the world?"

Rudy looked at him. "What is it?"

"There's writing on the back of each one. Looks like from a marker."

Everyone scrambled to look at the back of each piece of jewelry they were holding, and everyone acknowledged that, yes, each stone had writing. After some comparison, they discovered the writing was different, yet similar, on each one.

"Wait a minute." Gary looked more intently at them. "Do you suppose?" He looked up. "How many stones are in this set? An exact count."

Everyone counted the stones in their hands, and after the tally was done, they determined that there were sixty-four stones.

With a big grin, he asked, "Grandma, can we put these out on the dinette table?"

Rudy stood up looking at the back of the tiara in his hand. "Ahh. I think I see what you mean. It could be."

When they placed the jewelry upside down on the table, Gary sighed. "Grandma, we're going to have to take the stones out of their settings."

"What for?"

He pointed to a stone in front of her. "Do you see this?"

"Yes. What of it?"

"I think those letters and numbers could refer to positions on a chessboard."

Cora looked puzzled.

"Here, I'll look it up." He pulled out his phone and looked up the information. "See how each space on a chessboard has its own description? These match what is on the stones. I think if we arrange the stones according to this pattern, we might find out what the secret is. After all, her mother said there was a secret, and she made the jewelry. What do you think?"

Rudy nodded slowly. "I think it's worth a try. Do you think she'd mind if we did that?"

Cora's face pinched in thought. "I suppose it's okay if we remove them delicately so we could put them back in their settings."

Rudy reached into his pocket and pulled out a multi-tool gadget. He started opening the clasps and set them on the table while Gary placed them in order. When they were in alignment, he turned them face up, making sure they kept their original places.

Everyone stared at the mosaic in front of them.

"It kind of looks like some trees," Sharon suggested.

It was a hazy and irregular picture, apparently of one large tree and two smaller trees with patches of grass on the ground around them. A stream ran in front of them, and the sky had a couple clouds.

Callie gasped. "I've seen that place!"

"You have? Where?" Cora seemed shocked.

Callie put her face into her hands and moaned. "I can't remember, but I know I've seen it somewhere."

Georgia leaned over to Rudy and whispered in his ear, "Is she having trouble remembering because of her concussion?"

He shrugged. "Maybe?" he whispered back.

"Oh! Where was it?" Callie moaned.

"Hey, Cora." Ralph had returned from the bathroom and stood next to her. "Is Dr. Reynolds still our doctor?"

Everyone looked up slowly, clearly concerned.

"Why do you ask, Ralph?"

Callie looked at him suspiciously. She knew he hated going to the doctor and went out of his way to avoid a visit. He'd even go so far as to super glue his wounds shut. A sick foreboding wrenched at her gut.

"Ah was gonna drive over there."

Cora stood up and asked cautiously, "Why do you want to go there?"

He looked at everyone staring at him and blanched. "Well, Ah been havin' chest pains fer four days, and I ..."

Chapter 31

Cora was speechless, as if frozen. She couldn't even think.

Everyone jumped up from their seats.

Callie blurted out, "We're taking you to the emergency room right now! I'm not letting you drive yourself." Her pain pill was working, but she was more alert than ever.

Although everyone wanted to scramble out of there as quickly as possible, they tried to play it cool so they wouldn't alarm Ralph into a heart attack.

Mark drove the van with Ralph next to him. Jack and Sharon held Cora between them in the back seat, while Callie and Gary sat in the middle. Jack called his brothers to let them know their father was on the way to the ER.

There were no highways or freeways that would make the trip any quicker, so they just stuck to the main roads.

Ralph laid his head back with his eyes closed, and Callie looked worried. "Hold on, Grandpa, you're not dying on my watch."

"We all gotta go some time," he replied casually, like he had so many times before.

"Not today."

This time, hearing those words again, Cora closed her eyes hoping that wasn't going to happen. She felt the veins pounding in her neck, and a sinking sensation in her gut. *Why didn't he say something four days ago? Why did he wait so long?*

Callie saw Ralph's head slump forward, and his tongue seemed to have grown too big for his mouth. All she could think was that he wasn't getting air. That he wasn't breathing. She reached over and held his head up with her right hand.

Cora's voice trembled. "Is he okay?"

"I don't know."

Cora started to cry, and Sharon put her arm around her.

They were just a few minutes away when Ralph started to seize. Still holding up his chin, Callie yelled at him, "Grandpa! Please, hang on. We're almost there!"

Callie was still kicking herself for not knowing CPR when Mark screeched to a stop just outside the emergency entrance. Gary was by the door, so he jumped out and raced into the emergency entrance, yelling for help.

Two doctors rushed out, pulled Ralph out of the front seat, and laid him on the sidewalk. When the first one started chest compressions and the other placed a face mask on him to start pumping oxygen, Cora wailed hysterically. Sharon held her tightly.

Two more people in white coats ran out, one carrying an IV kit and the other pushing a lowered gurney. After the IV was started, they lifted Ralph onto the cart without missing a beat, and then they raised up the cart. The one doing CPR jumped onto the cart, straddled Ralph, again without missing a beat. One held the fluid pack above Ralph and ran alongside as the remaining two pushed the gurney into the ER.

Standing on the sidewalk with the rest of the family, Callie felt nausea come on. She assumed her blood pressure had spiked because the pounding in her head had returned. She bowed forward holding her head.

Gary put his free hand on her shoulder. "Are you okay?"

"No."

She realized Gary didn't look much better than she did. She wondered if he'd reached out to steady himself as much as to comfort her.

Jack parked the van while everyone else went into the ER. Sharon helped Cora to check in at the nurse's desk to give them Ralph's information. Mark helped Gary and Callie to a seat in the waiting room.

When Jack came in, Sharon and Cora were still at the desk. Apparently, Cora was unable to think, and Sharon had to find the information in Cora's purse. Jack offered to take Cora to one of the chairs in the lobby. As he guided her to the rest of the family, she started trembling and collapsed into the chair.

When Sharon finally finished at the desk, she brought Cora's things back to her. "They're working on him now."

Cora quickly looked up. "I have to go in there." She stood up and determinedly walked towards the keyed door.

Sharon caught up with her. "I don't know if they'll let you."

Cora glared at her. "They will," she declared. She tried the locked door and then marched over to the desk. "I have to be there with him."

The attendant looked at her. "Uh. I'll ask the doctor." She returned in a few moments and let her through. She led Cora to the bay where they were still doing CPR.

Watching for a moment, she seemed to slump where she stood. A nurse walking by guided her to a chair. Cora plopped down, staring at nothing. The conversations between everyone working on him became a dull drone in the background. The noises and lights of the busy ER faded as if someone had turned down a dimmer.

"Cora? Cora, you shouldn't be here." Sharon reached for Cora's hand. "Come on, you have to get out of here. You shouldn't watch this."

Cora slowly looked up into Sharon's distraught face. "I have to."

A nurse came back and quietly told Sharon, "Some people need to know that everything possible is being done. It's okay."

Holding back her tears, Sharon swallowed hard and nodded. She looked over and saw Ralph's limp body flopping like a rag-doll with each chest compression. "I just can't watch." She walked away quickly, shaking her head.

Cora returned to her blank stare, unaware of the passage of time and activity around her. Gradually, she thought about when Dean, their firstborn was brought home from the hospital. Neither of them knew exactly what to do, but they muddled through raising him. She smiled at the memory of Ralph telling her that Jack, their second son, being almost ten pounds, was going to walk himself home, he was so big. Funny how the bigger baby grew up to be smaller as an adult. For her, it was easier each time they brought home another one of their sons until by the time they had the fourth, it was old hat.

Well, almost easier. Art and Ricky, their third and fourth, were unplanned. That's when Ralph changed. He'd wanted to stop at two and then blamed their financial struggles on the fact that now they had twice as many mouths to feed. Ralph left their care to Cora, and that's when he'd started drinking in earnest. It wasn't until almost three years ago that the intervention happened, after almost 45 years of alcoholism, that he learned how his drinking, bad attitude, and bad treatment affected them. Alcohol had dulled his perception of what really happened for all those years. When he finally acknowledged what he did, became alcohol-free, and started reconnecting to their sons, Cora was so happy. Their family was finally healing. And now this!

She felt sudden remorse when she remembered how she snapped at him less than an hour ago. *Why did I do that? Is that going to be the last thing he'll hear from me?* She slumped over and covered her eyes. Tears trickled down her arms.

Somehow, she became aware that the monitor was not beeping. Someone counted to three, and then a strange bzzt sound rattled her nerves. The sequence repeated. And again.

Someone said, "Time of death, 1:14 p.m.

In the lobby, when the doctor came out to tell the family, Callie closed her eyes in remorse. "If I'd known how to do CPR, I might've actually been able to do something."

Sharon put her arm around her, "It's not your fault. None of us knew."

Suddenly, she hung her head and shook it. "No. I should've called for an ambulance when he first told us." She sobbed in her mother's arms.

The next two weeks were a bustle of activity. Jack and Sharon handled the details of Ralph's funeral. They were able to arrange for a Saturday viewing ten days after his passing. Georgia spent most of her time with Cora comforting her in her loss. Although Rudy worried that the stress might be too much for her, she had insisted. Callie and Gary spent this time recovering from their concussions.

Mark was busy setting up the last-minute details preparing for the grand opening of the kids' center. Since Rudy had funded most of the start-up costs, he had procured a lot of the equipment and was overseeing its installation.

But every day, throughout the day, it was strange and heart-wrenching, knowing that they'd never see Ralph again. Callie would never again hear him call out, "Trouble's here!"

She remembered a saying, and thought how true it was. She hadn't fully understood it before, but now it made perfect sense. "The day you lose someone isn't the worst; at least, you've got something to do. It's all the days they stay dead." How odd that such a truism would come from the ordinary sci-fi series, *Doctor Who*.

Chapter 32

It was after midnight when the two poachers locked their truck. They adjusted their night-vision goggles, loaded their rifles, and put on their packs. They had a practiced set of hand signals so that they wouldn't have to talk. They were skilled in moving in near silence through the forest, and they knew from experience where their prey might be. They quickly camouflaged the truck and took off.

Although the storm was over, the ground remained soaked. They counted on the water dripping from the trees to produce white noise that would diffuse any noise their boots might make in the soggy ground.

They were dressed for the weather, but that meant more weight to carry and less freedom of movement. They had to go out; their families were almost out of food.

Red got his nickname, not from his hair which was dirty blonde, but from his ruddy complexion. He looked the part of a mountain man, bushy beard, big hands, and burly build. He had repeatedly lifted the front end of a loaded pickup, just to show off. But he wasn't only brute force, he was also fast.

Ben had thick, bushy eyebrows that inched down to his hooded brown eyes. He was smaller than Red and not as strong, but he had a sharp wit.

Although Red was a little slow mentally, he was an excellent hunter and often saw things before Ben did. Because they recognized and respected each other's skills, Ben took the lead for where to hunt, and Red watched for their targets. Their system always worked out.

When they reached the first rise, they slowly scanned the area for movement. Seeing nothing, Ben signaled to head to the next rise. Moving cautiously, they had to go down one slippery slope and up another to reach it. As they reached the top, Red tapped Ben who was ahead of him.

Ben turned around hopefully, thinking Red had seen a deer or an elk.

Red pointed to a bluff on the other side of the ravine.

Ben saw the movement and nodded.

Red pulled up his rifle, but then he lowered it.

Alerted, Ben searched the area to find what he'd seen. He knew Red would never hesitate without a good reason. On the edge of the bluff, two men had exited a dually pickup truck that had apparently just backed up to the ravine. The shorter man shined his flashlight on the tailgate as he lowered it. The other man limped towards the back and then lifted himself up onto the bed of the truck. It looked like they were moving a barrel, probably a metal one. They tipped it onto its side which landed with a clang, and the man in the bed stepped behind the barrel to push it out of the bed. It rolled out onto the ground with a thump.

Ben huffed. *Well, with all that noise, they're going to scare away all the game.*

The two men started to roll the barrel towards the ravine. Just as they neared the edge, the shorter man slipped and fell forward. He scrambled to grab something, anything, but there was nothing to hold onto, and he went over headfirst. The taller man couldn't reach him, and all he could do was stand there as he hollered, "Dad!"

Cupping his hands around his mouth, Ben called out, "We're coming." He knew the man left behind would never be able to pull his friend out by himself.

The man stopped, desperately looked around in the dark, and then scrambled for the driver's door like a frantic dog on a tile floor. He started the engine and took off leaving the barrel at the edge of the cliff.

Ben used his scope to see the license number before it disappeared. He also noted that the truck was light colored, but the left front fender was dark, meaning that the fender had been replaced at some point.

Red spoke, "We've got to go down there to see if he's okay."

"Yeah, let's go."

Getting down the side of the ravine was tricky. But as they neared the bottom, they could see numerous barrels, hundreds of plastic bags full of who knows what, and rotting lumber. The scene was obviously a dump site.

They scanned the area and finally saw the limp body lying amid the trash, impaled on rebar. When they finally got to him, they could not find a pulse.

Red grimaced, "What're we gonna do?"

Realization hit, and Ben's mind spun with anxiety. "If we tell the authorities, we'll be exposed. We'll have to explain why we're out here. We can't afford the fines. If we had the money, we wouldn't be out here in the first place."

"We can't just leave him here."

Ben knew their consciences would torment them if they didn't tell.

Quickly Ben checked his map app. Then he checked his compass to get the heading. Now he knew exactly where they were. Finally, he checked the time. He had all the information they needed. Ben whispered, "We have to tell the cops. We'll have to call it in. We just won't tell them who we are."

"Yeah. Okay."

"We'll have to wait 'til we get back to the truck. There's no cell reception here. Since we're already out, we might as well try to bag a deer. Let's try another spot."

Red looked around. "What do you suppose all this stuff is?"

"I don't know, but it smells bad. Let's go." Ben led them north.

Red nodded as he followed silently.

Chapter 33

It was early March, and the sun was out in Newport.

Gary watched as Callie rested her elbow on the table, her chin in her hand. She gazed blankly at the table while picking at her breakfast. Dealing with her grandpa's unexpected death and funeral was hard for him, too.

In his head, he replayed the day of Ralph's wake.

They'd just returned to Grandma's house with the whole family after the funeral. Nobody but family would be there for the mini wake. Grandpa just didn't socialize and, therefore, didn't have any friends. Although Ricky didn't get to the ER, he did come to the funeral, and now he was at the house with the rest of Jack's brothers and their wives. Gary was grateful that everyone gave Grandma the gift of their presence. Their being there meant so much to her.

Everyone was piling into the living room. In the week after Ralph's death, there had been so much activity taking care of the necessary details involved with someone passing that nobody had the gumption to put anything away since that awful day. So, when Callie walked in, she sat on the couch right in front of the coffee table where the jewelry pieces were still assembled and still displaying the hazy jigsaw puzzle of trees, grass, and sky.

Jack had placed a dinette chair for Gary to sit on at the end of the coffee table, so Gary had a bird's eye view of what took place next. Not that he was fully functioning at the time, but he still remembered what happened.

At first, Callie didn't seem all that interested in looking at the picture the jewelry created. She apparently had another headache; he did too. He attributed it to stress. He watched her as she rubbed her temples. Her attention wavered between Jack interacting with their uncles, their aunts helping Mom with the food preparation, and Grandma staring at the fireplace while rocking in Grandpa's rocker, snuggled up in his blanket.

Georgia sat down next to him. "Can I help you with your pill bottle? It should be about time for the next dose." His attention was off Callie for that brief moment, but when Callie quickly leaned forward and stared intently at the puzzle, he looked up to watch. She stood up like a shot and exclaimed, "I remember! I remember where I saw this."

It had taken almost an hour for them to explain the situation to her uncles and aunts.

They had finally figured out where to look for Donna's secret – in the coat closet. After recognizing that the jewelry puzzle was the same as the painting in the closet, they realized that those two photographs with the arrows drawn on the back actually pointed to the wall where the painting was.

Although their concussions were healed, neither Callie nor Gary was up to par. They were both still grieving, and he felt helpless with his arm still in a cast. Instead of worrying about himself, he wondered if the stress was too much for her. But they didn't have the luxury to wait. Donna's trial was going to start next week, and they couldn't delay any longer. So, here they were in Newport to finish their jobs.

He had to help Callie come out of her funk. He put his good arm around her and asked gently, "Are you okay?"

Lifting her chin from her hand, she sat up a little straighter. "I'm sorry. I don't mean to be such a downer." She looked up at him, almost pleading. "If only he'd said something sooner. Why did he have to wait four days before saying anything? Stubborn old man." She snuggled into him as close as she could.

"I've thought about it, too. Maybe he thought the pain would go away? You know how he hated seeing a doctor. We've both seen him seal up a cut with super glue. Normal people get stitches. But in any case, I think maybe he waited for you to return because he wanted to see you one last time."

"That's a really sweet thing to say, thank you." She hugged him tightly. Then, she suddenly became alarmed and pointed her finger at him. "If you have any health issues, don't you dare hold out on me. I want to know right away so we can take care of them. Got it?"

Even through her sternness, he felt the love. Putting his hand on her cheek, he reassured her, "Of course, I will."

She kissed him hard and settled in under his arm. "I'm really glad uncle Ricky was at the funeral."

When she made that abrupt turnabout, he could see she had trouble focusing, but he wasn't going to mention it. Instead, he said, "Me too. I was a little worried whether he'd come since he didn't show up at the ER."

"He's still not over all those years he and Art had to endure. You know, from how Grandpa treated them growing up. That'd be a lot to forgive. I can't imagine having to live through all that abuse."

"He told me the only reason he showed up was for Grandma's sake. I don't think he'll ever let it go. But don't tell her, I promised him she'd never know. At least, not from me."

Callie shook off the mood and took in a cleansing breath. "Okay. Ready to go?"

"You bet."

They climbed into the new-to-her car. Again, she fumbled with the key. She huffed. "I'm still not used to this thing."

"If you ask me, I think Rudy got it right. It may not be as cool as the VW, but you won't be sticking out like a red flag anymore. Or should I say a yellow flag? Anyway, with you determined to be a detective, it's a good idea to blend in. I'm glad he picked it out for you. And no decals on the taillights, either." He winked when she took his good hand and smiled.

"I know you're right, but I still miss my Bug." Callie started the engine. "Have you talked to him about that suitcase?"

"No. I was going to ask you the same thing."

"I can't stop wondering if it came from ill-gotten gains."

"I don't think he'd do that." However, Gary knew in his heart that might just be wishful thinking.

"I sure hope not." With a sudden check to see if anyone was following them, she pulled away from the curb.

"The guy is in custody, remember?"

"Yeah, but whoever threw the rock through the window is still running around out there." When she got to the main road, she asked, "Do you think I'm really detective material?"

"Of course. Why do you ask?"

"When I first saw that mural, I should've known it meant something. You know, with it painted in the closet. That's just too weird to mean nothing."

"Well, you were distracted. Sheila wasn't cooperating very well. Patty had stolen things, and you were worried about the case."

"I know, but Rudy told me so many times to look for what doesn't fit." She huffed. "I wasted so much time because I didn't pick up on it." She turned to him fiercely and said, "I'm never letting that happen again."

"And I won't let you." He smiled, knowing her passion was returning.

She pointed a finger at him. "I'm holding you to that promise."

He gave her a mock salute. It was strange, allowing himself to look forward to being there for her for the rest of their lives. A wonderful kind of strange.

Because Patty had stolen all the tools in the shed, they brought tools from Rudy's garage with them to open the back wall of that closet. Because Donna's mother had painted it, they planned to remove that painting intact so Donna could keep it. They seriously hoped the secret was there and not be just another clue.

Although Gary's right arm was pretty much useless, he had insisted on going with her. He reminded himself that his cast would make a great weapon if things got rough. He also knew he had never been a fighter. *She'd probably wind up protecting me. I'm going to have to get Rudy to give me lessons after my arm is good.*

Even if they might find someone in the house, they had to go in. Gary was just as curious about this secret as the rest of the family.

Chapter 34

Callie stopped at Sheila's house to get Donna's key. Callie had sensed that Sheila was annoyed when she asked, and Callie wondered what was behind her attitude. Now, all they had to worry about was whether Patty would show up. It would be awful if Patty found the secret before they could get to it for Donna. Because they had been away from Newport for two weeks, that was a distinct possibility.

Callie drove up Donna's driveway and parked. It was early spring, and the deciduous trees were leafing out and blooming, flowers had begun to come up, and the grass was starting to grow. She turned off the key and smiled guiltily. "I'm sorry to bring you into all this drama…"

"Stop right there. You know I would have insisted on coming with you even if you hadn't asked. So, don't think you forced any of this on me."

Callie had no doubt that Gary was sincere. She reached across the console to take his hand. "I wish I hadn't taken so long to figure out my feelings, but when I thought I'd lost you…" She gave his hand a hard squeeze and blurted out, "Don't you *ever* do that again!"

"Not if I can help it. I wasn't too crazy about it myself." He looked at his cast. "Still not."

"I love you." She leaned over to give him a long kiss and lingered in the embrace.

"You know I love you, too."

"I guess we'd better go."

After pulling the tools out of the trunk, she didn't lock the car. If Patty came by while they were in the house, a locked door wasn't going to stop her from getting in the car. Callie would rather not deal with a broken window.

Going up to the porch, she noted that it wasn't as slippery as before, but there was still moss on the steps. She had already handed the key to Gary before loading her arms with tools.

They went inside, and Callie laid the tools on the floor next to the closet. She stood up straight, looked around, and saw that more things were missing from the living room. "Aw," she moaned.

Gary turned towards her. "What's wrong?"

"It looks like Patty's still robbing her blind. It's bad enough Donna didn't have much to begin with." She growled. "I can't believe she took the pictures! Why would Patty want pictures of Russell?"

"What do you want to do about it?"

"Sheila already tried the police, so I don't think I *can* do anything. I guess we just do what we came to do."

Gary opened the closet and pushed the remaining coats aside. "So, how do you want to do this?"

"I want to keep the mural intact, but I'm not too sure how to do that. Can you tell whether it's painted on boards, or if it's on plywood?"

Gary examined the back wall of the closet with a flashlight. "Looks like plywood."

"Awesome. That should make it lot easier. The mural should come out in one piece." She paused. "I think. Do you have any suggestions?"

He stood looking at it for a while. "Does Donna care what happens to the house?" He grimaced. "That sounded pretty bad, huh?"

"She's determined to discover the secret. Let's just be as careful as we can. Maybe restore the wall when we're done?"

"Yeah. That's what I was thinking. Sorry. Didn't mean to make it sound like we should bulldoze the place."

"I get it. We should probably find where the seam is and try to pry the plywood off from there."

"Sounds good."

The plywood was a 2'x2' section. She sat down and used the claw hammer to pull each nail out. Gary stood just outside the closet and held the flashlight for her. Working on each side alternately, she was finally able to pull out the piece with the picture on it and set it aside. When she turned around with it, Gary exclaimed, "What's that?"

She looked back and saw a vintage tin box in the space. She picked it up. "Do you suppose the secret's in here?"

"I don't usually bet, but I'd be willing to bet it is."

She could see the mounting anticipation on his face. She tried to pry it open. It was a little rusty, so it wasn't easy. She broke a fingernail in the effort, but the lid finally came off.

There were some folded documents and a sealed envelope addressed to Donna. She looked up. "I suppose we should let Donna open this?"

He looked disappointed, but he nodded. "You're right. She should be the first one to see it. It's her secret."

"Okay." She closed the box again.

When they went back into the living room, Gary asked, "Do we go back to Rudy's cabin to get some wood to fix the wall?"

"I don't remember seeing any plywood that size. Do you think we could use boards instead?"

"That would work."

Including travel time, they spent the next two hours repairing the closet. The only way anyone would know the difference was that the boards they just installed were about two inches narrower than the shiplap. And the mural was gone.

Chapter 35

It was lunchtime, so they stopped for lunch before going to take Donna her "secret." They made sure not to go to any diner they had eaten at before. They had locked the package in the trunk before walking up to the entrance. Callie noticed a metered newsstand next to the front door. She did a double-take when she saw on the front page a picture of Russell with his eyes closed.

Gary reached for the door to open it, paused, and turned to see what she was doing.

She bent closer to read what the article was about. The headline read, *Body Found in Forest.* "It's him," she blurted out.

"Who?"

"Russell. I recognize him from the photos that were in Donna's house."

Gary's mouth dropped open. "Are you sure?"

"Positive." Callie bought the paper and started to read it aloud right outside the door of the restaurant.

> *In the early morning of March 6th, an anonymous call to 911 alerted police to a body in the Siuslaw National Park southeast of Newport, Oregon. The caller gave GPS coordinates which led the officers to a ravine. After a careful search of the area, they determined that the body was lying at the bottom of the ravine. Using mountain gear to descend into the ravine, they had to return to the top when they discovered that someone, or several*

people, had been using the ravine as a dump site for hazardous materials. Rescuers had to put on hazmat gear to protect themselves from the toxic materials at the bottom. When they reached the bottom of the ravine, they discovered that the man had died on impact. There was no identification on the body, so the search is on to determine his identity. The man was 5'6", medium brown hair with graying temples, graying beard, and steel gray eyes.

The anonymous caller claims that there was a light colored dually truck with a dark front fender at the scene, and a second man drove away in it. Police have taken casts of the tread marks and footprints. They are actively looking for the driver for further information.

If anyone can identify the deceased or the driver, please call 541-555-6294.

She looked up wide-eyed. "We have to go find out what they know and tell them what we know."

They decided to grab sandwiches to go at the counter first and eat on the way to the police station.

She explained how she knew the identity of the corpse and then showed them the pictures of the photos she'd taken at the house. "So, that means Donna didn't kill him. You have to release her," she insisted.

The officer taking her information replied, "No. That only proves he wasn't the victim."

"But there's no motive now."

He stood rigid. "I'm sorry. I can't discuss the case with you."

Callie huffed in frustration, and they left.

The next stop was to visit Donna at the jailhouse. Callie had never been so excited to see her as she was right now. When Donna sat down, Callie asked her if Mr. Evans had talked with her since they were here last time.

"Yes. Since the trial starts Monday, we were going over the defense." She didn't look optimistic.

"Did his investigator find the comb and toothbrush at your house?"

"Yes. He said the test results would be in this week." She wrung her hands. "But he warned me that if they don't match, then it would look even worse for me."

Callie's mouth dropped open. "Why?"

"He said it would look like Russell and I planned it together to get the insurance money."

Callie chewed her lip as she glanced at Gary. "I have something to tell you, Donna. And I guess it's going to make things even worse for you." She pulled out the newspaper and showed it to Donna. "You were right, the body in your outbuilding wasn't Russell."

With furrowed eyebrows, Donna stared at the front page and swallowed. "So it looks pretty bad, huh?"

"The article said somebody called in anonymously. They said they saw another man drive away from there in a truck, a dually with a dark fender just after he fell," Callie added hesitantly.

Donna gasped. "Junior?"

"We think so. We just left the police station, and they said they'd look for him."

"I can't believe it." Donna grimaced. "Did he ..." She grimaced. "... did he kill him?"

"That's what we intend to find out. But I'm guessing the prosecutor is going to try and prove what your lawyer suggested might happen." Callie cringed.

Donna slumped down. "Well. I guess that's it for me then."

"I have some good news, though."

Donna didn't respond.

"We found the secret in the house."

Donna immediately came to attention. "What's the secret? Where was it? How'd you find it?" she eagerly asked.

"It was hidden behind the picture your mom painted in the closet. There was a tin box inside the wall. Here, I brought it." Callie pulled it out of the paper bag and gave it to her.

"I can't believe it. All those years. I always wondered why she painted it there." She looked up. "How did you figure it out?"

"Remember the jewelry you sent to Grandma?"

Donna nodded.

"Well, they had a clue. There were numbers and letters on the backs of the stones." She explained how the numbers and letters corresponded to a chessboard. "We had to piece them together like a jigsaw puzzle. I hope you don't mind that we took the jewelry apart."

"Don't worry about it. I always thought that set was hideous."

Callie chuckled. "Me too. When we assembled them, it looked just like the picture she painted, just kind of blurry. Then there were two photos with arrows on the back, one pointing to the wall in the kitchen, just on the other side of the wall of the closet, and the other in the living room pointing toward the closet. That cinched it."

"Did you have to destroy the painting?"

Callie smiled proudly. "No, we were able to save it."

"Thank you. I can't tell you how much that means to me."

"Glad to do it."

Donna looked like she was holding back a storm of emotions as she began prying off the lid of the tin box. When she saw the envelope with her name written in her mother's hand, she cried out, "All this time!" She shook her head as she carefully opened the envelope with trembling fingers. As she read the two pages, her expression progressed from joy, to shock, to horror. She slapped the letter down on the table. "I can't believe this!"

Callie and Gary looked at each other. Gary took Callie's hand under the table and held it.

Suddenly, Donna cried out in outrage, "How *could* she!" She covered her mouth, tears welled up, and she struggled to breathe normally.

Callie didn't know what to do. The desire to know this awful secret was overwhelming. She couldn't just pick up the letter and read it, and she would be embarrassed to ask. She'd have to wait.

Donna wiped away the tears, picked up the letter, and read it again. When she finished, her hands dropped to her lap, still holding the letter. She let out an anguished wail.

Her reaction reminded her of how Grandma reacted when she got Donna's letter. *What a weird coincidence.*

"You have to give this to Cora," Donna insisted. Looking at it again, she added, "You can't read it until she sees it. Promise!" She refolded the letter and struggled to put it back into the envelope with trembling hands. "As soon as possible. Today."

"I promise." A heavy foreboding seemed to weigh on Callie's chest. Whatever was in this envelope was something serious, but she couldn't imagine what. Flustered and wanting to change the subject, she asked, "Did you want to see what else was in the box?"

Tears were running down Donna's cheeks, but she managed to focus. "Oh, right." She reached into the tin box and pulled out the documents. As she looked at each one, she shook her head. Her lip started to quiver. "Give her these too." Her voice cracked, and she broke down sobbing.

Chapter 36

Keeping her promise to Donna to give that letter to Grandma without first looking at it was torture. Gary put the tin box into the trunk to keep them both from opening it. To keep their minds busy during the drive back to Portland, they considered possible scenarios about that letter. Neither one of them could come up with a logical answer. At least, not one that could elicit the response Donna had.

They burst into the house, scaring Cora so badly that she dropped the pot she had in her hand, spilling water all over the floor.

Callie regretted scaring her when Cora's hand flew to her chest as if she were having a heart attack.

"Good grief, what in the world?" Cora protested.

"We found the secret Donna's mother hid. Donna said you have to read the letter. Today."

"Letter?"

"Oh right." Callie had to refocus and explain what happened. "It was right where we thought it would be. There was a tin box with a letter and some documents. Donna insisted you read it before anyone else, so that drive back was torture." Callie practically forced the envelope into her grandmother's hands. She led her to the dinette table where she always read her mail. Then, Callie sat down next to her and leaned in. Gary sat down next to Callie and held her hand.

Cora opened it slowly. "So, it was in the closet like you thought?"

Callie wanted nothing more than for her to read that letter and tell her what it was about. And here she was asking questions. "Yes." She bit her lip to keep quiet.

Cora opened the pages and started to read. Just like Donna, her expression changed from joy, to sorrow, to outrage. But she was silent for several seconds. She quickly started to read the letter again.

Callie was holding her breath. Gary had to nudge her elbow to snap her out of her reverie. She gave him a grateful nod and quickly turned her attention back to Grandma.

Cora's mouth turned down, tears welled up, and she silently mumbled something indecipherable. Finishing the letter again, she silently looked out the window with a vacant stare.

"What is it?"

After a moment of stillness, Cora seemed to become aware of her surroundings. "Take me to Newport. I have to be there."

"Now?"

"Yes," Cora demanded as she stood up. "I have to pack." She headed for her bedroom, increasing the pace as she went.

"Grandma?" Callie called out, but Cora was in her room. Callie looked at Gary, and she whispered, "Do we dare look at it?"

"We'd better wait until she says okay."

Callie rolled her eyes before shouting down the hallway, "Can I read it, Grandma?"

"Yes, yes, just get ready to go as well."

Gary looked over her shoulder as she read.

> *Dear Donna,*
>
> *You've always known that you and Patty were adopted, and you've always had a special friendship with your cousin, Cora. I've marveled at how you two became so close. I tried hard to make sure you stayed connected and were happy, and I hope I succeeded.*
>
> *Since you are reading this letter, I am gone, and you must have figured out the secret in the jewelry I gave you. I'm relieved that I don't have to face you as you read this. It would have been awful to see the look on your face as the truth came out. I have an awful secret to tell you. I just hope you don't hate me for it.*

You have always believed that Phyllis was your mother, but that's not true. The day you were born, her child was small and died just after birth. Since I was the nurse on duty at the hospital, I did something unthinkable. Her sister, Hattie Kerns, gave birth to twins, you, just before midnight about the same time that Phyllis had her baby; and your twin, Cora, was born just after midnight. You were less than twenty minutes apart, just on consecutive days.

I placed Phyllis's baby on her stomach to sleep, but she stopped breathing during the night. I was convinced I'd caused her to smother. I didn't know what to do. When Hattie had you, I made the decision to switch you with Phyllis's dead baby. Phyllis was my friend, and I felt so bad for her and the sorrow she would feel. Phyllis had always told me that Hattie got all the breaks, but she actually always got the rotten deals. Then with what I'd done to her baby, I wouldn't be able to tell Phyllis what I did, and then be able to live with myself.

Besides, I thought it was unfair for Hattie to have two babies while Phyllis went home empty-handed. Hattie's twins were both small, so nobody noticed when I switched you with Phyllis's dead baby. I wanted Phyllis to have some happiness too. Hattie still had a living baby and a husband, so I felt like it wasn't a total loss for her. I guess that was just rationalization.

I immediately started having doubts about what I'd done, and I was troubled with awful guilt. Then two years later, when Patty was born with Fetal Alcohol Syndrome, I really grieved over the bad judgment I'd made. I'd always suspected Phyllis had lost her first baby because of drinking, but when Patty was born, I was certain of it. About six months later, Phyllis died from a drug overdose. That, you knew about. I thought if I adopted you and Patty, it might make up a little for what I did. I thought it was the right thing to do, but mostly because I was consumed by guilt. I guess I still am.

I made sure to let you and Patty stay in contact with your cousin, Cora. After all, she's actually your sister, your twin. I regret that I didn't have the courage to tell you before. I was afraid of the legal repercussions if what I did came out. I'm sorry I was such a coward.

I also wanted to explain why I willed the money to Patty and the house to you. I knew I couldn't count on her to keep the house, she'd just sell it. And I knew if I left it to you, you'd find my secret. I know she's going to want to contest the will. She's always wanted more than her share and then squandered whatever she got. Regretfully, she's more like her mother than I'd wish on anyone. That's why she can't hold down a job. But that's probably from the Fetal Alcohol Syndrome.

I hid this letter in the closet wall along with the original hospital certificates that have your footprints. I claimed to have lost them so replacements could be made to hide my deed. This way, you'll have the necessary proof after I'm gone. I'm sorry I didn't have the courage to do this when I was alive. After Patty finds out you aren't actually her sister, I don't know what she'll do. I apologize for that. I don't know where I went wrong in raising her.

My biggest regret is that I stole the time you and Cora could have spent growing up together, and there's no remedy for that. I am so ashamed of what I did, and I don't deserve your forgiveness.

I don't deserve your love either, but know this, I truly loved you. I hope you have happiness – somehow.

I love you, Mom

P.S. I guess I can't even sign this as "mom", can I? I'm so sorry.

Callie stared open-mouthed at the letter in her hands.

Gary stood up. "Well, I'll be."

Cora didn't take long to pack and came out wearing a look on her face that Callie had never seen before. Cora was fiercely determined, almost angry. Callie felt like she should step back to get out of her way.

Callie looked at her grandmother. "She's your sister?"

"Apparently. The documents are pretty conclusive, aren't they?" Cora straightened her shoulders. "Are we ready to go?"

"Uh, I guess we'll stay at Rudy's cabin." Callie stammered. "We've got to take food. We made sure there wasn't anything there when we left."

"Since I'll be there during the trial, we'd better go grocery shopping."

Chapter 37

By the time they got to Newport, it was evening. Cora took the main bedroom, and Gary and Callie set up their blankets in the living room as they had done before.

Cora knew they had to leave to talk to Sheila to find out what she knew about Junior, and Grandma agreed that they should go. They made sure she was settled in before they said their goodnights.

On the way there, Callie and Gary discussed the situation. Since the two families were close, Sheila must know about Junior. They just hoped she'd know how to get in contact with him.

It was almost eight o'clock when they knocked on the door. Sheila was surprised, almost irritated to see them since she'd already given Callie the key to Donna's house, but she let them in and invited them to sit.

Callie saw that the door, the same one that was ajar the first time she was here, was ajar again. Since it was late, she assumed that Ethan was listening again.

"I'm sorry to bother you so late, but I was hoping to ask you a few more questions. I know you and Donna were friends. And you saw Russell regularly too. I'm wondering if you know Junior." She didn't want to assume that Sheila knew him, and she didn't want to make her uncomfortable. Sometimes people with Asperger's can put people off.

"I've seen him and talked with him a few times." Sheila's demeanor seemed odd, as if she were hiding something.

"I'm hoping you might know how to find him."

"Why?"

Callie showed her the article from the paper and pointed out the section where she'd highlighted the witness's statement about the driver that was with Russell.

Sheila looked stunned.

"Didn't you hear about this?" Callie wondered.

"No. I don't pick up the paper, and I don't watch the news. It's too awful." She read the article and continued to stare at it.

"So, do you know how to contact him?" Callie asked again.

"Do you think he'll get arrested?"

"All we know is that the police want to ask him some questions."

Sheila stood up. "I have to go pick up Ethan. You'll have to go now."

That was abrupt. What does she know? Callie stood up and thanked her for her time.

She and Gary left, but decided to look at Donna's house one more time, so they went there next.

When they drove off, Ethan came out of his room. "Mom?"

"What, Hon?"

"I've seen the paper. I have to tell you something."

Sheila groaned inside as if she knew what was coming.

"Remember the day I was late for work?"

"Yeah. What of it?"

"When I went down the path, I heard those two talking by Donna's house. She was standing at the garbage can." Ethan swallowed hard. "She told him that Donna's bloody clothes and a rag with something on it were found in it."

"And?"

"I saw Junior putting a sack in that garbage can just before the fire started. I think that sack was the one with her bloody clothes."

"But, how… Wait, are you saying you think he did it?"

"I'm just sayin' what I saw."

There was another knock at the door.

Sheila huffed. "Oh, great, they're back." She jerked opened the door. "You!" She grabbed Junior by the arm and yanked him inside.

Junior's smile turned to bewilderment. "What's the matter?"

Sheila sat him down, held the newspaper in front of his face, and explained what was in the article.

He put his hands up defensively. "I ... I can explain."

"Well? Start talking."

As Callie and Gary looked around Donna's house, a knock at the door surprised them. She was puzzled to see Ethan standing there. *Well, Sheila lied again.*

"Can I talk to you?"

Callie realized he had a look of panic. "Of course." She brought him inside, and they sat around the kitchen table. Her mouth dropped open as Ethan explained that he'd seen Junior put a sack into the garbage can.

"I'm scared. I think my mom is helping him. They go off together a lot."

"Oh, you poor thing. You must be frantic."

He nodded quickly. "Yeah. And...," Ethan cringed. "He's there now."

Callie jumped up from her seat, knocking her chair back. "Right now?"

He nodded again.

Callie immediately dialed 911 and told the police where they could find the driver of the dually.

She put an arm around Ethan and told him they'd keep him safe, and they'd wait at Donna's house until the police came.

Chapter 38

Visiting hours were in the afternoon, so there was no hurry to get ready in the morning. Even so, Cora couldn't sleep in or take her time with breakfast. Nothing could calm her down. The entire morning, Callie and Gary tried multiple tactics to distract her, but nothing worked. Callie worried about her blood pressure.

In the jailhouse, Callie knew she couldn't do anything to alleviate Cora's emotional state. She watched as Cora wrung her hands as they waited for Donna to come through the door. Cora had insisted on being early for visiting hours, but that only increased her anxiety to see her twin. When Donna finally came into the room, Cora stood up, bawling. Callie had to hold her arm to make sure she didn't run up and embrace Donna, which would've forced the guards to escort them out and Cora would miss the visit.

Beaming with joy, Donna sat down with tears streaming down both cheeks.

Neither woman seemed able to say a word, but Callie could see the communication between them.

Finally, Donna rasped, "You came."

Cora, mirroring Donna's emotions, whispered, "Of course. Didn't you know I would?"

Donna quickly nodded. "Yes."

They seemed to say so much with their eyes, Callie almost felt like she was intruding on a very personal moment between them. She suddenly felt calm, realizing the joy her grandma and Donna were sharing. But, just as quickly, she was distraught. Donna's trial was not going to go well. Just as these two kind women found each other, they'd be torn apart, never to be together again. Callie started to cry.

Donna saw Callie wipe away a tear. "Don't cry. We have each other now. That's what matters."

Callie bit her lip; she didn't have the heart to bring them back to reality. She smiled as pleasantly as she could.

It wasn't long before the two older women were chatting and reminiscing. Neither of them broached the subject of Donna's certain prison sentence. Callie wondered if that was a defense mechanism to avoid ruining their time together.

Too soon, visiting hours were over. Both women cried at having to leave each other.

Chapter 39

Cora had insisted on seeing Donna during all possible visiting hours during the next two days until the trial started. On Monday, she made sure they were first in line to enter the courtroom.

Everyone stood up as Judge Isaac Murray was announced. His long face and hooded eyes made him look stern and harsh. Callie swallowed hard.

After some instructions to the audience, the bailiff announced, "Lincoln County versus Donna Turner."

Donna was led into the courtroom by a guard, and she smiled at Cora just before she sat down next to her lawyer, Mr. Evans.

The jurors were brought in and seated, and the bailiff read the charges.

Seeing Donna and Grandma here in the courtroom, Callie thought about the anxiety she had felt in the hospital when she thought she might lose Gary. This level of empathy made it hard for her to watch them. She felt Gary's hand grasp hers. She looked at him with anguish in her eyes.

Mr. Furman, the prosecutor, and Mr. Evans each gave their opening arguments. Callie cringed. Donna's case seemed so hopeless.

Mr. Furman was self-confident, forceful, and convincing in his argument. He stated that Donna and Russell Turner had conspired to commit insurance fraud. The high value of the life insurance policy, along with its very recent purchase, was the biggest red flag. He stated that the very vocal discussions in two different restaurants made it clear that Donna was the instigator of this purchase. He made it clear that he would present evidence that proved that the body found in the fire was not that of Russell Turner and that additional evidence would show that Donna

Turner murdered the man originally thought to be Mr. Turner. Furman finished by saying that Mr. Turner's untimely death only added to her guilt.

Mr. Evans stood up to speak; his argument was lackluster and weak. He sounded as if he was reading some boring material and not engaged in it. Callie assumed that since Mr. Evans thought she was guilty, that he didn't actually have an argument; so what was the point in trying.

She glanced at Gary who looked just as hopeless as she felt.

Mr. Furman brought in witness after witness. First, the firemen who found the body at the fire and then each of the detectives investigating the scene. Their testimonies took up the entire afternoon. As each witness was questioned and each piece of evidence was presented and explained, the family seemed to lose more hope. They knew the evidence was bad for Donna, and it seemed even more convincing to hear it. On cross examination, Mr. Evans' questions seemed feeble, at best.

Callie watched the jurors' faces as each answer was given, and as each argument was presented. Donna's chances didn't look good.

By the end of the day, Cora's initial excitement had deteriorated to despair. She was sullen at dinner and only picked at her food.

The medical examiner was called first thing the next morning. The poor, pre-death condition of the body was emphasized. Mr. Furman made the point that in his weakened condition, he would easily succumb to either man or woman using ether.

When Mr. Furman called an unfamiliar name as the next witness, Callie quickly glanced at Gary, and he shrugged. This name was not on the list they had received. He must have been added after they got the list from Mr. Evans. She sat up to listen carefully. It turned out to be the DNA technician who pronounced that the body from the fire was not Russell Turner and that the body found at the bottom of the ravine was actually Russell Turner.

Of course, Mr. Furman connected this testimony to his opening argument to the jury, the "fact" that Donna and Russell had conspired to commit insurance fraud.

The next witness was the operator that took the 911 call about the body in the woods. Mr. Furman presented the recording of the call, and the operator verified that it had not been tampered with. The recording and the witness both stated that the caller said it looked like an accidental fall and that there was a second party present, but they had left the scene.

The judge called recess for lunch.

Cora was despondent. "Do you think they'll find her guilty?"

Callie wanted to sound positive, but there wasn't much to go on. "I don't know," she lied. She tried valiantly to hide her worry.

But Cora was pretty savvy, and she knew that Donna's chance at acquittal looked bleak.

Chapter 40

Lunch recess felt like slow torture, and when it was over, Callie, Gary, and Cora were the first ones back to the courtroom.

One of the investigating officers had just finished his testimony, and Mr. Furman was calling his next witness when a man burst into the courtroom. He spotted Mr. Evans, rushed over to him, and whispered to him as he handed him some papers. Mr. Evans scanned them, stood up, and announced, "Your honor. I've just received new evidence. May I have a ten minute recess to look it over?"

Mr. Furman objected, saying, "This is irregular. Nothing has been submitted..."

"That's because it just came to my attention," Mr. Evans explained. "Please, your honor?"

Judge Murray paused and then said, "You have five minutes, and you'll have another five to present it to me in my chambers when you've finished. Court adjourned for ten minutes." He banged the gavel before heading toward his chambers.

"Thank you, your honor."

Obviously excited, Mr. Evans scanned the papers more thoroughly and headed for the judge's chambers with Mr. Furman close behind.

Gary leaned over. "What do you think that was all about?"

For the first time, Callie had a glimmer of hope. "You think it has something to do with Junior?" she whispered to Gary.

Eventually, the judge appeared with the two lawyers, and they took their places.

"Court is in session," Judge Murray said as he clacked his gavel.

The deflated attitude of Mr. Furman was countered by the increase in Mr. Evans' confidence. Mr. Evans announced, "I'd like to introduce new evidence." He brought it forward to the judge and placed the papers in front of him.

Judge Murray picked it up and said, "Any objection, counsel?"

The prosecutor glumly acceded, "No, your honor."

"Your honor, I'd like to call Russell Turner Jr. to the stand."

When Donna heard his name, she visibly flinched.

A guard entered the courtroom from the hallway bringing a man forward with him. He was about 5'8", in his early 30's, and had a husky build. He had straggly blonde hair, brown eyes, a pug nose, unshaven jowls, and he favored his left leg.

After he was sworn in, Mr. Evans approached. "State your name for the court, please?"

"Junior."

"Is that your legal name?"

"I don't know what you mean."

"What is the name on your birth certificate?"

"I don't know. I never saw it."

A few people in the audience chuckled. Callie knew he had to treat Junior with gentleness to keep him talking. Intimidation could have unexpected reactions. Even so, Junior looked like he was on the edge of breaking down. She saw signs of guilt, shame, and probably remorse, even though he wasn't to blame.

When she first heard about Junior and Russell having Asperger's Syndrome, she and Gary had done some research on it; but they discovered that the range of conditions varied widely, from mild to severe. And not everyone displays the same symptoms. The syndrome still isn't totally understood.

Mr. Evans took in a slow breath. "Why do people call you Junior?"

"So they don't get me mixed up with my dad."

"Are you saying you have the same name as your dad?"

"Yeah."

"And what is your dad's name?"

"Russell Turner."

"So that means your name is Russell Turner?"

Junior nodded.

"Please say yes or no so the court reporter can record your answer."

"Oh. Yes."

He sighed. "Where were you on March first around one in the morning?"

"I don't remember. All the days get mixed up to me."

Evans paused. "Do you drive a cream colored truck?"

"That's my dad's truck. He doesn't like me driving it much."

"Have you driven it?"

"Yes."

"When?"

"A few times."

"Do you drive it to the woods?"

Junior turned pale. "Sometimes. But only when Dad can't."

"What happened the last time you drove it in the woods."

He looked down. "Dad fell."

"Please explain what happened."

"It was real muddy. He slipped and fell."

"Didn't you help him up?"

"I couldn't. He fell off a cliff."

"Did he call for help?"

"No."

"Why didn't you tell someone?"

"I was scared."

"What were you afraid of?"

"He told me never to tell anyone about that place 'cause we'd get in trouble and go to jail."

"Why would you get in trouble?"

"'Cause we throw stuff over the edge, and we're not supposed to."

Callie could hear people in the audience whispering.

"Did you hear anybody after he fell?"

Junior turned pale again and nodded.

"Please answer with words."

"Yeah."

"What did that person say?"

"It was kinda far away, but I think he said he was coming."

"Why didn't you accept his help?"

"I was scared. I thought it was the police, and they'd put me in jail. Help was coming, so I drove away."

"Have you heard the news about your dad?"

Junior cringed. "Yes."

"You knew the police were looking for you. That they found your dad and needed to know who he was?"

"Yes."

"Why didn't you come forward?"

"I was scared."

"So, let's make sure the court understands. You were scared because you had been breaking the law."

Junior grimaced. "Yeah."

"You and your dad regularly dumped materials into that ravine?"

"Yes."

"Materials that were not allowed?"

"Yes."

"You do it in the middle of the night?"

"Yes."

"That night, he slipped and fell to his death?"

"I guess. I didn't know he died until later."

"Okay. Let's talk about something else. How did the police find you?"

"I don't know. They came to me."

"Where were you?"

"I was at my girlfriend's house."

"And who is your girlfriend?"

228

"Sheila."

"Her full name, please."

"Sheila Myers."

Donna flinched.

"What were you doing there?"

"I had to talk to her."

"About what?"

"About the police looking for me."

"Did you tell her why?"

"Yeah. I told her about the accident. Then I told her about us throwing that stuff over the cliff. I told her I was afraid I'd get arrested for that."

"That stuff you threw over the edge of the cliff, where did those materials come from?"

"We do odd jobs. When we remove stuff, Dad didn't want to pay the dump fees. So, we brought all of it there."

"What kind of stuff was it?"

"Bricks, tiles, drywall, roofing stuff. Whatever we took away."

"Does that mean asbestos, mold, and other hazardous materials were in it?"

"I don't know. Dad would know."

"Did you ever have to wear a protective mask?"

"A few times. I didn't like wearing it. It felt creepy, kind of like I couldn't breathe very good. But he made me wear it."

"Did he ever say why?"

"Huh-uh."

"Please answer yes or no."

"Oh right. No. He didn't."

"Where did you keep the tools for all that work?"

"We kept them at the barn."

"The police didn't find any tools. What happened to them?:

"We moved them. Well… We put them in the truck before the fire, but he didn't want anyone to see him, so I stored them at my place."

"Now about Sheila. Do you think she wanted you to turn yourself in?"

"I don't know. She didn't say that."

"Did she ask you to hide?"

"We were going to hide the truck. Is that what you mean?"

"How were you going to hide the truck?"

"We were going to drive out to the forest. I was supposed to leave the truck off the road, and she'd drive me back to my place."

"Why didn't you do that?"

"We were going to wait until Ethan was in bed."

"Who is Ethan?"

"He's her son. But he took off, so we had to wait."

Mr. Evans approached him with a pleasant demeanor. "You were waiting for Sheila's son to come back home. What happened while he was gone?"

"We were talking about what to do. Pretty soon, the police came banging on the door. I knew they wanted to talk to me."

"What did they tell you?"

"They wanted me to go with them for... they said it was for questioning."

"Let's go back to the night of the fire. Do you remember what happened?"

Junior blanched. "Yeah." His voice seemed to catch.

"We have a witness that saw you put a bag into the Turner's garbage can. What was in it?"

Junior turned to the judge. "Do I have to answer that?"

"Yes, answer the question," Judge Murray stated.

"Clothes."

"Do you remember what condition the clothes were in?"

He nodded.

"Answer aloud please."

"Yes."

"And what condition was that?"

230

"They had blood and gas on them. I didn't want to touch it."

"Whose clothes were they?"

"Donna's."

"And how did they come to be in your possession?"

"Huh?"

"Why did *you* have the clothes?"

"Dad gave them to me. Told me to throw them away."

The audience gasped and began whispering.

Judge Murray clacked the gavel. "Order in the court. If you can't be quiet, you'll be removed."

Callie saw a self-satisfied smile appear on Mr. Evans face. Then, she noticed Donna was trembling, and Cora had her hands over her mouth.

"Are you saying that Russell Turner, Donna's husband, gave her clothes to you?"

"Yes."

"Why did he have them?"

The prosecutor stood up. "Objection. Conjecture, your honor."

"Further questioning will prove the witness knew firsthand, your honor."

"Overruled. Continue."

"He was wearing them."

Again, the audience stirred, but with less volume.

"Do you know why he was wearing them?"

"He wanted it to look like Donna was the one that did it."

"Objection. Conjecture, your honor."

"It will become clear that Junior knew firsthand in the coming testimony, your honor."

"Overruled."

Mr. Evans turned to Junior. "To look like Donna was the one that did what?"

"To make it look like she killed the man."

"Who did kill the man?"

Junior started to wring his hands. "I didn't like it. I told him I didn't want to be there. He made me."

"I repeat, who killed him?"

A pitiful horror came across Junior's face. "Dad did it."

"Why?"

"He said something about insurance money."

Mr. Evans took a step back, and Junior seemed to be able to breathe again. "Was Donna there when your dad killed the man?"

"No."

"Why didn't you tell anyone?"

Junior shook his head. "I couldn't. Dad said if I told, he'd never see me again. I wouldn't be able to work or have a place to live. I knew it would be bad." Junior started to sob. "He said he'd tell everyone that I did it."

"Let's go back a little. Where did the man come from? Before your dad killed him."

"He said he found a good match. But I didn't know what he was talking about."

"Tell us what happened."

"He picked me up after dinner. He said we were going to do something important, but I needed to wear dark clothes. When I saw him wearing Donna's clothes, I asked him why. He said he had to do something to make sure the insurance would pay. I thought that meant it had something to do with that life insurance he got. So, I said, 'But Dad, that means you have to die.' He told me that he found someone that would take his place. I didn't know what he meant. I didn't know what he was going to do. Then, he explained that he was going to make the man sleep and take him to the barn. He parked a couple of blocks away from a place where homeless people camp.

"It was really cold outside. I had to put my hands in my pockets. He took me to a doorway in the next block where we could watch everyone. They were getting ready for bed. After a while, he pointed at a guy walking with a grocery cart full of stuff, and he whispered to me, 'He's the one. Now we wait.' He did kinda look like dad. The man stopped at a really big cardboard box. He got a blanket and newspapers out of his cart and put them in the big box, and then he crawled in under them. I couldn't understand why the man was going to sleep there 'cause it was so cold. I asked dad, 'How long do we have to wait? It's cold out here.' He sounded mad. He said, 'We talked about this. As long as it takes him to fall asleep.' I didn't like it. It didn't feel right.

"I looked at him and said, 'I don't know how you're not freezing in that getup.' He told me it was 'necessary,' He said, 'You don't have to wear it, so shut up.' He always talked to me like that." Junior looked hurt and embarrassed.

Mr. Evans' voice was empathetic. "What happened then?"

"He pulled me around the corner so nobody'd hear us. He said, 'I've been watching him for a week now. He's perfect. No one will miss him.' I told him I didn't like it and wanted to go home. He got mean again and said, 'Don't chicken out on me; it's all set up. Everything we've done means we have to do it *now*. Got it?' He grabbed my arm, real hard. He said, 'The bums will all be asleep, and everyone else with any sense will be indoors. Nobody will ever know.' That's when I figured something bad was going to happen."

"Why did you go along with it?"

"I didn't know what he was going to do."

"You said, it felt like something bad was going to happen. Why didn't you leave?"

Junior looked at him incredulously. "Nobody crosses Dad."

"Why?"

Junior sounded small. "'Cause when he's mean, you don't want to be around him."

"What do you mean?"

Junior cringed. "He hurt me once. That's why I limp."

"Are you saying he did it on purpose?"

"He said it was an accident. But it was when he got mad. Real mad."

"How long ago was that?"

He shrugged. "I dunno. Maybe ten years. I didn't want that to happen again, so I do what I'm told."

"Okay. So what happened after he pointed out the homeless man?"

"We waited in the truck for about an hour. Dad said he wanted to make sure everyone was asleep. That's when he told me what I was supposed to do to help him. We'd tiptoe to the cardboard box. He showed me a small jar and said he'd pour some of the liquid on a cloth. That's when I was supposed to pull the papers off his face. Dad would cover his face with the cloth, and I was supposed to hold the man's arms and sit on his legs. But it didn't go right. I didn't grab one of his hands fast enough. He was fighting, and he scratched my face before I could get hold of him." Junior pointed to his cheek. "Right here. I felt awful doing that to him. But he fell asleep real fast, so it wasn't too bad. Dad held that cloth for a long time. He said it was to make sure.

"Then, we carried him to the truck. That was hard. Dad kept letting one of his arms slip. I was glad I didn't do that. He would've gotten mad at me. We put him and his blanket in the back of the truck and went to the barn."

"Where is this barn?"

"It's behind Donna's house. Well, it used to be a barn, but dad and I made it into his office."

"So that's where the fire was?"

"Yeah."

"What happened when you got to the barn?"

"Dad made me help him carry the man into the barn. We put him down on the floor."

"Then what happened?"

Junior grimaced. "I couldn't believe it. It was so awful, I couldn't watch." His hands flew up to this face to cover his eyes. "He... he had a big knife on the desk. When he picked it up and went towards the man, that's when I turned away." He swallowed hard. "The sound... it made me want to throw up."

"What sound?"

"It made me think of when I was little and Mom would cut up a chicken."

Sick sounds came from the audience.

When he put his hands down, his lip was trembling.

"When did you open your eyes?"

"I don't know. Dad kept telling me to grow up and help him. He was mean again. I didn't know what he wanted me to do. All I could do was not cry. When I did look, there was blood all over." Junior started to sob again.

"It's okay. Take your time."

He nodded. "Dad started to pour gas on the man. I yelled at him, 'What are you doing?' He just looked mean and said, 'Shut up and help me.' I couldn't. I just wanted to get out of there."

"What then?"

"He was covered in blood and gas. He took Donna's clothes off and shoved them into a bag. He put that cloth in there too. Then he put on some regular clothes he had in the corner. When he told me to put the bag in the garbage can, I didn't want to touch it. It made me sick. But then he shoved it in my hand and said, 'Do it, now! I have to do something in the house.' Then he looked mean again and told me not to leave without him."

Junior looked down at his hands as if they were dirty.

"I don't know how he did it. He picked up that bloody knife. All that blood. It made me sick." He looked up again. "I asked him, 'How can you touch that?' He just said, 'Don't be a wimp,' like *I* was crazy."

"Is that when he went into the house?"

"Yeah. Then I looked at the bag in my hand. I couldn't get to the garbage can fast enough to get rid of it. Then, I sat on the back porch steps trying not to throw up."

"What happened then?"

"He came out and told me to get in the truck, so I did. He went back to the barn, and when he came running out, I could see a flickering light through the trees. He jumped in and drove us away. I asked him if he'd left a light on, but he just smiled. When I found out it was a fire, I knew he musta started it."

At first, Callie thought Donna was shuddering. No. She must be crying. Callie couldn't imagine how Donna felt on finding out her husband had gone through so much planning and effort to murder a stranger and frame her.

Then Mr. Evans gently asked Junior, "Why didn't you tell the police right away?"

Callie was anxious about how Junior was handling the trauma of seeing his father commit a murder and now the stress of telling about it in the courtroom. She noted a tremor in his voice as he continued.

"Dad's been telling me for years how much he hated having to take care of me." He looked spurned as he fidgeted. "He said that when the insurance money comes through, I'll have enough money to take care of myself. We'd just say nothing. Then, we'd split the money when they pay me. I didn't know how that would work, but I thought that if I could take care of myself, I wouldn't have to hear him be mean anymore. So, I stayed quiet."

"So, you didn't tell anyone?"

"No. Dad said it had to be a secret."

"Did you know that Donna was arrested?"

"Sort of."

"What do you mean?"

"I heard something, but I didn't know why."

"Don't you hear the news?"

"No. I don't like to read. And I don't have a TV."

"Didn't your girlfriend say something?"

"She said Donna was arrested. I remember she said she didn't like having to do all that stuff for Donna when she was in jail."

Callie saw Donna slump down. How awful not only to find out your husband framed you, but then to hear that your supposed friend begrudgingly helped you. Callie knew Sheila was in the audience so she turned to look at her. Sheila turned red and got up to leave, but she was stopped at the door by a guard. Callie wondered if she might've been added to the witness list, too.

On cross examination, Mr. Furman pushed hard to break Junior's testimony. Although he looked increasingly anxious and intimidated, Junior's testimony stayed the same. Repeatedly, Mr. Furman badgered Junior, prompting multiple objections from Mr. Evans. Even with the judge sustaining each objection, he continued. Finally, the judge warned him that if he continued, he would face serious sanctions. With a frown, Mr. Furman returned to his seat, stating, "No more questions, your honor."

Callie was right when she assumed that Sheila would be called as the next witness. Callie watched as Donna listened carefully. Callie was relieved that Sheila was unaware of Russell's plot, but devastated for Donna when Sheila admitted that she resented having to help Donna. Callie noted that Sheila never once looked at Donna. Apparently, she was too ashamed. Callie knew she'd be totally embarrassed if she had been called out.

It was a huge relief to finally hear the judge announce, "Case dismissed." An instant commotion from the audience flared up, prompting him to crack his gavel several times, with the mandate, "Order in the court! Order in the court!" The volume subsided enough that he could continue. He ordered that Donna be released, all charges against her be dropped, and that charges be brought against Junior for aiding and abetting. When Junior was escorted from the courtroom, the audience rushed out, led by the energized reporters who had to send in their reports and press for more interviews.

Cora rushed forward to embrace Donna. Donna was free, and they had each other now. Then, another worrying thought formed in Callie's head. *What is Donna going to do? Patty's robbed her of most of her belongings. Just when she gets some good news, she has to go to a house that's virtually empty.* She felt a hand on her shoulder.

"What's wrong?" Gary looked genuinely worried for her.

When she whispered her concerns to him, he held her with his good arm.

Donna took a long look at Gary and his cast. She leaned over to Cora, "What happened to him?"

"We'll tell you later. It's no biggie."

Callie hoped to exit the building peacefully. No such luck. There were a lot of reporters, and they were aggressive. However, Donna didn't mind stopping to give a short statement about justice prevailing and her happiness about being reunited with her family.

When they tried to walk out of the building, the cacophony of multiple conversations assaulted their ears. Gary pushed through the crowd with his casted arm. Multiple bumps made him wince, but he was determined to get Callie, Grandma, and Donna out of there. He practically had to drag Callie as she pulled Cora along behind her who was holding tight to her sister.

Callie worried about her grandmother and Donna having to snake their way through the crowd like this. She didn't want to think about them tripping over someone's foot. Progress was slow, especially whenever an occasional reporter tried to stop them with questions. Donna gave short happy answers as she was pulled through the crowd toward Callie's car.

Callie clicked her key fob so Gary could help Cora and Donna into the car. She jumped in and drove away, narrowly missing the daringly persistent reporters. The traffic was heavy with the media and rush-hour. Finally clear of the mob, she glanced at her grandmother to see if she was okay.

Gary shook his head. "I never would've guessed. That was pretty shocking, huh?"

Chapter 41

Everyone went out for dinner before going back to the cabin for the night.

Callie jumped when she heard the click of the lock at the cabin door. She and Gary looked at each other, wondering who it could be. Gary jumped up, although it was unclear what he could do with his arm in a cast. Seeing possible danger, Callie jumped up to try to hold the door shut, but it opened slowly just as she reached it.

Startled, she stopped in her tracks. "What are you doing here?" she blurted out.

Rudy chuckled, "This is my cabin, remember?"

Flustered, she muttered, "I know that. But why are you here?"

He walked around the cabin holding a device they'd never seen. He'd move it up, down, pointing in different directions as he went through each room. He covered the entire house, except for the bathroom where Callie said Donna was taking a bath while Cora sat in there talking to her.

Following him, Callie asked, "What are you doing?"

"I'm checking for bugs."

She was instantly alarmed. "Why?"

"One of the reporters followed you, and the cabin is all over the news now."

Both Callie and Gary looked at each other in dismay.

"I drove around everywhere before coming here. I didn't see anybody," Callie asserted.

Rudy shook his head. "Never underestimate a determined reporter. Nobody's safe here now. And I'm going to move the suitcase, so you don't have to worry about it anymore. Secondly, I've booked us all suites at a hotel for the next few nights. Get massages, room service, whatever you want, you've earned it. Just take a few days to relax. It's all on me."

"Are you going to tell us where the 'suitcase' came from?" Callie made the ironic air quotes around the word while rolling her eyes.

Rudy let out a slow exhale. "Right. Sit down, this may take a while."

Instantly anxious, Callie wondered about what they were going to hear, hoping nothing illegal was involved.

Gary and Rudy sat on opposite ends of the couch, and Callie sat in the rocking chair.

"Remember Pierre?" Rudy began.

"How could we forget? I still can't believe Alice was involved with him. And him being connected to the mob, too."

"It turns out that he had been stealing from the mob and had stashed the money in an overseas account."

"How did he get away with that?" Gary blurted out.

"The mob never found out. He was in charge of their finances, so he kept two sets of books."

"Then how did you find out?"

"He had hidden the second book in Alice's garage. I'm guessing he figured the mob would never look there if they got suspicious. It had all the information I needed to go to his bank and take the money out."

Callie sat forward. "You're kidding! And he didn't know you did that?"

"He knew somebody did, but he never found out it was me. When the police interviewed him, he let it slip that he thought Alice took his money."

"Wow!" Gary laughed. "Let me get this straight. Since the money was obtained from drugs and whatnot, that's why you're using the money to help kids? Because they were the victims?"

Rudy nodded. Then he smiled enigmatically.

Callie eyed him. "What aren't you telling us?"

"Well… I took money from the mob, too."

"You've got to be joking!" Callie's eyes widened in terror.

Rudy held his hands up as if to stop her. "It's okay. They never found out it was me. Besides, most of them are either dead or in prison."

"But…" Gary beseeched.

Rudy leaned back. "And they thought Pierre took it."

"What?" Gary laughed again. "Oh, that's priceless. How'd you pull that off?"

"Hey, I'm not telling all my secrets."

"Is that the reason for your trips to Switzerland?"

Rudy nodded. "The bottom line is I have to get that suitcase out of the garage before those reporters start snooping around and catch me in the act."

Puzzled, Callie frowned. "They'd do that? Breaking and entering?"

"I've seen it too many times."

Looking curious, Gary squinted. "So, how much did you steal?"

Rudy rolled his eyes. "A few million."

"What?!" Gary just about choked.

Callie's jaw dropped.

"I suppose you counted what's left?"

Callie and Gary both nodded.

"So, you see how important it is to get it out of here."

Cora had just emerged from the bathroom and was surprised to see him. "Rudy? What brings you out here?"

"I'm here to give all of you a treat. Tonight, we're staying at a nice hotel with room service. I'm paying for everything. It's just too cramped here for so many people."

By the time they packed their bags and settled into their rooms at the hotel, it was after ten. Cora and Donna had insisted on sharing a room; they still didn't want to spend any time apart. Callie was grateful for the soft bed after sleeping on the lumpy couch, but she missed being able to talk with Gary before nodding off.

Chapter 42

They all convened in one room for a loud, large brunch. Rudy wound up ordering half the room service menu, and everyone ate a little of everything.

It wasn't long before Callie started thinking about Donna's empty house again. This time, it was Donna who noticed Callie's anxiety. "Are you okay?" Callie saw the same empathy in Donna that always endeared her to her grandmother. When Callie finished telling her what Patty had done, Donna looked pensive.

Cora fumed. "I could've guessed. That   "

"Don't say it," Donna interrupted. "She doesn't deserve your anger."

"But what are you going to do?" Cora entreated.

"I don't know. I'm just glad the worst is finally over. Being released from that horrible place where everyone thought I'd committed murder, it kinda puts things in perspective, you know? It just doesn't seem all that important, having to replace furniture. I hated all of it anyway." She started laughing. "I actually like the idea of starting fresh."

"Stay with me!"

Everyone looked at Cora.

"But what about Ralph?" Donna asked.

Cora's hands flew to her mouth for a moment before she answered. "Oh. You haven't heard. I'm sorry I didn't tell you, with the trial and all. It happened when you were in jail." She started to tear up as she told the long story. Then, they all took turns telling about how Ralph waited so long to say something until it was too late. When Cora told her that they buried his ashes under the grapevine, Donna laughed hysterically.

Cora seemed confused.

When Donna recovered, she wiped away her tears. "Well, he was already mostly alcohol anyway."

Callie was surprised at the release of tension with her own outburst of laughter.

Everyone joined in.

Chapter 43

Donna huddled in the camp chair in the dark. In the cold. Nothing to read. No radio. Just silence. But, she was determined to stay awake. Her internal clock was resetting. This was the third day she was sleeping in the daytime and the third night just sitting, struggling to stay awake.

She had just looked at her watch for the umpteenth time when it happened; the door creaked open. She sat up alert, listening for footsteps, and readied her flashlight but kept it off. She saw a faint, moving light under the kitchen door. Faltering footsteps approached. The floor creaked, and she waited for the right moment. She knew the sounds of the house, so she listened for the squeak that announced when the figure was through the door.

Donna turned on the flashlight, shining it on Patty's face. Patty jerked. She knew Patty couldn't see her, at least, not until Patty aimed her flashlight into Donna's eyes.

"I knew it was you. How dare you steal everything I own?!" Donna stood up. She had originally wanted to throttle her sister. Now, she just wanted to scare her a little. Yes, stealing from family was just about the worst thing anyone could do. But the two previous nights had given her ample time to think. She thought about her missing belongings, but she found that she didn't care about them. The important things were still there, specifically a real sister, Cora. And she was thrilled about Cora's offer. Being able to get away from all the reminders of what her husband had done to her would be a welcome new beginning.

"Oh, you. Miss high-and-mighty. Hah, I already got the best stuff. You owed me, you know," Patty huffed.

"How do you figure that?"

"This house. It's worth a whole lot more than what I got. At least, you had a place to live." Patty struggled to look self-righteous.

"You know what. I agree. You deserve this house."

Patty's hand dropped, her flashlight pointing to the floor. "Huh?"

"I think you *should* have this house."

Patty said nothing, and during her stunned silence, she jerked again.

Donna turned on the overhead light. "Since the kitchen table is the only furniture left in here, let's go in there."

Patty suddenly became nervous. "Why?"

"You'll see." She didn't mind at all that Patty thought her demise was on the other side of that kitchen door. Make her sweat a little.

Donna walked through the door and stood at the table. "Are you coming?"

A rattling noise at the front door alerted Donna that Patty had not followed her, but instead was trying to escape. She dashed back into the living room and grabbed Patty by the arm before she could get the door open. "Come on, we have business to take care of."

Patty started to freak out. "Don't do it! You'll go to jail for real!"

Donna pulled harder. "Come on!"

Patty had a total meltdown, sobbing, and fighting all the way into the kitchen. But Donna was not impaired. She had all her wits about her and was easily able to haul her into the kitchen. "I'm not here to hurt you. Do you understand?" Several attempts to get through the fog in Patty's head finally made contact.

"Then what are you gonna do?"

"You want the house? I'm going to give it to you."

"Why? Where you gonna live?"

"Anywhere but here." Donna wasn't about to tell her about living with Cora. She pulled out a folded envelope from a kitchen drawer. "This is the deed to the house. I've signed all the papers giving you ownership. Take it to the county courthouse to have the title transferred." She smiled thinking about the fee Patty would have to pay for that.

Patty's confusion morphed into relief, then to triumph, and then to despair.

Donna became concerned. "Do you understand what I just said?"

"Yeah. You're giving me the house." She lashed out, screaming, "Why didn't you tell me earlier? I coulda kept all that furniture in here. Now there's nothing left."

It was a struggle, but Donna managed to stifle a laugh. "Here are the papers. Just make sure to transfer the title or you could get arrested for trespassing." Smiling, she turned around, walked outside, and sat on the porch, smiling. Contented now, she called Callie. "It's done. You can come get me."

Chapter 44

The next morning, Donna slept in. Callie joined everyone else in the hotel dining room for breakfast. They had never seen this side of Grandma; she was beside herself with anxiety and excitement. They had told her very little about last night because Donna wanted to tell her.

Because Cora refused to eat much, they took some food up to Callie's suite so that they could eat together when Donna got up. Gary had invited her to join in playing cards, but she couldn't concentrate. She paced. She tried to watch TV. Nothing worked.

Finally, at 11:30, Donna came into the room. Cora rushed to her with arms out. They hugged for what seemed an eternity. With joyful tears in her eyes, Cora led her to the couch, plopped her down, and sat next to her. "Tell me everything," Cora said, leaning in with eager expectation.

Donna rubbed her eyes. "Can I have some coffee?"

Nonchalantly, Gary and Rudy moved to a better viewing position. Neither of them wanted to miss seeing Cora's reaction.

Callie had already gone to the kitchenette and poured a cup. "Do you take cream or sugar?"

"Sugar, two, please."

"Cora, do you want a cup?"

Agitated by the delay, she snapped, "No."

Donna yawned as Callie handed her the cup.

Callie stood next to Gary and put her arm around his waist. Gary put his free arm around her shoulder.

Donna closed her eyes, took several gulps, and let out a satisfied, "Mmm." When she finally put the cup down, Cora grabbed her nearest hand and said, "Okay. Spill it."

Donna chuckled lazily. "I love you, but let me wake up."

Cora leaned forward and hugged her again. "I'm sorry. I got so caught up in wanting to know... I didn't think. You take your time."

Donna grinned. "Gotcha."

Cora gasped. "You're torturing me on purpose, aren't you?"

Donna nodded. "I've been awake for about an hour. I just had to give you a bad time." She giggled.

Cora stared at her. "You little dickens. So, when are you going to tell me?"

With a glint in her eye, she started. "Okay, here goes. I had resigned myself that this was the best way to go, just to let her have what's left. You know I didn't want the house anymore." She paused. "I always hated that house, except for Mom's painting of course." Donna looked down contemplatively, and then she looked at Callie, "I want to thank you again for saving it. It doesn't mean the same anymore. It means more. It's like a tree portrait of me with my twin." She looked lovingly at Cora. "I was so relieved when Patty finally sneaked in. I knew it was almost over, and I wouldn't have to lose any more sleep." She paused to drink more coffee.

"So what happened when she came in?" Everyone in the room watched the expectation in Cora's eyes.

"I was sitting in the living room with my back to the fireplace. That way I'd see if she came in either the front door or through the kitchen. Turned out, it was through the kitchen. She was trying not to make noise, but she was so high, she really didn't know how noisy she was. When she got through the kitchen door, I shined my flashlight into her face." Donna chuckled. "I wish I had a picture of that. I could tell she thought nobody was there. She must've thought the police were going to arrest her. When she found out it was me, she actually thought I was going to hurt her."

Cora's eyes flashed in delight as her hand flew to her mouth. "I wish I could've seen her face!"

Donna laughed. "It was priceless."

Cora inched closer. "Go on."

"I milked it. I let her sweat for a little while."

"Oh, you devil!" Cora pushed Donna's shoulder with mock chastisement.

Donna giggled. "It was so fun."

"When my back was turned, she actually tried to run out the front door. But she didn't have a chance. I hauled her into the kitchen, and she started begging for her life." Donna paused and hung her head. "Am I bad for enjoying that?"

"Oh no. Don't feel guilty, not after all she's put you through. I would've done the same thing. You were justified to give a little payback."

Callie nudged Gary and whispered to him, "I never would have expected that from Grandma."

He whispered back, "Me neither."

Smiling, Rudy mumbled, "Gotta love that feisty, little woman."

"What did she say when you handed her the deed to the house?" Cora asked expectantly.

"She thought it was a trick at first. I thought it might be hard for her to believe, I know I would've if I was her." She turned to look at Callie, "After I called you to pick me up, I remembered to give her a copy of Mom's, uh, Rachel's, letter." She turned back to Cora. "I'm pretty sure she's going to sell the house when she finds out she'll have to pay property taxes and utilities and all that. She'll probably end up mad at me for giving her the responsibility."

Cora looked somber. "I worry about what she's going to do with the money."

Donna pursed her lips. "I worry that she'll spend it all on drugs."

"I know. And that's what makes you so wonderful. But no one can stop anyone from squandering their money. No one can make a person do the right thing. You aren't responsible for her. Everyone has to make their own decisions." Cora sighed sadly. "I learned that living with Ralph."

"I'm just glad it's over. She has the house now, and I can move on. Although, I have practically nothing now."

Cora grinned. "You're coming to live with me. I'll take care of you. You deserve it after all those years dealing with Patty *and* Russell."

Donna clasped Cora's hands in her own. "We have so much catching up to do."

Chapter 45

The emotional roller-coaster ride was finally over. Cora and Donna were ecstatic with how things turned out, and now they were together. Donna was settled into one of Cora's extra bedrooms. Every day, they learned something new about each other: how much they were alike and how different they were. It was as if each of them was emerging from the emotional cocoons that their husbands had imposed on them and were finding out who they were now.

Callie no longer had reason to live at Grandma's home because she'd moved in to take care of Ralph, so she moved back in with her parents. Even so, she was happy to drive when Cora asked to take Donna to her favorite beauty shop and treat Donna to a makeover. When she arrived at the shop to pick them up, She saw Cora getting the final primp. Callie stopped in her tracks, thinking, *Wait, I thought it was Donna getting the makeover.*

When she saw Cora across the room getting a pedicure, Callie looked back and forth from the two Coras for a moment. "Pedicure Cora" had a contented and proud smile on her face. "Makeover Cora" was apparently Donna, and she looked thrilled with her results. Callie shook her head quickly. They looked so much alike now it would take a bit of time getting used to seeing Donna looking like Grandma.

As they got out to the car, Callie was still marveling at their similarity. "You two might need to start wearing name tags."

Cora and Donna laughed and sang songs all the way home. A peaceful calm came over Callie as she drove. *This is nice.*

Memorial Day was always an excuse for a big family shindig, and this gathering was no exception. It was an official welcoming for Donna. Normally, Rudy and Georgia held family dinners at their house because of their beautiful garden, but Cora and Donna had insisted on having it at their house, starting at noon.

Jack and his brothers had manicured Cora's large back yard because it had been neglected for such a long time. Everyone brought chairs, folding tables, barbecues, and canopies. Since Jack's youngest brother, Ricky, was the geek in the family, he set up music in the back yard with a playlist of Cora's and Donna's favorite songs.

Cora and Donna were so thrilled about looking so much alike, that they played up the confusion. Callie had been joking about the name tags, but when the sisters insisted on buying matching outfits, she insisted on the name tags. They were adorable.

The abundance of famous family dishes and barbecue specialties was nice. But more important was that everyone joyously came together with their support, enthusiasm, and camaraderie. Donna started to understand what family was supposed to be.

The food tables were set up under two canopies to keep the food protected from the direct sun. Chairs and tables were placed under the massive maple tree and additional canopies so everyone could eat in the shade. Croquet, volleyball, and horseshoes were available in the grass.

The tables were loaded with Jack's barbecued ribs, Rudy's barbecued chicken, Sharon's fried chicken, Dean's chef salad, Art's glazed ham, Callie's potato salad, Donna's fruit salad, Mark and Marci's deviled eggs and stuffed mushrooms, and Gary's chips and dips. Cora was proud to serve her special recipe of baked beans. Jack's brother, Dean, always told her, "They're better than dessert."

But everyone wondered if he'd still say that after seeing Georgia's masterpiece: an extraordinarily large, break-open chocolate egg with a chocolate mousse inside. "Donna broke out of a difficult situation to live the sweet life, so this is a tribute to her," she explained. Donna gave her a grateful hug. It had been a long time since she'd felt so peaceful and accepted. She realized that this family was better than anything she'd ever experienced, or even hoped for.

After dessert was served, Dean still loaded up on the baked beans. Turns out, he just wasn't a fan of desserts. Cora teased him, saying it was a good thing this party was being held outside. He replied, "And there's even a helpful breeze." He laughed and gave his mother a big hug and kiss.

When he walked away, Donna leaned over to her, "I love your family." Cora looked bewildered, "They're your family, too."

Donna got misty-eyed and whispered, "Thank you."

Donna asked Callie to tell everyone about the goings on in Newport so that she wouldn't have to tell the story over and over.

Callie stood up and tapped her glass with her fork. "I have been asked to fill you all in on what's happened since we left Newport.

"First, about Junior. He was arrested..." she looked at her notes to get the wording right, "for being an accomplice to murder and insurance fraud and for a few minor things: failing to report an accident, driving without a license, and vandalism.

"I know you've all heard that Donna was framed, but I want to explain a bit more. Apparently, a few of the homeowners that Russell did odd jobs for had started lawsuits against him. He decided to take out a large insurance policy on his life and fake his death. He made Donna the beneficiary, knowing that when she was sentenced for his murder, that she wouldn't be able to collect. He made Junior the contingent beneficiary. That way, Junior would collect when Donna was found guilty. The plan was for Junior to collect the money and split it with Russell, and they'd both disappear. He'd have money and not have to pay on the lawsuits. Also, when Russell's real body was found, the police didn't know who he was. Apparently, he had left his wallet in the truck. Junior said that Russell did that all the time because the wallet pressed on a nerve in his hip.

"Since Donna was cleared of all charges, the insurance company will be paying her the full amount, and she has arranged for an excellent lawyer to represent Junior. The lawyer is hopeful because Junior was unaware of Russell's plans until it actually happened. The mitigating factor is his Asperger's Syndrome; he wasn't able to respond in a normally responsible way. His lawyer is treating him as a victim. Donna has been in contact with the Newport police, and they have given her a say in how Junior's sentencing is to be handled. She has specified that Junior first be assessed for his abilities and disabilities, and he will most likely be diagnosed as disabled. That should have an impact on how the state wants to pursue everything. We'll keep you informed as we hear more." She returned to her seat by Gary.

Feeling emotional, Donna held herself with crossed her arms. Cora saw her distress and put an arm around her for support. "We're all hoping it turns out okay." Donna nodded in agreement.

Sharon sat down next to Callie. "Did you say Junior vandalized something? What was that?"

"Oh. I didn't tell you that part. It was when you were at Rudy's cabin. Remember the rock through the window?"

"That was him?"

"Yeah. He told the police he thought Gary and I were still staying there, and he wanted us to leave. He was afraid we'd find something out and he'd get arrested. That was before Russell died. He said Russell really let him have it when he found out what he did."

"That's so sad."

Callie sighed. "I really feel sorry for Junior. I hope the judge understands his limitations."

Georgia and Rudy congratulated Donna on her exoneration and gave her an additional hug to welcome her to the clan. Sitting down next to her, Georgia said, "I'm so glad you're able to live here with Cora. She was so distraught when Ralph died. I think you have given her the lifeline she needed."

"I think it's more like she gave me one. Everything I had in Newport is gone. My best friend turned out to be no friend at all. My house was worthless. And you know that my sister..." Donna hesitated and shook her head, "my unwanted sister, my *adopted* sister, she stole most of my belongings when I was in jail."

"About that, didn't you press charges?" Georgia asked.

"Nobody ever saw her take anything, so it couldn't be proven. But everyone knew it was her. Besides, what would I sue her for? It's not like she has anything I want."

"Well, she's out of your life now."

The biggest grin came over Donna. "Thank goodness for that."

"So, with everything gone, you're really fortunate to have Cora."

"Well. With what the insurance is going to pay me, I won't be a burden."

Georgia gave her a stern look. "Nobody would ever think that."

Donna was overcome. She had never before experienced people, other than Cora, who accepted her unconditionally. Tears threatened to overflow.

Just then, Cora came back with a refilled plate. When she saw Donna's tears, she stood over Georgia like an attack dog. "Georgia! What did you say to her?"

Donna reached out to take Cora's free hand. "It's okay. I just got sentimental. That's all."

"Okay, if you say so."

Georgia patted Cora's hand when Donna let go. "Now that's how sisters *should* be. They love and appreciate each other." Georgia got up and went over to the food tables. She stood there, her own memories flooding back like an impending storm. Facing away from everyone so nobody could see the tears she was fighting back, she stared gloomily across the yard.

Georgia's thoughts raced backwards in time, first recalling how Alice made the decision on how to kill their step-father. Then as a nineteen-year-old file clerk, Alice blackmailed Sharon's dad into divorcing his wife to marry her. Not only were Georgia and their mother not invited to the wedding, they were cut off after she got what she wanted. Later, Georgia saw a newspaper article about Alice, so she tracked her down to reconnect. Instead, she was met at the front door with a tongue-lashing to get lost. She groaned thinking about how Sharon told her all the ways that Alice made Sharon's formative years so miserable, and then cheated on her husband with Pierre, a member of a major crime family – just for the purpose of getting a good deal on art and antiques.

Georgia was about to cry when Rudy came up behind her and whispered, "Thinking about Alice?"

She jumped. "How'd you know?" her voice tight.

"I was eavesdropping. She was no sister, you know." He wrapped his arms around her. "But, you have a good family now."

Georgia wiped away a tear and nodded quickly trying to shake off the bad memories.

That evening, Cora sat with Donna so they could recount the events of the day. Overcome by the welcome she'd received, Donna cried some more. They shared more happy tears, laughing and joking about how the grandchildren fussed over having another grandmother. They giggled like teenagers.

Chapter 46

Time went by quickly. The two months since Donna came to live with Cora seemed to go by in a blink. Not only were they enjoying themselves, but also everyone was busy.

Donna's insurance payout had come within a month. She paid the lawyer, reminding him to make sure Junior got assessed properly. She had collected all the bills that Russell had run up and made checks out for all of them. Then she brought Callie to the dining room to write her a check.

Callie tried to object, but Donna held up a firm hand. "I don't want to hear it. If it wasn't for you, I probably wouldn't have ever got out. I found out that most of the people that did recognize Russell's picture in the paper were going to let it go. They figured it was justice. You're the only one that spoke up. So, I can't tell you how grateful I am that you did all that work to get me freed."

Donna looked down, and the tone of her voice became strained as she continued. "More importantly, finding Rachel's secret freed my mind, heart, and soul. What you did for me is worth far more than I could ever pay you."

Callie couldn't speak for several moments, so she gave Donna a long, tearful hug.

The next day, Gary jumped at the chance to go along when Callie said she wanted to visit Georgia. Callie was looking forward to spending some time in the kitchen getting cooking lessons, but that didn't explain why Gary wanted to tag along. She looked quizzically at him, "How come you want to come? Do you want to learn to bake, too?"

"I just thought I'd keep Rudy company." He shrugged. "You know, so he won't feel left out." *I hope that satisfies her. She's got a pretty good nose for ulterior motives.*

"You're so thoughtful." She smiled lovingly at him and gave him a long kiss. "But I'm guessing it's so you can stay close to me."

He gave an enthusiastic mm-hm. *Another good reason.*

When Rudy answered the door, he welcomed them in happily. "Come on in. What brings you two over here? I would've thought you'd be out having fun."

Callie started, "I have a confession. I was hoping to get some baking tips from Georgia. Classes start in September, so I've got some time to hone my skills a bit."

Rudy laughed. "You're in luck, she's in the kitchen now. Go ahead. She'll be glad to talk to you." When he led Gary to the couch, he noticed a pensive look in Gary's eyes. "So, what brought you along?"

"I'm not real sure how to..."

Rudy was instantly worried. "Are you having second thoughts about Callie? 'Cause if you are, that's just cruel. Just when you convince her to lo..."

"No!" Gary looked embarrassed. "Oh great," he whispered. "I sure don't want Callie or Georgia coming in right now. They're probably wondering why I'd be yelling at you."

"What's bothering you? Tell me."

"It was at the cabin."

Rudy's heart seemed to skip a beat at the thought that something awful had happened.

"You know how we're always pranking each other." He rolled his eyes. "Callie was out, so I thought it would be funny to give her a scare." His ears started turning crimson.

Rudy felt mostly relieved. He had a hunch where this was going.

"I hid behind a door so I could grab her when she came in." He sighed. "She had me on the floor before I even knew what happened. I was completely disabled."

Rudy tried, but he couldn't hold back the chuckle.

"Please don't tell Callie, but I gotta be able to hold my own with her, man."

Gary looked so distraught that it overcame any urge for Rudy to laugh more at Gary's predicament. "I'd be glad to help. But now that you and Callie are dating, what excuse will you make to be here?"

Gary looked uncertain. "Oh great. I didn't think of that."

Rudy put his hand on Gary's shoulder. "How about you tell her I'm giving you lessons in the business. After all, self-defense is one of the tools of the trade."

"That's brilliant." Gary's eyes beamed and he sat up straight. "Why *don't* you teach me everything? I'd really like to help Callie anyway. And then I could."

"We have a plan then."

In the kitchen, Georgia was busy loading the dishwasher when Callie walked in. She turned around, wiped her hands on her apron, and gave her a hug. "Hiya honey, what brings you over?"

"We'd been gone so long, I missed visiting. How are you feeling?"

"I'm fine. And yes, I'd let you know if I was concerned about anything. I'll pour some coffee so we can sit down and talk."

The reluctant look on Callie's face made Georgia wonder what was coming.

"I was hoping to get some cooking lessons from you. Mom tried teaching me some basics when I was growing up, but I wasn't interested back then; I preferred climbing trees and chasing after Mark. Grandma tried to pretend my food was edible, but I could tell she was just choking it down. And now that I know I'll be eventually getting married, I'd like to be able to cook us nice things, not just grilled cheese sandwiches."

When Georgia stopped laughing, she happily said, "Oh honey, of course I will! I'm so glad you came to me, I've always wanted to pass on my recipes to a daughter of my own, and you're better than I could ask for."

"Thank you so much!" Callie reached across the table to give Georgia's hand a squeeze. "Gary already told me that he'd like to come with me when I get my lessons, I think he wants to eat whatever we're cooking that day." Then a horrified look fell across her face. "Oh my, I hope I wasn't being presumptuous assuming you'd say yes."

Georgia laughed again. "Of course not. You had to know I'd be honored. I'll even show you how to make an impressive dish for Mark and Marci's reception."

Callie grinned. "He'll never believe it was me who cooked it." She panicked. "I know I have a year to learn, but still."

"Of course. It's not as hard to cook as you think it is."

"At least I only have the family to compete with. Not like it's actually a catering company I have to beat."

Georgia stared at her as if she was going to slap her hand.

"I'm sorry. I didn't mean to say none of you can cook..."

"Gotcha." Georgia laughed and then added, "Don't worry. You're going to be just fine." She got up to pour more coffee and asked, "So, have you heard anything new about everyone in Newport?"

"Donna just got an update about Junior. Remember, how Junior testified that his girlfriend was Donna's neighbor, Sheila?"

"Yeah. That was so weird," Georgia remarked. "You'd think she'd realize he wasn't husband material, especially with her being older. And why would he pick such a horrible woman?"

"Apparently, Junior got an inheritance when his mother died. Well, when Sheila found out about the money, she turned on the charm and convinced Junior to spend most of the money on that boob job. She treated him like her sugar daddy."

"That's disgusting. Taking advantage of him like that."

"Oh, there's more."

Georgia frowned.

"Apparently, she convinced her underage son to get a job telling him he had to contribute to the household expenses. Of course, since he wasn't old enough to legally work, Sheila arranged for him to work for a guy that would keep quiet. He'd pay in cash, and Ethan would work for less than minimum wage. No records. Even worse, she was collecting welfare money and state assistance. So, now she's being investigated for welfare fraud, breaking the child labor laws, along with whatever other laws she's broken."

"What a sleaze!" Georgia exclaimed.

"Yep, and I'm not even finished."

Getting really angry, Georgia crossed her arms.

"Making Ethan get a job wasn't just for the money. It was also to get him out of the house, so she and Junior could hook up. Later, when Donna was arrested and gave Sheila the key to her house, they'd meet over there for their trysts. She didn't realize that Ethan is pretty smart, and he had figured out what she was doing, especially when Junior would come to visit so often."

Georgia shook her head. "That's just sad."

"Ethan is in state custody while his mother's affairs are being sorted out."

"Aw, that poor kid. What's going to happen to him?"

"I don't know; I hope they find a nice foster home for him."

For a few minutes, Georgia watched Callie think about the situation. She knew there was nothing anyone could do, so she changed the subject. "You haven't told me yet."

Callie's eyes met hers instantly. "Told you what?"

"About you and Gary. You even mentioned that you knew you'd be married eventually, I'm assuming to him? How did you make your decision?"

"I just had this conversation with Mom, too." Callie blushed as she put her coffee cup down on the table. "You know, I'd been struggling for a long time. I made charts and lists; I was trying to be logical. I wanted to make the right decision."

Georgia smiled knowingly.

"It was in the hospital after the accident. All I could think about was, is he going to be okay? What if he isn't? I couldn't stand the idea of losing him. I don't know how to describe it. I just knew right then and there that I loved him. I don't know why I didn't see it before."

"That's because you don't get to decide about whether you love someone. Either you do or you don't. And I'm glad you two were such close friends first."

"Why's that?"

"Because you have to like someone first. People say they fall in love at first sight. But how can you know about that person? All that first sight stuff is based on physical attraction, not true love. True love is when you put aside your own feelings for the benefit of the other person. You go out of your way to please him. It's selfless, not selfish. True love starts when you are drawn to a man's respect for women, his ability to empathize, his diligence, his work ethics... there are so many qualities that make up a person. You just can't know about any of that until you see them function in real life. You have to like them as a person. Physical attraction is so temporary; we get old. Look at me and Rudy.

"How many times have you seen a drop-dead gorgeous man and then found out he was arrogant or an abuser or a drunk or a womanizer? Again, hundreds of repulsive qualities that you can't see, but you only learn about after you get to know him. Could you love a man like that? No. I'll tell you something that I learned from other women. I know at least two women who have told me that they love their husbands, but they don't like them."

Callie's jaw dropped. "Seriously?"

"Oh yes, and that's just the ones that have admitted it. What kind of a life is that?"

"I couldn't live like that." Callie felt like she'd just been gut punched. "Why did they stay?"

"There are a lot of reasons: for the children, they believe in keeping their vows, financial reasons, religious beliefs, and I could go on. That's why it's important to really know your man before you say, 'I do'. There's really no good reason to rush into a marriage."

"I see what you mean. I'm so blessed to have a man I really like."

Georgia smiled lovingly. "Me too! Now, what would you like to cook first?"

On the last Friday of June, Junior's new attorney contacted Donna with Junior's diagnosis. Not only did Junior have Asperger's Syndrome, but also he had Sensory Processing Disorder, dyslexia, and ADD. He was glad to report that since Junior was diagnosed as disabled and didn't knowingly break any laws, all charges were dropped in lieu of treatment. The judge gave Junior the option of living in his own home or in a group home with other young men living with developmental disabilities, and he chose to go into a group home.

He was granted Social Security Disability Income, food stamps, and a state-paid personal support worker to teach him how live as an adult, such as social skills, to be self-sufficient, hold down a real job, manage a checking account, pay bills, shop for groceries and necessities, cook for himself, and so forth.

Donna thanked the lawyer for letting her know that Junior would be taken care of. She regularly kept in touch with Junior to see how he was getting along. Junior was proud to tell her about each new skill he learned, and she was happy to hear about his progress, and told him often how proud she was of him.

That summer, Gary and Callie spent much of their free time visiting Rudy and Georgia for their lessons. By November, she was able to make several meals from scratch and without a recipe. Mark was skeptical, though. No amount of reasoning could convince him that this little sister could cook. Georgia's suggestion was brilliant. Everyone was invited to her house for a pot roast dinner, with roasted vegetables, and apple pie with a crumble top. Of course, everyone assumed that Georgia had made the meal, and Sharon chided her for doing so much work and not asking for help. Sharon and Callie helped load the table with all the dishes.

Mark had eagerly filled his plate with some of every dish.

Jack elbowed him, saying, "Hey, leave some for everyone else."

Mark waved him off. "Don't worry, Georgia always has leftovers. Besides, it's been a long time since we've had one of her dinners." He dove in. With the first mouthful, he leaned back and his eyes rolled back in his head, gracing everyone with the loudest groan of pleasure. He chewed slowly, getting every nuance of flavor. "Awesome! Even better than I remember. I applaud you, Georgia."

Georgia grinned slyly. "I didn't cook a thing. Callie did."

Mark practically choked. "What?" he sputtered.

"That's right. Nobody could convince you that she can cook. So, here's your proof."

Jack applauded, and soon everyone else did, too.

Mark sat with his mouth open for several seconds. When he finally processed what she said, he put his fork down, stood up, and bowed to Callie. "My apologies. I stand corrected."

Gary leaned over to whisper in Callie's ear. "I'm proud of you. It really is delicious." She smiled and kissed him on the cheek.

Gary's lessons at the Burke house were also progressing well. Rudy taught him not only self-defense, but also the art of interrogation, how to do a stake-out without being noticed, and most of all, fine-tuning his understanding of body language.

Whenever Callie and Gary visited Rudy and Georgia, they finished the day by doing yard work and home repairs for their teachers/hosts.

Because they spent so much time there, they bonded with Lucky, their dog. It wasn't long before they started talking about getting a dog after they were married.

Although Callie and Gary expected it, they were still unprepared for the summons delivered for the trial of Callie's angry stalker, Craig Whittier. The charges were two counts of attempted murder, destruction of property, and harassment.

To their surprise, there were multiple witnesses. First, the manager who terminated him testified to his outburst of rage against Callie for causing him to lose his job. A neighbor who had been walking his dog at night saw him as he was tampering with the step that Callie broke when she stepped on it. Gary testified seeing the license plate of his SUV just before he ran them off the road. Paint scrapings from his SUV matched Callie's VW. But the most condemning evidence was his confession after the arresting officer read him his rights, when Craig stated that Callie should have died.

Although the trial went fairly quickly, the judge decreed that the defendant have a psychiatric assessment before he would hand down his sentence.

The psychiatrist finally submitted a diagnosis of Bi-polar, Paranoia, Delusions, and uncontrolled anger. He was sentenced to the Oregon State Hospital for confined treatment since he had committed a felony. Callie was relieved that he'd be out of commission for a long while. Still, she made sure the court had it on record that she be kept in the loop about any future release date.

After the trial in Newport, Gary took Callie to dinner at a nice, romantic restaurant. They were seated in a remote corner. When the waiter came to their table, Gary asked for a bottle of champagne to start. The waiter bowed and said, right away, sir."

Callie's eyes popped. "That's really expensive."

Gary held up a hand. "It's okay. You just turned 21, remember?"

"But, that's…"

"No arguments. Okay? You deserve some spoiling." He smiled lovingly.

Callie reached across the table to take his hand. "I don't deserve you."

"You've got that all wrong. It's me that doesn't deserve you." He could see her eyes getting misty.

When Callie looked at the menu, she looked worried. "Gary. I don't think we should be here. This dinner is going to cost more than you make in a week."

He winked. "I told you. It's okay, stop worrying."

The waiter returned to the table with their champagne. He opened it ceremoniously, poured a serving into each of their glasses, and placed the bottle into an ice bucket.

Gary ordered for both of them, dilled salmon crostinis for the appetizer, Seafood Paella for the main course, and chocolate mousse for dessert.

The waiter bowed and left.

Callie tasted her champagne and gave him an okay. "This is really good."

"Glad you like it."

The waiter brought their appetizers.

"I love this place," Callie whispered as she looked around. "It's so romantic."

Gary smiled.

They took their time enjoying each course as it was brought out, but Callie mentioned at least twice how much she was looking forward to that chocolate mousse. When the waiter finally brought it out from the kitchen, Callie sat up straighter and picked up her spoon with anticipation. When the waiter set the dish in front of her, her lips parted, her eyes widened when she saw a diamond ring standing in the center of her mousse. She looked up quickly. "Is this for real?"

With heart pounding, Gary stood up, knelt in front of her, and took her hand in his. "I've loved you for as long as I can remember. I can't imagine living without you beside me. When we're apart, I'm not complete. I live to talk with you, tease you, support you, play with you, work with you. Every part of my life is centered around you. What I'm saying is that I want it to last for the rest of our lives. Please say you'll be my wife?"

Callie's free hand was trembling as she wiped away joyous tears. With eyes beaming and a lump in her throat, she nodded enthusiastically. She leaned forward and threw her arms around him.

His whisper of "I love you" seemed to drown out the patrons'
applause and cheers.

Chapter 47

One year later

Jack and Sharon insisted on paying for part of the wedding. Although Callie and Gary were both working, they still had tight budgets. Callie had taken a few PI jobs, but none of them had paid much, and those jobs were sporadic. She had received a nice payment from Donna a while back, but money goes quickly when you're in college. Although Gary had helped with the PI jobs, he kept his regular job as a part-time physical therapist to pay his bills.

It was late afternoon on the day after May Day, and everyone was arriving. The ceremony would be held in Rudy and Georgia's backyard, but they didn't have to do anything but attend. Jack and his brothers had spent that last month sprucing up the place. The couple was already in their 70's, arthritis had finally caught up with Rudy's knees, and although Georgia was still cancer-free, nobody wanted her to exert herself. When they were done, it looked even more spectacular than anyone remembered.

Looking outside while standing at the sliding back door, Georgia looked out on a stone patio which extended the full width of the house and out for over twelve feet. A new pergola covered the patio and was decorated with fairy lights. A mature plum tree in full bloom stood at the far left corner of the patio, and just to the left of that, she could hear the water gurgling into a good-sized koi pond with several water lilies and four orange-and-white koi. Low foliage grew around the waterfall hiding its water source. The garden bench next to it was decorated with satin bows and wildflowers.

Straight ahead, on the south side of the patio, stood an antiqued iron archway with a lush honeysuckle growing up through it. The scent of the blooms filled the air. It looked like a doorway to paradise, and that is where the minister was going to stand. Beyond the archway, a meandering path disappeared into the trees, bushes, and other native plants of the miniature forest on the double lot.

Chairs were set up under the pergola creating an aisle down the middle; and on the grass to the right, tables were lined up to hold the pot-luck buffet. A separate table held the wedding cake that Georgia meticulously designed for them.

Georgia smiled. Everything was beautiful.

Marci, Callie's matron of honor, helped her get prepared. Sharon was with them making sure of the details. They adjusted Callie's halo of blue wildflowers so that it sat perfectly on her head. Her red hair was loosely pulled up with ringlets that cascaded down the back of her neck. Her simple cocktail-length, georgette wedding gown had a sweetheart neckline, cap sleeves, and satin dusty-blue roses that cascaded from the left shoulder diagonally down to the hem on the right. The only jewelry Callie wore was her mother's antique pearl earrings.

"Callie, I'm so glad you chose now to get married. The blossoms on the trees are just gorgeous," Sharon cooed.

"That's why I worked so hard to graduate early," Callie explained.

"It's always May Day where you're involved," Sharon said with a glint in her eye. "so I understand why you didn't choose yesterday – didn't want to take any chances of added calamity?"

Callie laughed and gave her mother a huge hug. "I know, I know, all the calamity that follows in my wake is why you gave me my nickname, after Calamity Jane. But mostly because I wouldn't have been able to stand Mark running around shouting 'Mayday!' about everything on my wedding day. You heard him yesterday, right? He was saying it about the stupidest details! 'Mayday! We're out of butter! Mayday! Callie broke a nail! Mayday!' I finally had to just leave so he wouldn't drive me batty!"

Sharon hugged her daughter tightly. "A few years ago, you probably would've just punched him. I'm so proud of you, honey."

"Hey. You be careful. You're going to make my makeup run."

Marci fussed with the hem of Callie's dress. "I think you're ready." Marci's bronze skin glowed with happiness for her sister-in-law. Her dark chocolate eyes were misting, so she fanned at her face with her hands.

Sharon startled as she heard the band change songs. "They're playing the music for Mark to escort me to my seat. I'd better get going." She blew them a kiss.

Subtle music played in the background. A soft breeze brought the scent of blossoms. The sun lowered in the sky, creating a beautiful sunset.

Mark walked Sharon to her seat and then stood next to Gary beside the minister. "Nervous?" he whispered to Gary.

"Not at all. My dream is coming true," he whispered back.

"You sure, dude? You know she's a daredevil spitfire, right? Callie, Calamity Jane? It's not a coincidence Mom gave her that name. She's no walk in the park."

"No, not a park, she's more like a meadow of wildflowers that one could roll around in all day." He grinned at his best man.

Mark punched him in the arm, "Dude, that's my sister."

The audience snickered.

When the music began, Jack escorted Callie out of the house. Gary was stunned by her beauty for a moment before he grinned, nudged Mark, and whispered, "See? Wildflowers."

Mark clearly wanted to punch him again, but with Callie coming down the aisle, it had to wait.

Besides, Gary was instantly focused on the love of his life coming towards him.

At the altar, Jack gave Callie a hug and a kiss on the cheek, and then handed her to Gary. Proud as a peacock, he sat down next to Sharon.

Everything had been perfect so far, but the minister seemed to be in a hurry, saying their vows fast and in long phrases. As Gary or Callie tried to repeat them, they would invariably miss a word or scramble the sequence. The audience cringed for them, but when Callie and Gary both laughed at themselves, the tension was broken.

Gary gave her the longest kiss when the minister introduced them as husband and wife.

After the photographer took all the pictures, Callie and Gary had the first dance. They cut the cake, and Gary gently gave Callie the first bite.

Callie gave him a kiss. She cut a piece for him, and just as the cake was an inch from his open mouth, she quickly pushed it onto his left cheek and down onto his neck. The devil in her eyes changed when he leaned over to whisper in her ear. But instead of whispering, he held her tight as he rubbed his face against hers, and dipped her low to the ground to give her another long kiss. At first she tried a defensive move, but was unsuccessful because he had anticipated it. Rudy's training was spot on. So she reciprocated the kiss.

The audience applauded.

Mark walked up behind Gary at the food display and planted his hand on Gary's shoulder. "Pretty good potluck, huh?"

"Always," Gary agreed.

"Say. I've been watching your dad. He and Ethan seem to be getting along pretty well."

"They sure are." Gary concentrated on the food as he loaded his plate for the second time.

"Are you jealous?"

Surprised, Gary looked Mark straight in the face. "Of what?"

"You not having your dad growing up, and now this random kid getting all that love and affection that you missed out on, that you should have gotten. Jealous of that."

Gary smiled. "You know, not at all. Yeah, it was hard growing up, but it made me who I am. Your family took me in and we all became close. And it got me my wife. As for Ethan, I'm glad he's actually getting a break too. I see a lot of me in him. Kind of unloved by a single parent. That can tear you up inside and make you bitter. Ethan deserves this chance. What's more, I get a chance to see my dad being a good enough person to connect with now. He had some changing to do, like getting over the grief of losing mom. I'm just grateful that he's ready to love again. He just couldn't do it before." Gary scratched his head. "Don't worry, he's been giving me attention too." He chuckled. "You won't believe it, but I'm actually giving *him* advice on being a father, lessons I learned from Jack."

Mark gave him a bro hug. "I'm really happy for you."

Aunt Bonnie bounced over to congratulate the groom. "Hey there, new cousin, where are you taking my niece for your honeymoon?"

Cousin? Then Gary remembered her scatter-brained likability and chuckled. "We thought we'd go to the mountains."

"Oh. You know we went to the beach on ours. It's off season right now, you could get a good rate on a motel."

"I think we're a little tired of the beach right now. That's why we chose the mountains."

"Who doesn't love the beach?" Bonnie frowned cluelessly. "Anyhow, when's the next family reunion? Charlotte just asked me to find out on my way to get more of these delicious little egg pies!"

"Oh, the reunion will be the first Saturday in July, right here. But I think those are called quiches."

"Oh right! Thanks!" She waved happily before leaving.

Mark watched her as she bounced back to her seat. "She is always good for a chuckle, isn't she? I just love her optimism and lack of concern for what anyone thinks. I don't know how sisters raised together can be so different. Like her sister, Arlene; I think she's still mad at Mom. She's a no-show again."

Gary shook his head. "I don't get her. How can anyone stay mad that long? And it's not like what happened is Mom's fault."

"It takes all kinds. At least, everyone else is here."

Just before dusk, at Rudy's and Georgia's request, Callie and Gary saved their gift for last, partly because it was the largest one. When Gary opened it, there was another slightly smaller wrapped gift inside. He and Callie laughed. That gift had another smaller gift, producing another laugh, although they were a bit more puzzled. This process was repeated five more times, revealing smaller gifts, and producing increasingly frustrated sounds, until he revealed a 3"x3"x3" wrapped box. Gary looked at Rudy and commented, "If it gets any smaller, I'm going to think you didn't give us anything at all."

Rudy's deadpan face betrayed nothing. "Open it and find out."

During the whole episode, Callie watched with increasing amusement. She whispered in Gary's ear, making sure no one else heard, "Later, I'll make up for whatever isn't there."

Gary's ears turned red, and he cleared his throat, visibly trying to control himself. "Okay. Here goes." This time the box was wrapped in contact paper, completely stuck to the box. He pulled out his pocketknife to cut the wrapping and revealed a small jewelry box. But instead of jewelry, two keys were wrapped in tissue and tied with a bow. "What?" he wondered with curiosity.

"Surprise!" Georgia enthusiastically announced.

Gary and Callie looked at each other, totally confused.

Rudy explained, "I basically pulled you into this dangerous line of work, and I see it as my responsibility to make sure you're as safe as possible. We wanted to make sure you have a home that's going to give you everything you need; security, room to grow, and functionality."

"A house?" Callie asked. At that point, the newlyweds increasingly changed from amused to shocked as Rudy continued.

"Yep, those keys belong to your new home. It's an older house, but it's been remodeled to my specifications. There is an unattached studio which you can make into a large home office. It has a state-of-the-art security system covering the whole place. A raccoon wouldn't be able to enter your property without your knowledge. And there are enough bedrooms for you to take care of all the babies you'll have."

Gary and Callie blushed.

All of their guests applauded.

Chapter 48

Ten Years Later

Rico was barking frantically, so Callie looked to see what the emergency was. She stood up and yelled, "Rayne! Get down right now!"

Sharon laughed. "At least Rico gives you an alert when she's mischievous."

Callie rolled her eyes. "You actually laughed? This is the mother's curse, isn't it? All those years ago, you cursed me to have a kid just like me, and now here we are."

She shrugged. "I had to let you see what it was like being the mother of an active child."

"Active, uh huh. Thanks a lot. But I could've done just fine without that curse." Callie turned her attention to her four-year-old daughter up in the tree and walked towards her. "Come on. I'll help you down."

"Aww, Mom. Do I have to?"

"Yes," Callie stated firmly. She held her arms out knowing that Rayne would be glad to jump. Standing next to Callie, Rico wagged his stub tail as Callie reached up for her daughter's jump. After getting her rascal down safely, Callie led her to the patio with Rico following. "We still have chips." She was able to stroke Rayne's red hair just once before she got loose and ran to the picnic table with her victorious arms straight up as if she'd just made a field goal. "Woo-hoo," she cried gleefully.

Callie watched her daughter bounding towards the picnic table and marveled at the beautiful child she and Gary had produced. Rayne looked so much like her, the curly hair that frizzed around her face, the bright green eyes, and the rosy cheeks. But more than anything else, her mischievousness was almost entertaining. Almost. Like when Rayne climbed the counter to get into the top cupboard that held the hidden cookies. Afterwards, Callie wondered if hiding them was worth the time to clean up the broken cookie jar that had shattered on the tile floor. She grimaced as she remembered scrambling to prevent their dogs from trying to eat the broken cookies that were mixed with all the shards of ceramic.

Their two dogs became a blessing. Rico, the Boston Bulldog, was just as energetic as Rayne. He followed her everywhere. He seemed to enjoy the mischief she created, but he always gave that yapping warning whenever Rayne was treading on danger. Then there was Bennie. They'd gotten him as a pup ... was it only a year ago? He had grown so big, so quickly. He was a rescue dog, so nobody knew his breed, just a mix. Gary often wondered if the father was a horse. But the vet said he was probably a mix of Great Dane, Newfoundland, and Labrador Retriever. He told them the dog would probably be close to 200 pounds. Feeding him was a challenge, but he was worth all the effort. Although he didn't follow Rayne like Rico, he was just as protective of the two children.

Callie thought back to when she and Gary first moved into this house that Rudy had given them. Having just married and with getting organized after the honeymoon, it had been a few weeks before they looked into the studio. Not only did Rudy give them the house, but he had also donated all the equipment that he had collected over the years. Yes, most of it was out of date, but they still used most of it until they could update it. However, Rudy had not skimped when he installed the latest technology available for their security system.

Later, when Gary had joined her full-time in their investigation business, she became concerned. They were on a tight budget and losing that meager income from his part-time job as a physical therapist worried her. Yes, Rudy occasionally helped with finances, but she hated having to rely on him. Although Gary was a valuable asset as a physical therapist at the nursing home, he said he was glad to quit the job. The conditions there were stressful, his split schedule meant that he was unavailable Monday through Friday and wasn't able to help Callie in the field. His reasoning was sound. Even though Gary's take-home pay dropped at first, it wasn't long before together they earned even more than the meager paycheck from the nursing home.

She smiled thinking how quickly he had learned under Rudy's tutelage. Oh yes, that was an interesting discussion when she found out about those lessons. She still teased him, saying he was just trying to keep up, but she knew he had more to bring to the table than he was willing to admit. His photographic memory and ability to repeat verbatim any conversation was invaluable.

Gary turned out to be just as perceptive as she was, enabling him to have an equal part in their discussions with each case. At first, she had hated to admit it to him, but sometimes he saw things she had missed. She appreciated that he never threw that in her face. Instead, he treated her even with more love and respect. After a while, she found it easier to point out where he thought of things she hadn't, or tell him how much he made her life better. She smiled thinking how fortunate she was and embraced the fact that she loved him.

When their son, Austin, was born six years ago, Callie took time off to be with him. When she was about to go back in the field to work with Gary again, she found out she was expecting Rayne. Now that Rayne was about to enter preschool, she was preparing to rejoin Gary part-time. While she'd been mostly home these five years, she kept up the paper and phone work, did research, and handled business details. Thankfully, she had taken those business courses before getting married. Being in the background allowed her to spend most of her time at home with the children while they were little. Of course, Sharon helped enormously, especially if Callie had to be out of town. They all agreed that a mother's love and attention could never be replaced. It was so necessary in the formative years.

Callie's wandering mind returned to the present, and she sat down next to her mom on the iron bench and let out a tired laugh. "Was I that bad, mom?"

Sharon smiled knowingly. "Much worse."

Callie shook her head. "I'm so sorry. How many times have I apologized?"

"Numerous times." A wicked look crossed Sharon's face. "Although, I'm enjoying being the observer and don't have to do the chasing now. Well, at least, not all the time."

"Sorry to tell you, but it won't be long before I'm back in the field. You're going to have to do some chasing again when she's home from preschool."

"I know." Sharon chuckled. "It just reminds me that it's a good thing young people have children."

"Hey. You're not old."

"Tell that to my feet at the end of the day."

Callie laughed.

Gary sat down next to her holding a heaping plate of food and a beer. "What are you two gossiping about?"

Callie looked at him as if he missed the boat. "The usual."

"Rayne or Austin?"

Callie looked over at Georgia who was playing catch with Austin and smiled. "Who else? Rayne of course. Looks like Austin's okay. Unless you want to ask Georgia. I think she might be getting tired."

Gary chuckled, put down his plate, and said, "I'll go get him. I've got his favorite food-watermelon." He trotted off to get his son.

Sharon leaned over. "I'm content."

Puzzled, she looked at her mom. "What do you mean?"

"A lot of reasons. You have a wonderful family, a husband that takes good care of you. I know you can take care of yourself, but in this life, it takes two working together. Now don't get all Wonder Woman on me. I'm just grateful that Gary is ambitious, considerate, thoughtful, and really understands you." She smiled sweetly and added, "That's why I'm content."

Callie gave Sharon a long hug and whispered, "I love you, Mom. And thanks for all the advice you've given me through the years. I may not have told you at the time how much I appreciated all of it, but I did. And thanks for always being there for me." A tear formed as she winced. "I wish Alice had been a nice mom when you were growing up."

"That's in the past. What counts is what you do in the present. So let's enjoy it."

Callie gladly wiped the tear away. "Let's join the others."

Since Georgia and Rudy turned eighty, it had been decided that family get-togethers would be here, in Gary and Callie's back yard. The landscaping wasn't nearly as pretty, but they had the energy for the preparation and hosting.

Gary walked back with Austin in his arms. "I got there just in time," he said with a chuckle. "Georgia was just running out of gas." He pointed over at the picnic table where, fanning herself, she had just sat down.

Gary picked up his plate and handed it to Austin. "Think you can handle that, Bud?"

Austin nodded enthusiastically.

"We're going to sit over there," he said as he pointed to Ethan. "We'll let Mom and Grandma talk for a while."

Sharon smiled as she watched them walking together. "It's amazing how much Austin loves Ethan. I'm amazed at the progress Ethan's made."

"I know. I think it's wonderful. I'm really glad Gary's dad took him in. It's been good for both of them, especially Billy. When Billy went through rehab, Gary was worried about him. He'd been an alcoholic for so long, we all wondered if it would stick. But Ethan's given him a purpose. He actually told Gary that he doesn't even think about drinking anymore. And that was years ago."

"Is Ethan really becoming a lawyer?"

Callie beamed. "Yes. He wants to become an advocate for low-income families. He lived it, so he understands the frustration."

"How's his mother?"

Callie sighed. "She's out of the picture. Ethan's reached out to her several times, but she doesn't seem to want to work her way out of the welfare system. She's one of those people that only makes excuses. So Ethan's quit trying. It's a shame because it hurts him to see her not wanting anything better for herself."

Trying to change the subject, Callie suggested they move. "Let's go sit by Georgia." Callie picked up their plates, Sharon grabbed their drinks, and they headed for the picnic table. On the way, Callie took her hand and squeezed it. "I'm so glad Georgia became your mother figure. I really saw a change in you when she came into our lives. All for the better, of course." As the words were coming out of her mouth, she realized how awful it sounded and quickly added, "You were always a great mom, but you became…" she tried to think of the right word, and smiled peacefully as she added, "serene."

Sharon put her arm around Callie and gave her a hug. "That's because she filled that void that Alice created."

"Mind if we join you?" Callie asked when they arrived.

Georgia gave Callie a 'duh' look. "You don't have to ask, you know. We even saved a space for you." She patted the bench beside her.

Mark led his family up the driveway. "Sorry we're late," he called out. "Marci had another false alarm." He would have waved, but he had a fruit salad in one hand and was pulling a rolling cooler with the other hand. He looked back at Marci who was waddling along holding five-year-old Sara's hand. Inside the yard, Marci shut the gate and let Sara run. Mark set the fruit salad on the food table as Marci landed in a chair by the picnic table.

Callie looked at Marci's huge stomach and cringed with sympathy. "How many false alarms have you had now?"

"Too many." She sighed. "I can't wait for this to actually happen. The doctor told me yesterday that he was going to induce me on Monday if I don't have it by then." She looked exhausted as she rubbed her stomach.

"Remember, when it's the real thing, you call me, and I'll come get Sara right away."

"Don't worry, Callie. I won't forget."

Callie looked at her for a few minutes. Even though Marci's bronze skin tone was beautiful, she had begun to look pale. The circles under her dark eyes betrayed a lack of sleep. Her ankles had started to swell, and she could see that Marci had no room for a deep breath. She thought back to her own pregnancies and remembered those last two, long weeks just before the birth, desperately wishing it was over. She felt bad for Marci, but relieved that it won't be much longer.

Mark sat in another chair as he watched Sara running around encouraging Rayne to chase her. He smiled. "I've said this before, but Rayne's the spitting image of you, Callie. And it's more than just how she looks. She acts just like you did, too."

Sharon grinned. "I was just telling her that. Remember, the first time I called you Callie?"

Callie frowned. "Are we going down that road again? Just how many times have you reminded me?"

"Okay. I get it. But you have to admit you were a wild one. Calamity Jane seemed to fit so well."

Georgia chuckled. "Wait a minute. I don't think I've heard that story. What happened?"

Sharon smiled and shook her head at the memory. We were renting a little house in Sellwood at the time. Callie had just turned ten. Are you familiar with the monkey trails by Oaks Bottom?"

Puzzled, Georgia shook her head. "Did you say monkey trails?"

Sharon chuckled. "That's what the kids called them. At the edge of Sellwood park there's a pretty steep drop-off that goes down to Oaks Bottom. A lot of the kids go down those trails instead of walking a half-mile south, and then back, to get to the bottom." Sharon rolled her eyes. "I was making dinner and all of a sudden, Callie burst in the front door holding one hand under her bleeding forehead and the other hand under her bleeding elbow. Then Mark came in saying he brought the bikes home. When he said the wheel was bent, my stomach sank.

"When we finally got the bleeding stopped and bandaged, they told me what they'd done. My heart almost stopped when Mark explained what happened. Of course, Callie had led the way down a trail on their bikes. He said he saw her front wheel hit a rock, and he stood up and used his arm to show the arc she made as she and the bike went sailing. I about smacked him when he laughed. He didn't understand why I was so angry. He said, 'Don't be mad, she's okay.'

"Then he said the bike actually landed on top of her. I couldn't breathe when I heard that." Sharon shook her head. "That's when we started calling her Calamity Jane. Callie for short." Sharon shook her head. When she looked up, she added, "You know, I think a good nickname for Rayne would be Stormy. What do you think?"

Callie's jaw dropped, but after thinking about the suggestion, she conceded, "You know. You're right. A stormy rain does give me chills. And the things she gets into…. I like it. We'll call her Stormy from now on."

Callie looked up and ran to rescue the punch bowl that her daughter was about to dump.

Georgia turned to Sharon. "Have you heard from Cora and Donna?"

"Just last night. Cora texted me that they are having the time of their lives. You know, this is the third cruise they've gone on. Alaska is beautiful this time of year, and they've actually seen quite a bit of wildlife." She leaned in as if to share a secret. "She said that they've been approached by at least three older gentlemen trying to get acquainted."

Georgia visibly cringed. "I hope they don't get taken in. There are a lot of con men out there."

"Oh, no. She said she's fully aware of that and not to worry. She and Donna are enjoying the attention, though. And a few gifts too. It almost reminds me of my mother. She always flirted to get what she wanted."

"But this is different, right?"

"Oh, of course. They have no intention of getting a husband or even dating for that matter. They're having too much fun. Besides, they're almost ready to publish that book they've been writing."

"Remind me, fiction? Or a tell all?"

"Fiction. But there is a lot of fact in it, just with a spin on it."

"How'd they get started anyway?"

"Since Cora had already written a family history, she encouraged Donna to do the same. Cora said it was therapeutic for her and helped her to understand some of Ralph's emotional issues. She thought Donna might be able to face some of her demons too. So Donna did. At first, it was an exercise to help her face and reconcile the guilt, shame, disappointment, and humiliation that she had endured, but it really helped her let go of all that negative stuff.

"Cora told me that when she read the finished product, she cried a lot. She had no idea how hard it had been for Donna, even with all the letters and phone calls between them. She admitted that she had been struggling herself, and apologized to her for being so distracted. Donna told her she hadn't told anyone about the extent of how bad it was. As a kind of therapy, Donna took a creative writing class to help her express in words what she'd gone through. After the class, Cora asked if she could play with one of the short stories she'd turned in. That short story took on a life of its own and they decided to work on it together. As they did, they addressed their emotional issues, held each other, and allowed their past to be in the past. They let go of their guilt so they could focus on each other. They agreed that if something haunted them, they'd share their feelings.

"Eventually, that short story turned into a novel based on their history. They used some of the qualities of themselves for the heroines and aspects of Russell, Junior, and Ralph in their characters. Of course, they changed the story line several times until it was almost unrecognizable from the first draft, but they always put in the emotions. They let me read it before they left for the cruise. I knew instantly which family member they'd based a character on. But the story! Believe me, it's an expression of empathy, survival, determination, and pride. Pride that the heroines had come out of their ordeal intact, and stronger. I think it'll be a best seller. With all of their history, it could even turn into a series."

Georgia's eyes glistened. "I can't wait to read it."

The kids were finally asleep. Callie snuggled under Gary's arm as they leisurely rocked on the porch swing. The clouds were reflecting the setting sun's rays into a glorious kaleidoscope of gold, orange, and red. She smiled contentedly. "You know, I've always loved this big porch. When the sun sets like this, I feel like everything is going to be okay. Rudy couldn't have chosen a more perfect house for us."

"I have a confession to make." He looked at her with a glint in his eye.

Callie looked at him. "What do you mean?"

"Remember way back when you were recording the walkthrough at Donna's house?"

"What about it?"

"When you let me see the recording, I made a mental note of the fact that you couldn't see the sunset from her front door."

"That's the confession?"

"Hold on, I'm not there yet." He cleared his throat before continuing. "When we announced our engagement, Rudy told me about his plans to find a house for us."

"You mean you knew ahead of time?"

"Uh-huh."

"You stinker. Why'd you wait so long to tell me?"

He shrugged. "It never came up. Anyways, I helped Rudy find a house that had a front porch facing West just so we could do exactly this, spend our lives watching sunsets on our front porch."

"I don't know how you still surprise me with what you remember."

"I remember everything I ever learned about you."

"I can't believe it," Callie whispered tenderly. She sat upright. "No... I mean, yes I believe it. But you remembered that little detail? From so long ago?" A tear started to form. "I can't believe how lucky I am to have you. I love you so much."

"I love you, too. More than you'll ever know."

The sunset turned purple as they lingered in a tender kiss.

List of Characters

Callie Cooper – Heroine
Gary Rawlins – Neighbor
Mark Cooper – Callie's brother
Roy Jackson – Callie's ex-boyfriend
Vera – Acquaintance pg 2
Marci Collins – Mark's girlfriend
Rudy Burke – Callie's great uncle by marriage
Cora Cooper – Callie's grandmother, Jack's mother
Ralph Cooper – Callie's grandfather
Sharon Cooper – Callie's mother
Corinne – Hospital Liaison
Donna Turner – Cora's cousin
Jack Cooper – Callie's father
Georgia Burke – Rudy's wife, Sharon's aunt
Russell Turner – Donna's husband
Charlotte Knapp – Sharon's half sister
Arlene Rand – Sharon's half sister
Bonnie Parker – Sharon's half sister
Sheila Myers – Donna's neighbor
Patty – Donna's sister page 29
Uncle Dean – Jack's older brother
Alice – Sharon's mother
Ethan Myers – Sheila Myer's son
Diane – Callie's given name
Paul Myers – Sheila's ex
Kiki – Waitress
Aunt Bonnie – Sharon's half-sister
Phillip Evans – Donna's lawyer
Craig
Drake Furman – District Attorney
Dr Reynolds – Ralph's doctor
Art – Jack's younger brother
Ricky – Jack's youngest brother
Red – 1st hunter
Ben – 2nd hunter
Isaac Murray – Judge
Pierre – Alice's crime partner
Rico – Dog

Rayne – Callie's daughter
Bennie – Dog
Austin – Callie's son
Billy – Gary's dad
Sara – Mark and Marci's daughter
Stormy – Rayne's nickname

About the Authors

Sandra Denbo and her daughter, Tamarine Vilar, live in Portland, Oregon, which is the setting for their stories. Sandra has five children, Tamarine being the youngest. Sandra has had a wealth of experiences and has met a wide variety of personalities, each with their own idiosyncrasies. This fertile bed is the source of ideas for creating the characters you will learn to love and hate. Sandra has always had the ability to clearly describe ideas and feelings.

Tamarine Vilar has one son and also lives in Portland. She has a Bachelor's degree in English with a minor in writing from Portland State University. Because Sandra loved to read, she read to Tamarine from infancy. As a result, reading became her favorite way to relax. Professors and fellow students alike have enjoyed her natural ability to evoke emotion, even tears, with her writing, and have encouraged her to continue writing.